# RICOCHET

John Everard is a cold, ruthless businessman. When he returns home from a business trip he discovers that his Spanish wife Juanita and baby son Tommy have disappeared, his house has been burgled, and his firm's payroll stolen. Moreover, it was his wife who was seen driving the thieves away in Everard's own Jaguar. Has Juanita been kidnapped — or is she implicated in the robbery? And where is Tommy? Now, with little police co-operation, Everard begins his own investigation . . .

J. F. STRAKER

# RICOCHET

*Complete and Unabridged*

**LINFORD**
*Leicester*

First published in Great Britain

First Linford Edition
published 2009

British Library CIP Data

Straker, J. F. (John Foster)
Ricochet.—Large print ed.—
Linford mystery library
1. Kidnapping—England—Fiction
2. Detective and mystery stories
3. Large type books
I. Title
823.9'12 [F]

ISBN 978–1–84782–569–8

Published by
F. A. Thorpe (Publishing)
Anstey, Leicestershire

Set by Words & Graphics Ltd.
Anstey, Leicestershire
Printed and bound in Great Britain by
T. J. International Ltd., Padstow, Cornwall

This book is printed on acid-free paper

*To Margaret, Dot and Gerald*

# 1

Grant Rossiter stirred the hot sand with his foot and ran a hand down the dark hairs on his chest, feeling the sweat ooze from his skin and trickle over his stubby fingers. The gay umbrella shielded him and his companions from the direct rays of the sun, but it could not shut out the heat; it beat up at them from the sand, pressed in on them from between the baked bodies massed around them on the Playa. There was no breeze. Behind the houses and the cafés even the towering mass of Santa Barbara, its yellow rock contrasting vividly with the deep blue of the Mediterranean and the paler blue of the sky, seemed affected by the heat, its stark outlines blurred by the shimmering haze.

'God, but it's hot!' Rossiter removed his dark glasses and wiped the sweat from forehead and brows. 'Why the hell did I pick on Alicante? We should have gone to

San Sebastian. It may be farther from base, but it's a damned sight cooler.' He sucked at his dry lips. 'How about a beer, Emilio?'

Emilio Ginachero rose lazily to his feet, his slim body beautifully co-ordinated.

'You all want beer?' he asked.

'Please.' On Eve Corbett's lips the word was a caress. So was the accompanying smile.

Her husband nodded, frowning. Andrew Corbett was tall and thin, with a long stringy neck and a lined face that looked incapable of a smile. Under the bathing shorts his knobbly knees and spindly legs were a greyish white, the left leg twisted and shrunken. His face and torso were brick red.

They watched Emilio pick his way between the sprawling bodies, making for the bars and cafés that lined the back of the Playa. He walked smoothly and easily, his bare toes curling to grip the sand, his body erect. For Eve his boyish grace had an irresistible appeal, but to the crippled Corbett it presented a taunting challenge. On Rossiter it had no effect at all. He did not see Emilio as a person, only as an essential cog in the machine he had created.

He said, 'So the cash angle doesn't interest you. Is that it?' He had a deep, rich voice that rumbled up from the pit of his stomach. 'Well, it makes a change.'

'I didn't say that.' Corbett's frown deepened. 'Everard owes me plenty, and anything I can take him for I will. But my main concern is to make the bastard sweat. I want — '

'It isn't *my* main concern,' his wife interrupted, smiling at Rossiter, her blue eyes wide. There were smudges on her cheeks where the mascara had melted and run. 'We need every cent we can get. It's all very well for Andrew to gloat on revenge, Mr Rossiter; but living takes money, and that's something we happen to lack.' She sighed and stretched, arching her body voluptuously. 'An awful lot of money if one wants to do it well.'

Rossiter nodded. Andrew Corbett, with his impotent plaints and stupid jealousy, irritated him. But he sympathized with

Eve. Her materialistic outlook, her directness, appealed to him; she was a woman who knew what she wanted and went all out to get it, scornful of subterfuge. In the four days they had been in Spain she had made it clear that her immediate objective was the young Emilio, and Rossiter suspected that the conquest, if not already achieved, was unlikely to be long delayed. It was an objective he understood — a desire to prolong the youthfulness already slipping rapidly away — and under other circumstances he might have aided her in it. It would amuse him to see the gloomy Corbett cuckolded. But not yet. He must warn Emilio to play it cool. They were engaged in a difficult and dangerous operation, and he wanted no warring factions disrupting his team.

'You'll get your cut,' he told her, purposefully gruff.

Emilio returned with the beer, ice cold from the fridge. Rossiter threw back his head and poured the liquid down his parched throat; the others drank through straws, direct from the bottle. As Emilio sat down Eve moved her chair closer to his, so that their knees touched; her hand rested on his thigh, white against the brown. Noting the move, Corbett's eyes narrowed. He sucked viciously at the straw until the beer gurgled in the bottom, and then dropped the empty bottle on to the sand.

Eve handed her bottle to Emilio and stood up, adjusting the too scanty briefs. She was small and plump, and the bra of her white bikini supported without covering the full breasts. Her hair, cut in a Cleopatra bob, was a rich chestnut, although the roots betrayed that it had not always been that colour.

'Who's for a swim?' she asked, looking at Emilio. 'I need cooling off.'

That you do, thought Rossiter — although I doubt if the Mediterranean will cool what's heating you. 'Off you go, Emilio,' he said, noting with sardonic pleasure the scowl on her husband's face. A little dalliance in the sea would present no danger to his plans. 'I want to talk to Corbett.'

Eve smiled at him, appreciating once

more his broad physique. Although his skin glistened in the heat, its creamy pallor seemed unaffected by the sun's rays. With less fat and a few more inches, she thought, he'd be quite a man.

She turned to pull Emilio to his feet.

Corbett watched them as they threaded their way between the packed bodies under the umbrellas. The sea was only a few yards away, but they did not hurry. As they moved apart to avoid a prone sunbather he saw that their hands were clasped.

She never walked that way with me, he thought. And swore.

'Stop interfering, Rossiter, damn you!' he said impulsively. 'Leave my wife alone.'

Rossiter chuckled. 'Relax, man, relax. She'll come to no harm out there.' He selected a cigar and lit it, puffing luxuriously. 'I'm flying back to England tomorrow.'

'Oh?' They were in the water now, with Eve clinging to the young Spaniard's arm and taking advantage of each little ripple to lurch against him. 'It's on, then? When?'

'Friday. Sure you've given me all the dope?'

'All I can. If it isn't enough — well, I'm sorry.'

'We'll all be sorry,' Rossiter said grimly.

Reluctantly Corbett switched his gaze from the sea to look at him.

'No-one gets hurt, do they? No-one else, I mean. Of course, if Everard happens to be there and tries to interfere — if you have to rough him up a little — well, that's good. That's very good. But I don't want — '

'I know what you want.' There was contempt in the rich voice. 'You want us to hand out the kicks you were too scared and incompetent to deliver personally. O.K., we'll do that. We'll also cut you in on the cash. But don't start telling me how to run the show. This isn't a private war any longer, chum. I'm in charge now, and anyone who tries to louse me up is liable to get hurt. Anyone. And don't you forget it.'

Corbett's cheeks were too red to flush, but his body tautened in protest.

'You don't have to threaten. I'm not

7

lousing you up; this is a damned sight more important to me than to you. Damn it, man, I've waited the best part of two years for it!' He bent to massage the twisted leg. It might be the heat, or it might be that he had used it too much, but it ached more than usual that morning. 'And I wasn't scared. Not of him. I did what I could.'

'Not you,' Rossiter said. 'The others. And that was chicken-feed.'

'Maybe. But then we're not professional crooks.'

Rossiter saw a compliment, not an insult, in the words. But contempt for his companion was replaced by curiosity. He said, 'You really hate this guy, don't you?'

Corbett's fists clenched, and he caught his lower lip between his teeth as the image of his enemy seemed to float before his eyes like a mirage in the heat. Even Eve was momentarily forgotten. He had disliked John Everard from the start; Everard had been too impersonal, too arbitrary, too savage a new broom. Yet he had never expected dismissal; not after all those years with the firm. It had shocked

8

him so badly that for months he had been ill. Brooding on injustice, it was then that the bitterness had germinated. Some day, he had told himself (as he had told himself many times since) he would have his revenge. Intensified by Eve's open revolt against their new poverty, the bitterness had become a purpose, the purpose an obsession — until it seemed that his whole existence was directed towards that one essential end. And now, if Rossiter was right, that end was very near.

'Yes, I hate him,' he said. 'I want the bastard to suffer the way he made me suffer.'

Rossiter drew on his cigar until the end glowed through the ash.

'He'll suffer,' he said casually.

An aeroplane was circling over the sea, scattering leaflets that gleamed in the sunlight as they fluttered inland. Brown bodies leapt from the water to snatch at them, others scrambled for them on the beach. One leaflet escaped a clutching hand and drifted gently into Rossiter's lap. It was an advertisement for a local bar.

'Why did you bring us to Spain?'

Corbett asked. 'It doesn't make sense. You don't need us here, do you?'

Rossiter didn't want it to make sense. He had no intention of explaining that the scheme had expanded since he had taken charge. If the fool were naïve enough to believe that a gang of professionals would be satisfied with small pickings when a rich reward was offered elsewhere, so much the better. He could take his little cut, and be off to gloat on his revenge.

'I may do. And I'm not risking your getting cold feet at the last minute and busting the job wide open. I want you out of England. People like you have consciences, and consciences sometimes work.' He reached for a towel and wiped the perspiration from arms and torso. 'Anyway, what's wrong with a few days of Mediterranean sun for free? I don't hear any complaints from your wife.'

Corbett turned to look at the sea, trying to distinguish Eve from the throng of bodies that was almost as thick in the water as on the beach.

'What happens after you leave tomorrow?' he asked, narrowing his eyes against the sun.

'You stay here until Emilio says to go, and then you drive to Granada. You're booked in at the Alhambra Palace.' Rossiter chuckled. 'Nothing but the best for my friends.'

Corbett ignored the sarcasm. He needed Rossiter, but he feared him even more than he disliked him. Yet he could not keep the antagonism from his voice as he said sharply, 'I don't trust that bloody dago. He's too smooth by half.'

'I don't give a damn whether you trust him or not. We need Emilio, so don't start anything there.' As an afterthought he added. 'Besides, he'd eat you.'

'Perhaps. But tell him to lay off Eve.'

'I'll tell him.'

Not that there would be much point to it, Rossiter thought. It was the eager Eve who needed telling, not Emilio. Emilio might condescend to take what was so persistently offered, but he could not be so devoid of female admirers that he had to lay siege to a woman at least ten years his senior.

The aeroplane was back, dropping little plastic bags of sweets that spun as they fell. Watching them, Corbett said, 'When do we meet you at the airport?'

'Saturday. And it isn't an airport. It's a disused runway, built during the civil war. Emilio will show you.' Ash from the cigar fell on to Rossiter's chest, but he did not bother to brush it away. He had donned the dark glasses, and was staring over Corbett's shoulder. 'Ah! Here they come. Let's get back to the hotel. I'm bloody well roasted.'

They did not come from the sea, but from the far end of the Playa. Eve was chattering gaily, laughing up at her companion; but the smile on Emilio's face was fixed, and he did not look at her when he spoke. Rossiter guessed that he was bored. But Corbett saw only his wife's happiness, and that her hair and costume were dry, and knew that it was some time since they had left the water.

They collected their belongings and plodded across the beach to where Emilio's car was parked on the Paseo de

Gomis, picking their way round the prone bodies, their feet sinking in the hot, dry sand. Eve walked between Rossiter and Emilio, an arm linked with the young Spaniard's. Corbett, lagging behind, slowed by his twisted leg and the futility of a heavy stick in yielding sand, watched her with a gnawing love-hate emotion. He had never been a happy man, and the sense of injustice that had been with him for the past two years had intensified his inherent gloom. He had thought that in revenge he might find peace; now he doubted that. It seemed that one source of bitterness was to be exchanged for another. In the past he had shut his eyes to Eve's amorous affairs, but he could not shut his eyes to this. It was too blatant, too overpowering; the warmth and sunshine of Spain had induced her to abandon all restraint. And although he might take her away from Spain when their mission was accomplished — might even separate her from Emilio — the damage would have been done. This was something that neither he nor Eve would be able to forget.

Yet it was against Emilio that most of

his anger was directed. His grip on the stick contracted as he saw the linked arms tighten, bringing Eve's lightly tanned body closer to the golden warmth of the Spaniard's. If I catch them at it I'll kill him, he promised himself savagely. I'll bloody well kill him. Then the grip relaxed, and his jaw slackened in a sigh. The promise was an idle one. There would be no killing. Not of Emilio. Emilio, as Rossiter had said, would eat him.

By the time the others had reached the car he was some thirty yards behind. He paused to watch Emilio help Eve into her wrap, scowled as he saw her hand caress his arm, and then limped sullenly on. He would talk to her when they returned to the hotel. It would not stop her — nothing would stop her now — but at least it would make him feel less impotent, more of a man.

Eve was on the front seat, her head thrown back and her eyes closed; with her chestnut hair and her green wrap she was a flourish of colour against the drab grey of the upholstery. Rossiter had drawn

Emilio some distance from the car and was talking to him. It seemed to Corbett that there was something furtive and conspiratorial in their attitude, and he was immediately suspicious. What were they plotting that they wished to keep from him? Was it himself they were discussing? Or Eve?

He was careful not to use his stick as he stepped on to the Paseo and crossed to the car. The two men had their backs to him, and his canvas shoes made only a soft slurring sound as he dragged his bad leg over the tarmac. They kept their voices low, so that it was not until he was within a few feet of them that he was able to hear the words.

Emilio said doubtfully, 'But — against her own husband, Señor? Are you sure she will do it?'

'I'm sure,' Rossiter said. 'I'd say it's a bloody certainty.'

# 2

On most evenings the Everards dined by candlelight. Juanita preferred it; she had had candles in Spain, and she wanted them in England. But that evening there were no candles, and electric wall lamps shone brightly on polished mahogany and crystal glass and gleaming tableware. John Everard knew the reason for the change. Juanita was angry; and when there was friction between them she arranged things his way, not hers, so that he could find no opening for reproach. She became the dutiful wife, not the gay companion and lover. Only when the friction broke into words did her warm Spanish blood take over. Juanita had a talent for words.

He eyed her covertly across the table as they ate. The mood that was on her did not detract from her beauty. One day she might grow fat and ungainly like that obese Spanish aunt of hers, but now it was difficult to believe that that slim, tiny figure could ever be otherwise. Perversely she kept her head bent, not looking at him, the light glinting on jet-black hair swept smoothly back to the nape of her neck. But he could see the long, curling lashes, the tiny nose, the warm glow of flesh at throat and shoulders, and despite his own ill-humour he longed to rise from his chair and take her in his arms and tell her that he loved her.

But he did not. He went on with the meal, venting his mood on the cutlets with such savagery that presently Juanita looked up from her plate and said quietly, 'Is the meat tough? I am sorry. I will ask Mrs Chater to speak to the butcher.'

Her English was good, if often stilted. The daughter of a wealthy Spanish landowner and a Welsh mother, she had spent her childhood in Spain and most of her adolescence in England and Paris. It was in Paris, at a reception at the Spanish Embassy three years before, that she and John Everard had first met. Despite opposition from her father, they were married a year later.

He said curtly, 'It isn't tough.' And

then, because he had become impatient of their polite fencing and wanted to bring the quarrel to a head, he added, 'There's nothing wrong with the cutlets, and you know it. It's I who's at fault; isn't that what you're thinking? All right, then, say so.'

'Very well.' She had a quiet voice, speaking slowly and precisely. 'You have been irritable and contentious for weeks. Why? Is it something I have done that has upset you?'

'I've had good cause to be irritable.' He avoided the last question. 'That damned burglary, for a start.' He speared a sprout, eyed it balefully, then put down the fork and pushed his plate away. He was in no mood to relish food. 'What the hell do the police get up to when they're not handing out parking tickets? It's over three weeks since it happened, and I bet they haven't a clue to where the stuff went. I'm not so worried about the silver — the insurance company will pay up on that — it's the loss of the pictures that gets me down. They weren't insured.' He poured himself some wine, ignoring his wife's empty glass. 'It took me twenty years to collect that lot. Now they're gone — and probably for good.'

'How sad.' Three weeks ago she had been full of sympathy. Now sympathy had worn thin. She had heard the plaint too often, and had come to realize that it was the value of the pictures, not the pictures themselves, whose loss he regretted. 'But must you vent your bad temper on me? It was not my fault.'

'One can't turn a mood on or off at will.'

Neither the burglary, nor the inefficiency of the police, nor the fact that nothing had seemed to go right at the works of late, was the main cause of his ill-humour. There was more to it than that. But pride would not permit that he should tell her so.

'But are you not being unfair to the police? What are they supposed to do if the clues are not there? Invent them?'

He reached for his glass, gulping down the wine as if it were *vin ordinaire* rather than a *château Burgundy*.

'I can't stand inefficiency,' he muttered.

'I know,' she said quietly. 'You make that very plain, John, both at home and at the works. You despise people for their frailties — no es así?' It was seldom that she broke into Spanish. 'Yet we cannot all be as perfect as you.'

He looked at her sharply. It was not her sarcasm that troubled him, but the thought that her own particular frailty might be the one he suspected and feared.

'What do you know about the works?' he asked.

'A little. I have not been there so often since Tommy was born, but before that — ' She paused. There was a new earnestness to her voice as she looked at him, and her dark eyes were sad. 'They dislike you, John. Did you know that? No-one has said it to me — but I am not a fool, I know what they are thinking. There is an edge to their voices when they speak of you. They think you are hard, ruthless — and they are afraid. They remember what happened to poor Mr Manning and those other two men. One little mistake, and you dismissed them. It made no difference that they had worked so many years for the firm.' She sighed. 'The others — they know it could happen to them.'

'So it could. Mistakes cost money. We can't afford them.'

'We? The directors, you mean. But they dislike you too, John. Not one of them is your friend. They support you in what you do because it makes them rich, but they do not like you for it. Not as a person. I have heard them speaking to one another at those dull parties they give, and I know.'

He was about to reply that he did not need their friendship, only their co-operation, when the housekeeper came into the room. Mrs Chater was a good-looking woman in her forties, but her severe mode of dress and hairstyling did not do justice to her looks.

'Mr Laroche is on the telephone, Mrs Everard,' she said. She had a prim way of speaking, with only a slight movement of the lips. 'He'd like to speak to you.'

'Thank you.' Juanita stood up. 'I will take it in the sitting-room.'

As Mrs Chater cleared plates and dishes from the table and brought in the sweet, Everard sat staring moodily out of the window. Peter Laroche was the main cause of his ill-humour. He had moved into a neighbouring bungalow some five weeks previously, and had quickly wormed his way into their small circle of acquaintances. Everard had taken a dislike to him at sight — an effete, effeminate creature whom he suspected of being a homosexual until he observed his interest in Juanita — and did his best to ignore him. But Laroche was not easily ignored. He was constantly on the telephone or calling at the house, inviting them to the bungalow or suggesting an evening at the local; and he made no effort to disguise the fact that it was Juanita's company he wanted, not her husband's. At first Everard had regarded him as something of a joke. But of late he had begun to wonder. Juanita made no secret of her pleasure in the young man's admiration and attention. But was she as honest about what might so easily follow? What did the two of them get up to when he was away — as he so often was?

Pride had hitherto prevented his putting these questions to his wife. But pride was wearing thin under the constant friction of suspicion.

There was a faint smile on Juanita's lips when she returned. It seemed that the telephone conversation had temporarily erased their quarrel from her mind, for she said, almost gaily, 'Peter hoped to organize a party for this evening; he mentioned it when I saw him earlier. Something out of the ordinary, he said; a *chef d'oeuvre*.' She caught sight of her husband's face, and the smile faded. As she picked up her spoon she said flatly, 'He rang to say it was off.'

'As far as I'm concerned it was never on.'

'No? You used to enjoy parties.'

'I still do. But I'm particular about the company I keep.'

She put down the spoon, her face flushed. 'Meaning that I am not?'

'Meaning that you see far too much of that young pup.' His voice had thickened, his face and hands felt hot. He knew that

23

he was nearing the verge of indiscretion, of direct accusation. Yet although suspicion had blunted his pride he would not admit outright to jealousy. It must still be disguised, however thin the veneer. 'Most unwise. I should have thought that with your upbringing you would have known better.'

'We are not in Cordoba now, John.'

'No. But an English village can be equally censorious. What the hell do you see in him, anyway?'

'He amuses me.'

'H'm! I find him repulsive. All those 'dears' and 'darlings' and impossible 'r's. And the scent — ugh! Like a bloody queer.' He gulped at the wine. 'And what do we know of him? He calls himself a writer — but have you read anything he's written?'

'He is a critic, not an author.'

'Even critics write, don't they? But whatever he is or does, I still say you're overdoing the matiness.'

'Am I? Perhaps.' She plucked nervously at the brooch that narrowed the gap in the plunging neckline of her dress. 'Has it never occurred to you that I might be lonely here?'

'You have Mrs Chater.'

'Yes, I have Mrs Chater. But she is twice my age, and . . .'

Too late she realized the hurt she had done him. For John too was twice her age, although she had never thought of him as such. His body was as hard and as strong as his character, the thick brown hair showed no sign of grey. Only his face hinted at his years. There were lines in it that no young face should possess.

'Don't bother to spare my feelings,' he said bitterly. Juanita was twenty-two, he forty-three, and that gap in their ages had troubled him since the first weeks of their marriage. It had provided a hot-bed in which jealousy might flourish. 'You were about to imply that a young man's attentions are more acceptable than my own. All right. But it was me you married, not Laroche — although your behaviour of late might suggest to some that the reverse is the case.'

She glared at him across the table. Then she stood up.

'You know that is not true.' There was subdued fire in the quiet voice. 'You say it because your bad temper makes you want to hurt someone, and I am the obvious victim. Or is it that you are actually jealous?' She caught her breath at the thought, studying him wide-eyed. Slowly she shook her head, light glinting on the long emerald earrings. 'No, of course not. That is too human a weakness for John Everard.' She pushed her chair against the table with a slam that made the glasses rock. 'I am going upstairs. You have insulted me enough for one evening.'

As she walked from the room, head high, her slim body very straight, he longed to call her back and apologize, to admit that his accusations were unfounded, to tell her that he loved her. But he remained silent. Apologies were foreign to him, and love was a topic on which he had never been articulate. Even on their honeymoon the words of love had not come easily to him. He found them embarrassing, even slightly emasculating.

He was on his third brandy when Mrs

Chater returned to clear the table. She was a quiet, unobtrusive person, not given to chatter, and although she eyed him thoughtfully when she believed herself unobserved she did not speak. Neither did he. He was too angry, too miserable, to indulge in idle talk. He sat on in the dining-room after she had left, brooding on love and marriage and wondering where the latter had gone wrong. There had been too many such quarrels of late. Yet his own love had not faded; did it follow that Juanita's had? The possibility frightened him, for it was beyond his control and he would not know how to cope with it. If she should transfer her affections to Laroche . . .

He shook his head violently to clear the unwelcome thought from his mind. Then he drained his glass and stood up, not entirely steady on his feet but determined on a showdown. He would have it out with Juanita right now, while the mood was on him. Even if the truth should prove unpleasant it was better to know it than continue in uncertainty.

The house was quiet, nothing moved

on the lane outside; the stairs creaked faintly under his tread, as if in protest at this intrusion on the stillness. The silence had an unfriendly quality that sapped his confidence, and to combat it he walked heavily and purposefully along the landing. But outside their bedroom door he paused, uneasily aware that for once in his life he was uncertain how to handle a situation of his own creating. Yet it was too late now for planning. He opened the door and went in.

Juanita was not there.

He was so surprised by her absence that it took him some time to realize she might be with Tommy. But when he tried the nursery she was not there either. For a little while he stood watching the sleeping child. Then he went downstairs to the kitchen.

Mrs Chater sat at the table, writing. She looked up quickly at his entrance.

'Sorry to disturb you,' he apologized. 'I thought my wife might be here. She's not upstairs.'

'Mrs. Everard went out a few minutes ago,' she told him. 'She needed some fresh air, she said.'

'Oh? I didn't hear her.'

'She went out the back way.'

Everard hesitated, aware of an alien urge to confide in someone; and Mrs Chater had a strong if rather sad face, which hinted that she had known tragedy and had learned to live with it. They had first met her in the village pub, and in the course of conversation had discovered that she was leaving her post in London to look for one in the country; town life was not for her, she said. About a week later had come the burglary; and although they had been away at the time it had made Juanita nervous of being alone in the house at night, and they had agreed that she should engage a resident housekeeper. But he had not been prepared for the haste with which she had acted. How about references? he had asked, when he had returned home two days later to find Mrs Chater already installed; and Juanita had retorted that she was not interested in references, she preferred to trust her own judgment. It had annoyed him that she could be so imprudent, and he had made his own inquiries, hoping to confound her. But it was he who had been confounded; Mrs Chater's former employers, of whom he had some knowledge, had been liberal in their praise. He had not mentioned this to Juanita, however. It might encourage her to further imprudence.

He came out of his reverie to see Mrs Chater eyeing him with undisguised curiosity.

'I'm sorry,' he said. Somewhat regretfully he abandoned the idea of confiding in her. It would be difficult to unburden himself to a close friend, let alone to a woman who was a comparative stranger. 'I was day-dreaming.'

She smiled faintly. 'That doesn't sound like you, Mr Everard.'

'We all step out of character occasionally.' He mustered a smile in response. It seemed rude to hurry away, and he said idly, 'I hope you like it here.'

'Oh, yes. You've both been very kind.'

He shrugged off the compliment. 'I can't think how we managed without you. You don't find it lonely?'

'Not a bit.'

He had not meant to probe. But now he realized that the opening was there, and he decided to take it. Mrs Chater was at home more than he. If there was anything to know it was possible that she would know it.

'Sometimes I think my wife does,' he said. 'In fact, I've been wondering whether we should move into town. I'm away so much, and she'd be nearer her friends.'

'She doesn't seem lonely to me, Mr Everard. Quite the reverse. As for friends — well, she has Mr Laroche. They get on famously.'

'So I understand,' he said, hoping for detail. 'Odd, that. I wouldn't have thought they had much in common.'

'Perhaps not,' she agreed. 'But they're of an age, aren't they? That counts for a lot.' He looked at her sharply, but she seemed unaware of her *gaffe*. 'I think that sports car of his is part of the attraction. Didn't she used to drive in trials or something?'

'Rallies.'

'Yes, of course. Rallies.'

The probe seemed to have died on him. Seeking to revive it, he said, 'Well, I'm glad she has someone to amuse her when I'm away. And with you here she isn't tied to the house so much, of course.'

She gave that faint, tired smile of hers.

'I'm always glad to look after Tommy for her,' she assured him. 'And when she wants company she just rings up Mr Laroche, or pops down to see him. Through the woods, usually; it's quicker than by the lane. I'm sure there's no need for you to worry, Mr Everard.'

No need to worry!

He bade her good night and returned to the dining-room for a final brandy. Juanita would be home shortly; he would talk to her then. But when, twenty minutes later, Juanita had not returned, a new thought came to plague him. She had left by the back door, Mrs Chater had said — and from the back door one could cut through the woods to the bungalow. Was that where she had gone?

Had she, in her anger, sought consolation from Laroche?

He did not allow the thought to plague him for long. Because he did not know the way through the woods he went out by the front door and along the lane. The bungalow stood back among the trees, and he walked quickly down the winding path, despising himself for what he was doing and yet impelled to do it. As he rounded a bend he saw that the lights were on in the living-room, the curtains drawn. And then he stopped. Two figures had moved into silhouette behind the curtains. And one of them was a woman.

Later he was to reflect on his actions that evening; they were completely foreign to the controlled, impregnable person he considered himself to be. But he wasted no time on reflection now. Abandoning discretion, he ran to the front door and banged the knocker furiously. When no-one answered his knock he banged again, and kept on banging until, after what seemed like an age, the door was suddenly opened and Peter Laroche stood there, staring at him in bewilderment.

'What the hell? Oh, it's you, John.' The door opened wider. 'Anything wrong? You looked chuffed.'

Everard scowled at him. The familiar, unauthorized use of his Christian name by this baby-faced youth, with his long hair and his rosebud lips and fine, curling lashes, never failed to annoy him.

'Is my wife here?' he demanded.

'Juanita? No. Should she be?'

Everard pushed past him and stalked into the living-room. Laroche closed the door and followed.

'Come on in,' he said. 'Don't wait to be asked.'

Juanita was not in the room, and he could see no evidence that she had been. Yet some woman had. A woman, too, whose presence would have been embarrassing to Laroche — or why had she so suddenly vanished? Where had she gone? Had she left by the back door? Or was she hiding in one of the bedrooms until he should leave?

'Sorry.' The apology came reluctantly to Everard's lips, but he would not give

Laroche the satisfaction of learning the truth. 'My wife went for a short stroll after dinner — said she'd be only a few minutes. That was some time ago, and she hasn't returned. It got me worried. I thought she might be here.'

If Laroche needed an opening to admit to Juanita's presence in the bungalow he did not take it.

'Sow-wy.' He lisped the syllables slowly, wandering idly round the room, his fingers caressing walls and furniture. 'But not to wow-wy, my deah. She must have gone farther than she intended. You know how impulsive the dahling is. Have a dwink?'

Everard did not answer. He was staring at a small china ornament depicting a rustic youth clutching a large red heart in his hands. Juanita had given it or its fellow to him the previous Easter, after Tommy was born. 'That is you, my darling,' she had said, 'and that is my heart you are holding. Be careful not to break it.'

Her *prenda de amor*, she had called it. Her love token. And now she had given it to this disgusting little squirt.

'Where did you get that?' he demanded.

'Lover boy?' Laroche strolled over to the ornament and examined it. 'Howwible, isn't it? Or do you like it? Take it, my deah, if you want it. It does nothing for me.'

Everard clenched his fists. 'Where did you get it?'

'Where?' Laroche pursed his little mouth into a circle. 'I don't wemember. A girl, I suppose; I wouldn't have bought it, would I?' The lips parted in a knowing smile. 'The dahlings lose their taste in art when they're stuck on a man. They just want to be expwessive.'

Everard wanted to hit him. But that would solve nothing, and he pushed him roughly aside and strode angrily out of the bungalow without another word. Laroche could wait. It was Juanita he had to talk to now.

She was at the dressing-table when he walked into the room, leaning forward to peer into the mirror as she rubbed cream into her face with the tips of her slender fingers. It was a nightly ritual he knew

36

well. Her hair was down, a dark cascade that fell below her shoulders. Sometimes, in the winter evenings, she wore it that way to please him. In the summer it was too hot, she said.

She looked up at his entrance. 'Have you come to apologize?' she asked quietly. 'Or do you still think I have behaved badly?'

Even with the cream on her face, and in the voluminous negligée that hid her supple form, she managed to look seductively feminine. There was an appeal in her dark eyes that belied the coolness in her voice. But Everard saw neither the femininity nor the appeal. He had eyes only for that corner of the dressing-table where the china ornament had always stood.

It was not there now.

# 3

For some time Emilio had been silent, concentrating on the road. But as they came down the long winding descent and entered the straight stretch that vanished ahead into a line of low hills and jagged peaks he turned to Eve and smiled.

'Guadix,' he said, pointing. 'We stop there.'

Eve looked where he pointed. The town stood on a hillside, aloof and lonely; its walls hotly red in the afternoon sun, and in vivid contrast to the snow-capped Sierra Nevada beyond.

'It doesn't look very inviting,' she said.

Corbett stirred in the back. He said hoarsely, 'Rossiter said to go direct to the hotel in Granada. Why stop here?'

'I am thirsty,' Emilio told him. 'So are you, eh? And in Guadix I have friends.'

Corbett did not protest further. After the long hot drive a drink would be welcome, even if it had to be taken in the company of Emilio and his friends.

Eve had enjoyed the first part of the journey. This was her first trip abroad, and there had been plenty to arouse her interest: the vast palmery of Elche, the towers and coloured domes of Murcia, the steep streets and white-washed houses of Lorca. There had been novelty too in the roadside hedges of aloes and prickly pear, in the groves of oranges and olives and pomegranates, in the stately avenue of palms that led to the *albergue* at Puerto Lumbreras, where they had lunched. But soon the road had climbed into a wilderness of flat hills, its bare monotony relieved only by the stunted crops and fruit trees of an occasional *barranca*, or by a group of cave dwellings hollowed out of a high cliff face. For mile after uneventful mile she had sat beside Emilio, with her husband watching them suspiciously from the back. She had hoped that Andrew might sleep; then she could have moved closer to Emilio, made him more aware of her. Since Rossiter had left he had been less responsive, which annoyed and distressed her. But

Emilio drove fast; and although the road was for the most part good, at times it deteriorated unexpectedly into a series of ridges or pot-holes which caused the Seat to bounce on its axles, making sleep impossible. Now, bored and hot and uncomfortable, she welcomed the news that they were to stop.

It was even hotter in the town than on the road. They drove into an arcaded square and parked the car where a group of mules and donkeys stood dejectedly, as though they too found the heat oppressive; heads down, flanks quivering and tails swishing spasmodically against the swarming flies. The houses were shuttered, the few people in the square eyed the visitors stolidly. But the air was not still. A hot wind blew, and as they left the car and climbed the hill it came swirling down the street, picking up dust from the dry, gritty soil and flinging it in their faces, offending their nostrils with the smell of garbage and decay. The street deteriorated to a track, the track to a rocky path which threaded its way between small, one-storeyed houses. And then the houses ceased, giving way to caves cut into the soft rock, with white-washed fronts and small courtyards and pots of flowers at the entrances, and an occasional vine growing on crudely constructed trellis-work.

Emilio had been helping Eve up the hill, a hand at her elbow. Near the top he paused to wait for her husband. To Eve the wind here seemed even hotter and smellier, and she took the scarf from her head and tied it round nose and mouth. She felt messy and irritable; but she managed a smile for her companion as she said, her voice muffled, 'Not exactly attractive, is it? What a place to live!'

'Is Barrio,' he said. 'Barrio de Santiago. Very famous place.' He pointed vaguely to the south. 'Over there the *gitanos*.'

Corbett came up to them, limping painfully. His face was still red from the sun, but the lines in it looked deeper, etched in the dust of Guadix.

'What the hell are you playing at?' he demanded. 'Do we have to come this far for a bloody drink? What's the game?'

'No game, Señor,' Emilio told him

blandly. 'And not far now.'

They went on over the crest of the hill, and as the track dipped again Eve paused in astonishment. So did her husband. Below them a vast rocky amphitheatre stretched to the far hill peaks — a lunar landscape of cones, pinnacles and ravines, red and yellow and orange in colour, and criss-crossed by tracks. It was as though a sea of molten lava had swept over the escarpment, cutting innumerable channels in the soft rock and solidifying as it went. And everywhere were the cave dwellings; row upon row, tier upon tier, scooped out of the antheap-like pinnacles or cut into the cliff face, the flat roof of one forming the courtyard of another, its cowled chimney projecting like a small, squat lighthouse. Most of the cave fronts, their courtyards and roofs, even the chimneys, had been white-washed; and against this backdrop of white the potted plants at the entrances, the dark squares of the windows, the goats and pigs tethered to the chimneys, were sharply defined. A few sad-looking trees, an occasional cactus or prickly pear, the thin haze of grass which clothed some of the rock pinnacles, were the only signs of vegetation.

The stench that came from a myriad open drains caused Eve to wrinkle her nose in disgust and pull the scarf tighter over her mouth as she followed Emilio down the hill. The dark-skinned men and women who stared at her from the cave entrances made her uneasy, but she forgot them in the crowd of shouting, pestering children who came running from all directions to swarm around them and impede their progress. A few looked reasonably clean and well-dressed, but many were in rags. Some of the smallest were naked. A girl in a tattered frock, with the snake-like locks of the gypsy and the filthiest face Eve had ever seen, caught at her dress and held it. Terrified, not daring to touch her, Eve stood still — until Andrew with his stick, and Emilio with a loudly abusive tongue, drove the children away.

'They are a nuisance, los niños,' Emilio said equably, taking her hand.

Eve thought they were horrible. She

disliked all children, and some of the faces she had seen there looked demented as well as dirty. It was a blessed relief when Emilio led her across a courtyard lined with potbellied jars of olive oil, skirted an inquisitive goat, and ducked through a porched doorway into the shadowy interior beyond.

It was cool inside. The room was large, with white-washed walls and a tiled floor. At one end bottles were stacked on a wooden bar, and beyond that an opening led to another room in which electric light glowed feebly behind a beaded curtain. A fan spun lazily in the arched roof.

Two men rose from their seats at a table and embraced Emilio. To the Corbetts he introduced them as Federo and Antonio. Apart from a lean, handsome woman who brought them wine and then retired behind the curtain, they were the only people in the bar.

The five of them sat together at the table and drank the wine from narrow, heavy glasses. It was strong and sour, and despite her thirst Eve only sipped it. So did Andrew; but the others drank freely, conversing in rapid Spanish. For the most part they kept their voices low, leaning across the table, their heads close together. Occasionally Antonio's harsh, rasping voice would grow loud with excitement, quickly to be hushed by Emilio. Eve wondered at this caution; there was none to hear them. She understood Spanish better than she spoke it, although her vocabulary was limited; and at first she listened idly to their talk. They were discussing plans for the week-end. Soon, however, she abandoned the strain of trying to translate and concentrated on their appearance. Neither of Emilio's friends impressed her favourably. Both wore lightweight suits, with draped jackets and pointed shoes, and flat caps on their heads. Antonio was in the middle forties, squat and hairy; a rough, tough-looking man with a black patch over one eye and the other bloodshot and watery. Federo was some twenty years younger; unlike Antonio he wore a tie, bright red and food-stained. Eve decided he was a gypsy. He had a swarthy skin, and a mass of greasy black hair that flopped over his face, partially hiding the sharp button eyes. When he moved he moved jerkily, like a puppet. He looked at her frequently, his bright eyes lingering frankly on the plump, well-defined figure in the gay summer frock. But it was not a look to which she was accustomed. It contained appraisal rather than admiration, as though he were assessing the merits of some beast at a fat-stock show.

It was Federo's glances which reminded her that she could not be looking her best, and she reached for her handbag. Making up her face, intent on her mirror rather than on her companions, she found herself listening again to their conversation. But it was Emilio's use of the word *mujer* which drew her full attention. He's talking about me, she thought, flattered — and was thankful for Andrew's complete ignorance of the language.

She soon realized she had been mistaken. This was another woman they were discussing; a woman who, according to Emilio, would be arriving with Grant

Rossiter. That puzzled her. Andrew had told her that only three people would be on the plane; Rossiter and two of his accomplices. Because they were unusual, she could even remember the two men's names: Albemarle Johnson and Constant Smith. Rossiter had referred to the latter as 'Connie'. Did that account for Emilio's mistake? Had he assumed that 'Connie' was a woman?

She wanted to ask him. But she was reluctant to admit to her smattering of Spanish; he would expect her to employ it when they were together, and it was so much easier to be ardent in a familiar tongue. She would also be admitting to eavesdropping, and from the appearance of Emilio's friends she suspected that the admission would not be kindly received. Even Emilio looked different; his handsome face was no longer smiling, and the occasional quick glance he gave her showed no recognition. Indeed, there was a furtiveness about all three of them which made her uneasy, even a little afraid. They looked more like a bunch of conspirators than a reunion of old friends.

She put away the lipstick and the mirror, and snapped the bag shut. Federo was staring at her again. It was wrong to judge people (and foreigners in particular) by their looks, and she smiled at him nervously, content now with her appearance. Apparently it made no impact on Federo. He stared for some time, unsmiling, and then said something which made his companions laugh. Furious — Federo's remark, she was sure, had concerned her — she turned to her husband. But Andrew was gazing morosely at the tiled floor, and her attempts to engage him in conversation were met by a series of grunts. There was no comfort there.

Avoiding Federo's eyes, she sipped her wine and listened, wishing she had bothered to learn more of the venture on which they were engaged. Until now her sole interest had been in the promise of a large sum of money, with no risk to herself and little to her husband. She had not concerned herself with the mechanics of the venture, or the moral aspect, or with Andrew's fanatical desire for vengeance. But money was always interesting, no matter how acquired.

Presently Antonio mentioned a name — it sounded like Alamadilla — and as they talked she realized it was the name of a place to which Rossiter and his companions would be going on their arrival. But they used the word *escondido*, and that puzzled her. According to Andrew, Rossiter had been emphatic that none of them need go into hiding. Why, then, this talk of concealment?

Suddenly she was afraid again. For she remembered how Rossiter had assured them that Emilio was the only Spaniard in his confidence — and that Emilio knew how to keep his mouth shut. Yet here he was, discussing Rossiter's plans with these two villainous-looking Spaniards, and discussing them in a manner that made it plain, even to her, that Antonio and Federo were not to be mere spectators. Somehow, somewhere, they intended to participate.

Did Rossiter know this? Or were Emilio and his friends hatching some sinister counterplot?

# 4

At a quarter to eleven that Friday morning the three closed vans came down the road from the town, dead on time. There were always three — that had been one of John Everard's innovations on becoming managing director — but only one carried the money from the bank. Joe Sharpe, the gateman at Anstey and Rylance's, knew the procedure. As the convoy drew level with the entrance, the van with the money (it differed each week) would turn off the road, he would open the gate to let it through into the yard, and close the gate again. The two other vans, their security mission accomplished, would move on down the road to the firm's main car park.

The convoy was still a hundred yards away when a black Jaguar overtook it and came on at a smart pace. Joe Sharpe, always alert to possible danger at this moment, watched it anxiously. As it slowed and turned into the entrance he reached for the gate telephone. Then he recognized the driver, and relaxed. Saluting smartly, he opened the gate, and held it while both Jaguar and van drove through. With a wave of greeting to the van driver, he closed the gate and turned to watch. The sight of so much money being unloaded never failed to fascinate him, even though he never saw the actual cash. Twenty-five thousand pounds, someone said it was. Every week. What couldn't he and Milly do with just one of those weekly deliveries!

The two vehicles crossed the yard and stopped outside the office block. The four occupants of the Jaguar seemed in no hurry to leave it; they sat talking while the van driver and the guard alighted and moved round to unlock the rear doors. But as the first cases were unloaded came swift and violent action. Three men leapt from the car and made for the van behind. For a moment Joe hesitated, unable to believe that anything could be wrong. Then he saw the coshes, and hesitated no longer.

The men from the Jaguar moved fast. As Joe shouted for help and started across the yard the coshes rose and fell, and he saw the van driver and guard go down. Other men, alerted by his shouts, were emerging from the workshops and running towards the office block. But Joe had a good start. He was less than twenty yards from the scene when he saw that one of the robbers had a gun — and that it was pointed at him.

'Stop right there!' the man shouted. The others were bundling the cases into the back of the car. 'Stop, you fool!'

He tried to stop. But impetus carried him on, and the man with the gun did not wait. Joe did not see him press the trigger, did not hear the shot. There was just a sudden, searing pain in his leg; and with a cry that was half-agony, half-anger, he crumpled and fell.

★ ★ ★

Seated in the corner of a first class compartment, with a full brief case and a pile of unread newspapers beside him,

Everard shut his mind to business affairs and pondered what he should say to Juanita when they met. He knew that he should have stayed another night in Bristol; the programme had been too full to crowd into a day and a half. But for the first time in his life a personal problem had taken precedence over work. He had to get home.

He thought back to Wednesday evening, when he had returned from the bungalow to question Juanita about the china ornament. He had been prepared for a scene of heated and bitter wrangling; but Juanita had seemed genuinely puzzled and distressed by its disappearance, and at the sight of her tears he had not the heart to accuse her of having given it to Laroche. Somewhat stiffly he had done his best to comfort her, had even managed an inadequate apology for his earlier behaviour. Yet later, when she had fallen asleep in his arms, doubt and suspicion had returned. Tears were a woman's first line of defence. Had hers been genuine?

They had seemed genuine. So had her behaviour the next morning, when outwardly at least she had been the warm, loving wife — getting up early to breakfast with him, packing his suitcase, driving him to the station. She had even found time to question Mrs Chater about the missing ornament. But Mrs Chater, it seemed, had never noticed it on the dressing-table and could supply no explanation for its disappearance. Juanita had decided that Mrs Long, the daily woman, must be the culprit. 'Perhaps she broke it when she was dusting, and forgot to tell me,' she said, kissing him goodbye. 'She would not know it had a sentimental value. But I will buy you another like it, darling. They still had a few left in the shop when I was there last week.'

That final item of information had given him some comfort, since it provided the possibility that the ornament he had seen in Laroche's bungalow was not the one Juanita had bought. He had departed on his journey with a lighter heart. But that had been thirty-two hours ago; and in that time, and without Juanita's glowing presence to confound it, doubt had returned. Much as he wanted to believe her, jealousy would not permit.

At his home station he was surprised to see Mrs Chater alight from the train. She seemed equally surprised to see him.

'We weren't expecting you until tomorrow,' she told him.

'I finished earlier than I anticipated. Is my wife meeting you with the car?'

'Oh, no. She and Tommy are spending the day with a friend. A Miss Walker. Do you know her?' Everard nodded. 'I took the opportunity to do some shopping in Town. Mrs Everard said it would be all right.'

They took a taxi from the station. As they neared the house Colclough, the local police constable, stepped out from the hedge to watch them pass, then reached for his bicycle and pedalled off down the lane.

Everard frowned. 'Very zealous, the police, now that we have nothing left worth stealing. Did you tell them the house would be empty this afternoon?'

'No. And I'm sure Mrs Everard didn't. Perhaps it was Mrs Long.'

Juanita and Tommy had not returned.

'I'll see about dinner,' Mrs Chater said, removing her coat. 'Mrs Everard expected to be back by six, and it's nearly that now. She said not to bother about a meal, seeing as she'd be on her own. But a poached egg won't do for you, will it?'

He agreed that it would not.

Despite his disappointment that Juanita was not at home to greet him, it was a relief to know that for that day at least she had not been with Laroche. Molly Walker had been a friend of her mother — an eccentric, middle-aged woman who lived in a converted stable and collected junk. Or what Everard considered to be junk. Molly called it Victoriana.

With his mind more at rest he settled down to study the documents in his brief case. But an hour later, when Juanita still had not returned, he began to feel uneasy. Seven o'clock was not late, but it was late for Tommy. He was always fed at six. Had Juanita had trouble with the car?

He decided to ring Molly.

'Why, hello, John!' Molly had a bark like a sea-lion. 'Nice to hear from you. What's your problem?'

'Has Juanita left yet?' He wasted no time on pleasantries. 'She told the housekeeper she'd be home by six.'

'Eh? I don't get it. Left where?'

'Hasn't she been spending the day with you?'

'Heavens, no! Haven't seen her for weeks. What made you think she was here?'

'Just a guess,' he told her. 'Sorry.'

So that was it. Supposing him to be in Bristol until the morrow, Juanita had spent the day with Laroche. She might even be intending to spend the night with the little bastard. At any moment the telephone might ring, and it would be Juanita calling Mrs Chater to tell her that she would be staying overnight with Molly Walker, that she would be home some time the next morning. The tears and protestations of Wednesday night, the wifely care of Thursday morning, had been utterly false. And he, blind fool, had almost been persuaded by them.

He went into the dining-room and poured himself a whisky, his hands so unsteady that much of the spirit missed the glass. He drank it neat and then another, the tears smarting in his eyes. Only after the fourth whisky did he feel sufficiently composed to confront Mrs Chater.

She was puzzled but not alarmed.

'I can't understand it,' she said, busy with the mixer. 'She said Miss Walker had telephoned to ask her over, and that she'd be out for lunch and tea. That was last night, after Mr Laroche had left.' Everard's fingernails dug into his palms, and he unclenched his fists. 'She must have changed her mind. I wonder why she didn't tell me.'

'What time did she leave?' He had not mentioned that Molly had telephoned no invitation. Only that Juanita and Tommy had not been there.

'About nine-thirty. She was going to do the shopping on the way.' It was warm in the kitchen, and she wiped her brow with the back of a hand. 'Shouldn't you ring the police, Mr Everard? They may have had an accident. It's not like Mrs Everard to keep Tommy out so late.'

Everard hesitated. He had been imagining them together in some hotel room, with Tommy in his carrycot at the foot of the double bed. But wasn't it as likely that they were at the bungalow? No-one, they must have supposed, would be looking for them. The bungalow would be as secure a place of assignation as any hotel.

'I'll speak to Mr Laroche first,' he said. 'You say he was here last night. My wife may have discussed her plans with him.'

If they had been at the bungalow earlier they were not there now. The building was unoccupied. He walked all round it, peering in at the windows. The beds were made, the rooms as tidy as if they had never been lived in. Even in his anger and misery he was puzzled by that. Why should Laroche have put his house in order if he intended to be away for one night only?

Mrs Chater was waiting for him in the hall when he returned.

'There's a policeman to see you, Mr Everard,' she said, a note of anxiety in her prim voice. 'He's in the study. I do hope nothing has happened to Mrs Everard.'

The policeman was a tall, smartly dressed man of around fifty, with a ruddy complexion and heavy jowls. His thick neck, broad shoulders, and massive chin gave the impression of considerable strength, but his voice was soft and musical. He introduced himself as Detective Superintendent Morgan, and the grip as he shook hands was muscular.

'It's about the wages snatch at Anstey and Rylance's this morning, sir,' he said. 'Perhaps you can tell me — ' He saw the look of astonishment on Everard's face, and paused. 'You haven't heard?'

'I've heard nothing.' It was a relief to have a new focus for his thoughts. 'I got back from Bristol less than two hours ago. What happened?'

'They cleared the entire payroll. Around twenty-three thousand pounds, I understand.' The superintendent mopped his brow with a silk handkerchief, ran a well-manicured finger round the inside of his collar, and carefully adjusted his bow tie. 'Warm, isn't it? Mind if we have a window open?'

Everard did not find it particularly warm, but he opened a window. 'I don't understand,' he said. 'I thought my precautions were foolproof. And incidentally, why wasn't I informed? I'm the managing director, dammit! My secretary would have told you where I was.'

'She did, sir. She also told us you would be in Bristol until tomorrow. We tried to get you at your hotel, but you had already left. It wasn't until the local police informed us you were back that we knew where to contact you.'

So that, thought Everard, explains Colclough's unaccustomed zeal.

'All right,' he said impatiently. 'What went wrong?'

'Something you hadn't allowed for, apparently. A robbery inside the gates.'

'Inside? You mean some of the firm's employees were involved?'

'No. Just that the gateman admitted the thieves' car at the same time as the van, and as soon as unloading started the blighters took over. I'm afraid the gateman got himself shot in the process; when he saw what was happening he tried to interfere. However, I understand he's in no danger. Just a flesh wound.' The soft voice hesitated. 'Is your wife at home, Mr Everard?'

'No.' What had Juanita to do with this? 'But what the devil did that fool Sharpe think he was doing? He had strict instructions — '

'I know, sir. But it seems that on this occasion he decided it would be safe to use his discretion. You see, he recognized both car and driver. A black Jaguar — driven by your wife.'

Everard stared at him. What was the man saying? Juanita and Tommy had been with Laroche, were presumably with him still. Why else would Juanita have lied to Mrs Chater about Molly Walker?

'Impossible,' he snapped. 'Quite impossible. Sharpe must have been mistaken.'

Morgan shook his head. He had a big head, with small ears and a wide mouth.

'Others recognized her too, Mr Everard. What's more, we've identified the car. It was found abandoned a few miles from the works.'

'And my wife and son?'

Morgan shrugged. 'I was hoping they'd be here.'

Improbable as it seemed, Everard knew it was true. Inefficient the police might be, but it was unlikely they were mistaken in this. Not with positive identification of car and driver. And mingled with this new anxiety was a sensation of relief that at least Juanita was not with Laroche. She and Tommy would have been on their way to meet him when the thieves hi-jacked them.

'It must have been very carefully planned,' he said, frowning.

'Such raids usually are, sir.'

'I know. What I mean is, they didn't pick on the Jaguar by chance. It wasn't so much the car they needed as the driver. Without my wife at the wheel they'd never have got through the gates.'

'Or out again. Once in, the gates would be closed. They'd know that. But I'm told there's a temporary exit at the rear which anyone familiar with the site would know.'

Everard nodded. 'By the new buildings. Tricky for a car, but my wife has used it once or twice, I believe.' Where did Laroche fit into this? Or didn't he? But right now neither Laroche nor the robbery was his main concern, and he said sharply, 'What has happened to my wife and son, Superintendent? Can you tell me that?'

'No, sir, I can't. We're doing all we can to trace them, but so far we've drawn only blanks.'

His apparent complacency angered Everard. He said heatedly, 'Dammit, man, it's over eight hours since the robbery! The thieves wouldn't hamper their escape by taking them with them. They've probably dumped them somewhere.' He frowned. 'Why didn't they leave them in the car, I wonder?'

Morgan said blandly, 'They'd have their reasons, I expect. Tell me, sir — where was your wife going when she left here this morning?'

Everard's anger vanished. Pride was back. It forbade that he should mention Laroche, and Molly Walker was out. The police could easily check that Molly had issued no invitation — and that he knew it.

'Friday is her morning for the week-end shopping,' he said.

'Taking the baby with her?'

'I don't know. I'm not usually here.'

What was the man getting at? What did it matter where Juanita had been going? But the interrogation had taken an awkward turn. Swallowing his dislike of all policemen, he said, 'I'm being inhospitable. May I offer you a drink?'

'No, thank you, sir.'

'Cigarette?'

'I'm a non-smoker.' The invitation seemed to remind Morgan that he lacked something. There was the rustle of a paper bag as he rummaged in his jacket pocket, and he popped an acid-drop into his mouth. 'You wouldn't know if Mrs Everard took a suitcase with her?'

'How the hell should I? But it seems highly unlikely. Does your wife usually go shopping with a suitcase?'

'I'm a bachelor, Mr Everard.' There was regret in the superintendent's voice. 'And we haven't yet established that the shops were your wife's objective, have we? Perhaps your housekeeper could help us there.'

'Perhaps. But as my wife never got to wherever it was she was going, I can't see that it's important.' He poured himself a generous whisky. 'It's where she is now that matters. Can't you chaps concentrate on that?'

'We're as anxious as you to find them, Mr Everard.' The superintendent sucked hard on his acid-drop. 'Now, sir — how about the housekeeper? No, don't fetch her — ' as Everard moved towards the door. 'Isn't that a bell push by the fireplace?'

Mrs Chater answered the bell promptly; so promptly that Everard wondered if she had been listening in the hall. Before Morgan could speak he said quickly, 'The superintendent wants to ask you about my wife's shopping expedition this morning.'

Morgan frowned. But Mrs Chater took the hint. She had not actually seen Mrs Everard leave that morning, she said. She had been in the kitchen, and Mrs Everard had looked in to say she was off. She had not mentioned the shops; but they had made out the list the previous day, and where else would she be going? As for Tommy — well, sometimes she took him and sometimes she didn't. A suitcase?

Mrs Chater couldn't say. But it wasn't likely, was it?

Everard nodded approval. One could rely on Mrs Chater.

'Satisfied, Superintendent?' he asked.

'No, sir.' Morgan crunched the remaining sliver of acid-drop and swallowed hastily. With unaccustomed diffidence he said, 'I'm sorry to be insistent, but I've reason to believe that your wife *did* take a suitcase with her this morning. So would you please check if any of her clothes are missing? Oh — and your son's too, while you're about it.'

Everard stared at him. Then, stifling the indignant protest that sprang to his lips, he left the room and went upstairs. As he reached the landing his steps slowed. The robbery, the way Juanita and Tommy had become involved, his anxiety over what might have happened to them since, had pushed jealousy into the background. Morgan's talk of a suitcase had revived it. He did not know what was in the superintendent's mind, but his own was full of misgiving.

The bedroom confirmed his fears.

Juanita's toilet accessories had gone from the dressing-table, some of her dresses from the wardrobe; and without bothering to look further he sat down on the bed and held his aching head in his hands. She had taken more than would be needed for a day and a night; this was no escapade, she had been leaving him for good. Had the thieves not interfered she and Laroche would have been starting a new life together. Perhaps that explained the state of Laroche's bungalow. No doubt with Juanita's assistance, he had put it in order before leaving because he knew he would not be returning.

For some minutes Everard stayed on the bed. Presently a new thought occurred to him, and he went over to the small bureau and searched it feverishly. That was where Juanita kept her passport. It was not there now.

He did not go to the nursery. The state of Tommy's wardrobe would tell him nothing. He went directly to the study and confronted the superintendent.

'You were right. Some of her things are missing.' With difficulty he kept the tremor from his voice. 'I don't know how you guessed — perhaps you found her suitcase in the car — but before you start jumping to all sorts of conclusions I had better explain that my wife and I quarrelled before I left for Bristol yesterday. It was only a trivial matter; but my wife is Spanish and impulsive, and she must have brooded on it while I was away.' He found the superintendent's unblinking gaze disconcerting, and began to pace up and down the room. Mrs Chater watched him from the window, her faded grey eyes expressionless. 'I can only suppose she decided, on the spur of the moment, to take Tommy on a visit to her father in Spain. Her passport is also missing.'

Morgan shook his head.

'There was no suitcase in the car, Mr Everard. And if your wife has gone abroad I doubt if it is to visit her father.' He took a brown envelope from his pocket and showed it to Mrs Chater. 'Have you seen that before, ma'am?'

'Why, yes!' she said. 'I recognize the colour. It came this morning. I took it up to Mrs Everard with her breakfast.'

There was compassion in the superintendent's eyes as he handed the envelope to Everard.

'You had better read it, sir,' he said. 'We found it in the Jaguar, tucked under the driving seat.'

The stamp and postmark had been torn off, and with them part of the surname. But there was no doubt that the envelope had been addressed to Juanita. As he withdrew the single sheet of paper and saw the unfamiliar writing Everard wondered unhappily what new blow was about to be dealt him.

'Okay, bring the kid with you,' the note ran. 'We can dump him, or we might even use him as camouflage for the gateman's benefit. That's up to you. But once the job's done we're splitting up. You and the kid will be on your own. You'll get your cut later.'

There was no signature.

# 5

They sat on the wide terrace of the Alhambra Palace, high on the hillside, and drank their gin. Each was careful to avoid the eyes of the other two. The city of Granada lay spread below, the Genil River a dark blue ribbon in the sunshine; in the distance the tall range of the Sierra Nevada glowed warmly under its mantle of snow. Yet none of the three showed much interest in the view. Only Emilio looked relaxed; he sipped meditatively, apparently lost in contemplation of his long, pointed shoes. The others drank compulsively, as an antidote to speech. Eve was particularly nervous. She wished now that she had not told Andrew what she had overheard in the Guadix bar; it had increased his enmity towards Emilio to the point where it almost equalled his hatred for John Everard and his former employers. Without shifting her gaze she could see the knuckles white on his lean fingers, drained of blood as they clenched the heavy knob of his stick, and guessed that he was remembering the previous afternoon in the Alcazar. That had been a mistake; she must be more careful in future. Yet his jealousy excited at the same time as it disturbed her. Jealousy was not new in Andrew. But it had never been so intense. It added spice to the richness of her desire for the young Spaniard.

Had Andrew not been present she would have watched Emilio now. The dark beauty of his profile fascinated her. She no longer suspected him of duplicity. In one of the brief moments in which she had managed to be alone with him she had told him how the word *mujer* had caught her attention. That was a Spanish word she knew; had he been discussing her? She had managed to sound aggrieved; and Emilio had smilingly assured her that he never discussed his lady friends. This was another woman, he said, one who would be arriving in the aeroplane; Rossiter had told him to find somewhere for the woman to stay, and Antonio and Federo were arranging it.

Because she wanted to believe, because every fibre of her body clamoured for him, she had accepted his explanation unreservedly. Emilio had become a challenge she found irresistible. That he was a somewhat reluctant lover only made the challenge more potent. She was too experienced, too practical, to expect that she could hold him. She did not even know that she wanted to hold him. It was the thrill of conquest, not the dourness of retention, that possessed her.

Andrew Corbett was tired, physically and mentally. They had reached Granada on the Thursday evening; now it was Saturday. He had not been allowed to rest on the Friday; Eve had been bent on sight-seeing, and jealousy would not permit that she should go with Emilio alone. He had spent the morning following them around the city, inspecting a cathedral he was too weary to admire, and visiting innumerable shops in search of souvenirs. But it was the long climb back to the hotel for lunch that had tired him most. Eve had insisted on walking, and he had laboured painfully up the hill, constantly dropping behind and spurring his aching body for fear that he might lose them. He had almost welcomed Eve's guarded account of the conversation in the Guadix bar, had disregarded completely Emilio's interpretation. He believed in Emilio's duplicity because, unlike Eve, he wanted to believe in it. It galled him that he could take no immediate and decisive action. But he got a grim satisfaction from the prospect of exposing the traitor to Rossiter.

He was to get no other satisfaction that day. They had toured the Alhambra in the afternoon, with Eve exhibiting a restless energy which her husband recognized only too well. It was born, he knew, of the heat which was in her blood and which he had never been able to assuage. Yet because in his bleak, unhappy way he loved her, he did not largely blame her. His anger was for the man.

Emilio had disdained the services of a guide; he knew the fortress well. Eve was more interested in him than in his information. She had exclaimed fitfully at the solid red walls, at the view from the

Alcazaba tower (Corbett had almost lost them there), at the exquisite tracery and slender columns and elegant Arab baths of the Alcazar; but always her eyes had returned to Emilio's face, with her body close to his, demanding recognition. The beauty of the surroundings seemed to intensify his youthful grace, and she had hurried him from room to room, discretion gone, seeking to lose her husband and be alone with her demigod for a brief, ecstatic moment.

It was in the Patio de Los Leones that she succeeded. As usual Corbett had dropped behind. A group of sight-seers hindered his progress, and by the time he had elbowed his way through them Eve and Emilio had disappeared. For a few frantic minutes he searched, to find them eventually in the Patio de la Reja. The sound of his stick must have warned them of his approach, for he did not see the embrace; but the slackness of Eve's mouth as she turned, the wild look in her eyes, told him all he needed to know. From Emilio he learned nothing.

Emilio had smiled enigmatically and had continued the tour as though nothing untoward had happened; and Corbett had swallowed his rage and his pride, and followed. He had even gone with them late that night to watch the gypsy dancing at Sacro Monte — so that when, at two-thirty in the morning, he had crawled into bed, he was too tired to sleep. But he no longer cared. For hours he had lain awake, listening to Eve's heavy breathing and gloating on the satisfaction that the morrow would bring. Tomorrow, unless their plans had misfired, Everard and his damned company would be the poorer by some twenty-five thousand pounds (poorer, because the money was not insured), and Everard himself in a welter of anxiety and suspicion. And Emilio . . .

He smiled to himself in the dark at the thought of what Rossiter and his companions would do to Emilio.

Now it was mid-day. He had drunk too much, and he knew it. But he did not feel light-headed. His hatred and his weariness were too intense.

Emilio said, 'Es hora. We go, eh?'

They had been silent for so long that the sound of his voice startled the others. Eve jerked her gaze from the mountains, turned to smile at him, and then, mindful of her husband's presence, cancelled the smile. They would be taking two cars. She had been pondering, without success, how she might contrive to travel with Emilio.

Corbett swallowed the last of his gin and struggled to his feet. His twisted leg felt strangely heavy, and he leant more weightily on his stick.

'Tell the desk clerk to have our luggage brought down,' he said curtly. 'We'll wait for you by the cars.'

The Spaniard frowned at the tone of the order, but did not protest.

'Muy bien.'

They took the Murcia road. Emilio led in his Seat, with Eve at the wheel of the hired Simca; Corbett had protested that his leg was too painful to drive. As they climbed the tortuous hairpins that wound up and over the mountains, with the red fortress and the city falling away to their right, Emilio drove slowly; there were roadworks and crawling lorries to baulk him. But once through the pass he speeded up, and Eve had difficulty in staying with him. The road twisted and turned as it followed the contours, and again there were the sudden, unexpected potholes. Sometimes these were preceded by warning signs, more often not. Then it was the body-racking jolt, the loud protest of shock absorbers, that gave the first intimation.

For nearly two hours they travelled east, into arid country dominated by mountains, the dark leaves of the infrequent olive groves grey under the dust, the vines drooping in the heat. Occasionally there were villages, the buildings an assortment of Moorish and modern architecture, of red brick and sandstone and dazzling white. Lulled into drowsiness by the heat and the monotony of the landscape, his jealousy temporarily dormant, Corbett's body clamoured for sleep, his eyeballs felt on fire. But only sporadically did he allow his heavy lids to droop. Some inner force compelled him to stay awake. He would sleep later.

A winking trafficator at the rear of the Seat warned Eve that Emilio was about to turn left. She slowed and followed, and they bumped their way along a track which led, barely distinguishable in its dusty redness from the surrounding terrain, towards a distant *barranca*. Emilio had pointed out the track to them on their journey from Alicante, but it had soon been lost to Eve's memory in a succession of similar tracks. She knew that she could not have found it unaided.

Enveloped in a cloud of dust, she followed the Seat blindly. They traversed the *barranca* and climbed tortuously over a mountain spur, to find themselves travelling alongside a dried-up river bed, in which the channels of dead streams were clearly defined. Some distance from the main road, in a sudden clearing of the dust, they had passed through a village, where hens had run squawking and brown, wrinkled faces had peered at them curiously from dark interiors. Since then there had been only a man on a donkey, sitting side-saddle and impassive behind a small herd of goats.

The cloud of dust dwindled and vanished, and they found themselves on the airstrip — rutted and pitted now, but comparatively level. The mountains were closer, their terraced lower slopes sprinkled with olive trees, their summits bare and rugged. Corbett wondered how any pilot could find his way to such a lost and barren area, still more how he could land his aircraft safely.

Eve stopped the car at the far end of the runway, and they wound down the side windows. Emilio left the Seat and strolled back to them.

'Now we wait,' he said, removing his dark glasses and poking his head through the off-side window so that his face was close to Eve's. He smiled at them both impartially.

'How long?' Corbett demanded.

Still smiling, Emilio withdrew his head and shrugged.

'Quien sabe? One hour — perhaps two.'

Eve sighed, wondering what the dust and heat had done to her complexion.

Her husband slid lower in his seat, stretched his legs, and thankfully closed his eyes. He had no intention of sleeping, to allow them freedom for this final hour. But his heavy lids would have needed matchsticks to prop them open.

From the depths of sleep he struggled back to consciousness to find himself alone. The far door was open, knocking gently against the jamb in a faint breeze. Perhaps it was that which had awakened him. Or perhaps it was the pain in his leg. His body had twisted awkwardly in sleep.

He fished his stick from the rear seat and limped the few yards to the Seat. But that too was unoccupied, and he moved away from it, turning on his sound leg to examine the landscape. It provided no answer; nothing moved within his vision, and the scrub and the widely scattered olives could provide no cover for the truants. Yet with Rossiter expected at any minute they would not have gone far. Eve might be prepared to abandon caution, but not Emilio.

He began to climb the nearest spur, hoping that height would enlarge his view; they could be hidden behind some outcrop of rock, in some fold in the ground. With every painful step his anger grew, so that presently pain ceased to matter and his mind dwelt only on what he would do when he found them. He forgot his physical handicap. It no longer seemed incongruous that he should deal with Emilio himself, instead of waiting for Rossiter to exact retribution.

He was some way up the spur before he saw them. They half-sat, half-lay in the river bed, close to the bank that hid them from the runway. Emilio's back was towards him, and all he could see of Eve was the line of her side in the pale blue dress, a glimpse of chestnut hair, and her bare arm round the man's neck, her fingers lost in the thick darkness of his hair. He watched them for a few moments, convulsed in a wave of rage and hate and jealousy; then he went back down the spur, picking his way carefully so that they should not hear him. He wanted to come upon them as they were. This time they should be given no warning.

He followed the line of the bank until he judged himself to be opposite where they lay, and then limped cautiously to the edge. They were almost directly below him. The blue dress had slid farther up Eve's thigh, had been pulled from one brown shoulder; the fingers entwined in Emilio's hair twitched convulsively, clenching and unclenching in the fierceness of their embrace. Something snapped in Corbett's brain. His eyes misted over, and he slid the stick through his hand and grasped it at the ferrule end.

It was then Eve opened her eyes and saw him. He seemed to tower above them like an avenging angel, and she uttered a strangled cry and took her hand from Emilio's head and tried to push him away. His reaction was to clutch her the tighter. It was the woman who had proposed that they snatch this opportunity — Andrew slept, she had said, he would sleep long enough — and reluctantly, knowing it to be unwise but flattered by her obvious desire, he had gone with her. Now, when his ardour had been aroused and he sought to bring the affair to a logical conclusion, it seemed that she was protesting.

Only when she cried out again and he saw the fear in her eyes did he look up. It was too late. As he pushed her roughly away and sat up the heavy knob of the stick descended with a crushing blow on his head. He stayed there, stunned, blood starting to trickle from nose and mouth, his eyes glazed. Then the stick descended again, and he collapsed on his side and lay still. To the crazed Corbett it seemed that in falling his enemy was escaping him, and he slithered down the bank and belaboured the head again and again, beating it to a pulp, heedless of the blood that bespattered him. Dimly he was aware of his wife's screams; they merely intensified his rage, and he went grimly on with the work of destruction. Not that he consciously sought to destroy. It was pain and humiliation he needed to inflict, not destruction; and not until Eve caught his arm and clung to it did he desist. Breathing heavily, he stood immobile, the sickly smell of blood in his nostrils. Then the mist lifted from his eyes, and he saw clearly what he had done. It was an ugly sight. Emilio Ginachero was no longer recognizable. His body had twisted unnaturally, the once handsome head had become a sticky mess of bone and flesh and blood.

Eve still clung to him, screaming hysterically. Corbett was only vaguely aware of her. When eventually the screams ceased, and he felt the weight leave his arm as she slid to the ground in a faint, he lifted the stick once more and gazed in horror and disbelief at the blood-stained knob. Then his stomach heaved, and he leant against the bank and vomited.

# 6

To John Everard that Friday night was the introduction to a nightmare that was to remain vivid in his memory for the rest of his life. Added to his misery and anxiety was the unsympathetic attitude of his fellow-directors. At a brief board meeting held early on the Saturday morning they had made it plain that they held him responsible for the company's loss (it was he, they had pointed out, who had decried the necessity to insure the money while in transit), and had requested that he hand over as managing director until such time as the extent of his wife's complicity in the robbery had been finally settled. There had been no expressions of condolence, no offers of help. He had gone home from the meeting with the unpleasant reflection that Juanita had been right; he was a man without friends. Hitherto he had not felt the need of them. Now, unexpectedly, he did.

For most of the day he had stayed in the house. Once, heedless of the rain, he had trudged down the lane in the hope that some fresh information might be gleaned from the bungalow; it had been a fruitless journey, and the insistent swarm of reporters who had met him on his return had dissuaded him from venturing outside again. Occasionally the telephone rang. One of the early callers had been Colin Sievewright, a young Canadian who ran the Vauxhall Gymnasium which Everard frequented. Colin had expressed his sympathy and offered help ('I mean that, Mr Everard — and no holds barred. Just give the word.'), and Everard had felt strangely warmed and moved. He had not looked on Colin as a friend. The other calls had been from newspapermen or the idly curious, so that by the afternoon he had grown reluctant to answer the telephone. But answer it he did. There was always the hope that it might bring news of Juanita and Tommy, and a solution to the mystery surrounding their disappearance.

The police saw no mystery, he reflected bitterly; to Morgan it was all as plain as the nose on his face, which was about as far as a policeman could see. Juanita had taken a lover: the lover was a member of the gang, and had persuaded her to take part in the robbery: and, together with Tommy, they had now gone to earth in some prearranged hide-away, where for a while they could live comfortably on the proceeds of the crime. That, it seemed, was Morgan's interpretation. Who, he had wanted to know, was the lover?

With that damning note in his hand Everard could not deny the lover, but he had pretended ignorance of the man's identity. To admit to his wife's infidelity was ignominy enough; he could not bring himself to acknowledge a creature like Laroche as the man responsible. He felt no guilt at this deception. Laroche fitted the description of none of the men who had participated in the robbery. And it was the robbery, not his own matrimonial troubles, that concerned the police.

'I suppose a husband is often the last person to learn the identity of his wife's lover,' he had told Morgan. 'I assure you, Superintendent, all this has come as a terrible shock to me.' And Morgan, somewhat to his surprise, had not pressed the point. He had even expressed sympathy — which Everard had coldly rejected.

Mrs Chater had swung from optimism to pessimism. Hitherto she had not doubted the innocence of Juanita's friendship with Laroche; now she did not doubt its guilt. 'Youth calling to youth, I suppose,' she said, with unusual and infuriating candour. 'Mind you, I doubt if it will last. That Mr Laroche is the fickle kind, if you ask me. Even so, I can't see Mrs Everard coming home with her tail between her legs, begging forgiveness. She's too proud, wouldn't you say?'

He knew that her pessimism was a

misplaced form of kindness, that she was trying to dissuade him from building false hopes. But it was a kindness he did not appreciate, and he kept out of her way as much as possible.

And then, shortly after five o'clock, came a telephone call of a different kind.

'Mr Everard?' The voice was muffled and obviously disguised, and so falsetto that he could not decide whether it was male or female. 'What are you prepared to pay for information about your wife and son?'

Everard's heart skipped a beat. He had not anticipated this.

'Who are you?' he asked, his voice hoarse.

'Never mind that. Can you make it a thousand?'

'Yes.' He did not hesitate. If the caller had demanded more he would have agreed. 'Where are they? Are they all right?'

'Easy, easy. About the money. Send it in a parcel addressed to Shalford, Poste Restante, Oxford. In one-pound notes, please. And we don't want the police in on this, do we? That would bitch it for both of us. Let's keep it to ourselves, eh?'

'But — '

'No buts, Mr Everard. Just do as I say. When I have the money I'll contact you again. O.K.?'

'No.' It was not only the knowledge that this could be a hoax which prompted the denial. 'I can't get the money until the banks open on Monday — which means it will be Tuesday at least before I hear from you. Three days is too long to have to wait.' It was foreign to him to plead, but he was pleading now. 'Let me meet you tonight with what money I can raise. You shall have the rest later. That I promise.'

There was a pause. Everard thought he heard whispers at the other end of the line, as though a consultation was taking place.

'Sorry,' said the voice. 'No can do.'

There was a click and the line went dead. Perspiration started on Everard's brow as slowly he replaced the receiver. Then he snatched it up again and waited impatiently for the operator to answer.

'Number, please.'

Striving to keep the agitation from his voice, he explained that he wished to telephone the caller who had just rung. Unfortunately he had neglected to ask the number. Could it be traced? 'I'm not sure, but it might be in the Oxford area,' he added.

'One moment, please.'

It seemed incredible that anyone could speak so impersonally at such a time. He wanted to beg the girl to hurry, to impress on her the urgency of his business. But he merely thanked her and waited, with the receiver close to his ear and the fingers of his free hand drumming on the hall table.

'The number is Melwich 259.'

He had never heard of Melwich. He wanted to ring the number, to catch the caller off guard and hear his voice undisguised. But that might frighten him off. He got through to Directory Enquiries and requested the name and address of the subscriber. Again he waited — longer, it seemed, than before.

'The subscriber's name is Tasker,' came

the information. 'The address is End Cottage, Melwich.'

His hand was trembling as he put down the receiver. Tasker! Cyril Tasker was one of the men he had sacked, along with Corbett and Manning, shortly after his appointment as managing director. Both board and employees had resented his action, there had been talk of a strike; and when Manning had committed suicide the blame had been laid squarely on him. But he had ignored criticism and antagonism then as he had ignored it before and since, and the storm had blown itself out. Or so he had thought. But had he been wrong? Was this sudden spate of disaster a repercussion of his action — with Cyril Tasker responsible?

He shut his eyes in an effort to conjure up a mental image of the man: a self-opinionated mule, as he remembered, suspicious of change and resentful of advice. Physically the image was less clear. Had it been Tasker who was bearded? Or was that Corbett? Both, he was sure, had been in their early fifties and above average height, which seemed to exonerate them from participation in the robbery; the thieves had been younger and shorter. Yet that did not necessarily eliminate Tasker from all complicity. With his inside knowledge of the firm and its security arrangements, he would be in a position to organize the whole damned scheme. So, for that matter, would Corbett.

But had either of them done so? That, Everard decided, was a problem he would decide for himself. This was not for the police. This was for him.

He made no reference to Tasker when he told Mrs Chater of the telephone call. The name would be unknown to her; she would expect him to explain its significance, and that he was reluctant to do. He had felt no guilt in dismissing Tasker and the others; there was no room for sentiment in business. But Mrs Chater might not see it in the same light (women were funny about such things) and he could not afford to alienate her sympathy now.

'You don't think it's a hoax?' she asked.

'It could be.' He clenched his fists as he imagined what he would do if it were. 'But it's a possible lead, and I can't ignore it. I'm off to Melwich this evening. At least it will give me something to do. If I sit around here much longer I'll go crazy.'

She nodded understandingly.

'I know. It's agonizing, isn't it?' She hesitated. 'A thousand pounds is a lot of money, of course. But if you think this is genuine wouldn't it be safer to pay? If you tackle him empty-handed he might refuse to talk.'

'He'll talk,' he said grimly, relieved that she had not suggested consulting the police. 'If I have to choke it out of him, he'll talk.'

Because the police still held the Jaguar he had to telephone for a taxi. A few reporters still waited by the gate, and to put them off the scent he went out to them before the taxi arrived. In the heavy rain they looked an unhappy lot.

'I'm going for a walk,' he told them. 'Any objections?'

'In this weather?' one asked.

'In any weather. I need exercise.'

Curbing his irritation, he added, 'And if it's all the same to you fellows, I'd like to take it alone.'

'Is there any news of your wife and son, Mr Everard?'

'None, unfortunately.'

They let him go then. Some way down the lane he looked back, and smiled grimly when he saw that they had disappeared. If they hoped for more success with Mrs Chater they were in for a disappointment. Mrs Chater knew how to keep her mouth shut.

He passed the Laroche bungalow with no more than a brief glance down the wooded path, and walked on briskly to meet the taxi.

Dusk was turning to dark when they drove into Melwich and inquired for End Cottage. It stood back from the road, a mile out of the village, looking solitary and unfriendly; hedges untrimmed, the grass long, flowerbeds a tangle of weed and bramble. But lights shone behind curtained windows, and Everard pushed open the squeaking gate and almost ran down the uneven path to the front porch. There he paused. Inside the cottage a gramophone was playing pop music, and he turned the handle gently, hoping for a surprise entry. But the door was locked. He abandoned surprise, lifted the old-fashioned iron knocker, and banged it down heavily.

A door slammed on the first floor. There was the sound of footsteps on uncarpeted boards, and moments later the music stopped. As the footsteps approached the porch and he heard the bolts being withdrawn, Everard's heart beat faster. Now he would know. And if this was Tasker the man was in for a nasty shock.

It was not Tasker. Silhouetted against the light as the door opened was the slim figure of Peter Laroche.

The two men acted simultaneously. As Laroche tried to close the door Everard put in his foot and forced it open, pushing the other back. Once inside, he kicked the door shut and locked it.

'Now talk!' he snapped. 'Where are they?'

The front door opened directly into the

single living-room. As Everard stretched out an arm to grab him Laroche leapt agilely aside and retreated behind one of the two large settees which dominated the room. From there, long hair flopping over his face, he regarded his angry visitor with nervous defiance.

'They — they're not here,' he said.

Everard looked round the room. It was poorly furnished, with only a couple of threadbare mats on the floor. Over by the fireplace was a second door. Wooden stairs, unrailed and ladder-like, led to the floor above.

'You're a bloody liar,' he said. He wanted to grip the other by the throat and choke the truth out of him. But he had just sufficient control to resist the appeal of force. Incredible as it seemed, Juanita had chosen this baby-faced, flop-haired youth for her lover. Well, she could have him. Undamaged, if the pup behaved himself. But not until she had told him herself that that was what she wanted. 'They're here, and I'm going to see them. Are they upstairs?'

'No.' Laroche had expected force. But

apparently this was to be a battle of words, and with words he considered himself the other's equal. Emboldened, he lit a cigarette. 'They were here, certainly. But they've gone.'

'Gone? Gone where?'

'Well, now — ' He pursed his lips daintily, tilting his head back to watch the smoke dribble from his mouth. 'Silly of me, wasn't it, to forget that a telephone call could be twaced? But it doesn't weally matter. Have you bwought the money?' Everard felt a pulse start to throb in his temple. 'I know we said a thousand, but I'm weady to settle for five hundwed. How's that?'

Everard's control snapped. He hurled himself at the settee so suddenly that, before Laroche could move, he had grabbed him by his sweater and yanked him forward.

'You'll settle for a broken neck,' he growled. 'Talk, you bastard!'

Laroche could not match him in strength. But he had a certain courage, and despite the fact that the back of the settee was being forced into his stomach he did not answer at once. Cursing throatily, he tried to break away. Everard slapped him across the cheek and then relaxed the pressure.

Laroche had had enough. 'They've gone to Spain,' he said sullenly. 'With the others. Or Juanita has. I don't know where Tommy is.'

Everard let him go, thrusting him away with such force that Laroche stumbled and fell. He knew that the youth was lying, but the form of the lie puzzled him. Spain, of course, was obvious; but why the distinction between Juanita and Tommy? Juanita would never leave Tommy behind. Not willingly. Adulteress or not, she was a good mother — and Laroche knew it. The others, presumably, were the thieves. But was it credible that Juanita would desert her lover the day after she had eloped with him?

'You'll have to do better than that,' he said grimly. 'I'm not — '

He stopped abruptly at a noise overhead. It sounded like a tread on a loose floorboard. Apparently Laroche heard it too; he picked himself up and moved sluggishly towards the stairs. Everard followed.

'Upstairs, are they? I thought so,' he said. 'You and your damned lies!'

'No, no! You — you're wong.' Laroche's voice was shriller, his face grey. He seemed to have difficulty in speaking. 'It isn't — '

As he tried to bar the way Everard hit him. He put all his strength into the blow, and as his fist connected with the other's chin he grunted with pleasure. He should have done that weeks ago, he thought. Yesterday and today and tomorrow might have been different then.

Laroche fell against the stairway, slid to the floor, and lay still. Everard stepped over him and ran up the stairs, feeling them sway under his weight. As he reached the top landing the telephone in the living-room started to ring, but he ignored it. Two doors gave on to the small landing. The first was ajar, and the room beyond in darkness; but a line of light showed beneath the second door, and he threw it open, knowing that this was the one. Then he stopped. At the foot of a large double bed, nude except for a pair of briefs, stood a girl.

It was not Juanita.

Too startled to retreat, Everard stared at her. She was young and nubile, with small pointed breasts and a slim body, and hair that was dark and lustreless under the electric light. She neither exclaimed nor sought to hide her nakedness, but stared back at him with a mocking smile on her elfin face.

'Who are you?' she asked, smoothing her hands down her flanks. 'I don't think we've met.'

He went out and shut the door, too bewildered to speak.

Laroche still lay where he had fallen. Everard went slowly down the stairs and stood looking at him. He felt no compunction for the blow. But the man had not told him what he wanted to know, and he bent to shake him by the arm.

'All right, so they aren't here,' he said sternly. Vaguely he was aware that the telephone had ceased to ring, and wondered if he should have answered it.

'Now let's have the truth. What have you done with them?'

Laroche moved limply under the shaking, unfolding slowly on to his back as the arm was released. His face was drained of colour, the eyes closed. Alarmed, Everard knelt to put an ear to the pale lips. No breath fanned his cheek, and feverishly he pulled up his blue sweater and felt for the man's heart. For a full minute he waited. Then slowly he withdrew his hand and leaned back.

Peter Laroche was dead.

He was still on his knees by the body when a knock sounded on the front door — a loud, imperative knock that startled him into full awareness of what he had done. This was murder. No matter how Laroche had provoked him, it was still murder; and if he were discovered here the police would be informed, it could be only a matter of hours before his arrest. The events of the past two days had turned the Everard family into headline news; their photographs had been on the front page of every newspaper that morning, and anyone who saw him could hardly fail to recognize him. Tom Lever, the taxi-driver, could probably be fixed. He was that sort of man. But a stranger . . .

The knock came again. There were voices in the porch, someone tried the latch. Everard stood up. The girl upstairs would expect Laroche to answer the summons, but if the knocking continued she might come down. Before that happened he had to get away, and he tiptoed across the room to the far door, trusting to the curtains to mask his progress from the visitors, swearing under his breath when a floorboard creaked. He knew that the time must come when he would have to answer for what he had done. But it must not be now. Until he knew what had happened to Juanita and Tommy he had to be free.

The door led to a small kitchen. He fumbled his way through it and out by the back door. The yard was brick-paved and uneven, the night dark and wet; fearful of making a noise, he moved carefully westward, stumbling across the kitchen garden to round the house at a safe distance. Now he could see the front porch. He crossed the lawn towards the gate, bending low so that he was below the level of the hedge. Once there, he paused to consider. The visitors' car stood immediately beyond the gate, facing Tom Lever's taxi; he could not leave without being seen, perhaps recognized, by anyone in the car. Did that matter? Until the body was discovered no-one would know that a murder had been committed, no-one would seek to detain him. The one essential was to remove himself as soon and as far as possible, to find a bolt-hole before the hunt was on. And it could not be long delayed. Even if the visitors left before gaining admission to the cottage, the girl might raise the alarm at any moment.

He was about to walk boldly out by the gate when he saw the two men. They came out from the porch and started to walk round the house, and as they passed the window they were silhouetted against the light within. One was a uniformed policeman. The other was Superintendent Morgan.

Their presence shocked and dismayed him. Had Morgan trailed him to the cottage, or was it Laroche they were after? Whatever the reason, he could not now leave by the gate. A police car meant a police driver, and the man would almost certainly detain him. Pulling the collar of his raincoat tighter around his neck, he waited until the men had turned the corner of the house and then started to make his way along the hedge. Speed now was essential, and he began to run, with the briars catching at his clothing and his feet sinking into the damp soil. A chain-link fence barred his way, and he clambered over it into a field of uncut corn. Here the tall grasses hampered his progress and soaked his socks and trousers, and he cut back to the hedge and went stumbling on until he came to a gate that gave access to the road.

Out on the road he looked back. The cars were some sixty yards away, and in the diffused glow of their side-lights he could see Tom Lever chatting to the other driver, his backside resting against a mudguard, apparently unbothered by the rain. There was no sense of urgency in their attitudes; if Morgan had discovered the body he had not yet alerted his driver. Everard hesitated. He had only to call out, and Tom would climb into his taxi and come to pick him up. But could he take the risk?

He decided he could not. Reluctantly abandoning the taxi, he turned and ran off down the road into the night.

# 7

'You crazy fool!' Rossiter said. 'You bloody, crazy fool!'

Corbett made no comment on this unusual reaction to murder. Along with Emilio Ginachero had died the angry jealousy which had tormented him for the past week, and without it he felt weak and empty and strangely peaceful. It was as though he had been exorcised of a devil. Vaguely he was aware that he should be filled with remorse; but as he gazed down at the mutilated body of the young Spaniard the only sensation he experienced was one of revulsion.

'You don't think I meant to kill him, do you?' Despite the new-found peace he was still trembling, his body felt boneless. 'But catching them together like that it — well, I just saw red. All I could think of was to pay the bastard back for what he'd done to me.'

'And a thorough job you made of it,'

Rossiter told him. 'Added to which, you've bitched the whole bloody set-up. The Lord knows what we do now!'

The aeroplane had come and gone. On the runway stood the two cars, with Eve huddled, alone and frightened, in the back of the Simca. Corbett had tried to take her arm when she recovered from the faint; partly to help her, partly to comfort himself. But she had shrunk away from him, and he had watched her half-run, half-stumble to the car: When he had passed it some minutes later on his way to meet the plane she had looked at him as though he were a stranger. He had not seen her since.

Emilio had been right in one thing; there *was* a woman on the plane. One of Rossiter's men had hurried her away to the Seat on landing, and Corbett, distracted by his own problem, had barely glanced at her. The knowledge of Emilio's rightness did not trouble his conscience — Emilio had been punished for his association with Eve, not for intended treachery — and he felt no need to justify his action to himself. But he needed to justify it to Rossiter, and he said bluntly, still gazing in fearful fascination at Emilio's body. 'He was planning to double-cross us.'

'Emilio? Don't be a bloody fool. He had a damned sight more to gain working with us than against us. He knew it, too. What put that crazy notion into your head?'

Even to Corbett the case against Emilio sounded thin as he told it, and he tried to bolster it by stressing the villainous appearance of the young Spaniard's friends. But Rossiter angrily repudiated the accusation; Emilio had been arranging accommodation, which was what he had been told to do. 'You and your blasted woman!' he said, scowling. 'What the devil did it matter if Emilio gave her a tumble? He wasn't the first, I'll be bound.'

Corbett shivered. He was too empty to feel anger. But the insult fed the animosity he already felt for his companion.

'Leave her out of this,' he said sullenly.
'I will — when you stop knocking off

her boy friends.' Rossiter shifted his feet, and a little shower of stone and sand trickled on to the body below. 'But to hell with that! What do we do with Mrs Everard now? That's what I want to know.'

'Mrs Everard!' Corbett was shaken out of his trance. 'So that's who the woman is! But why bring her here? It wasn't on the agenda.'

'Not on yours, perhaps. It was on mine.' Rossiter glared angrily down at the river bed. He had not intended that the Corbetts should figure in this part of the operation; the Everard woman was to have been kept out of sight until they had been sent packing with their share of the robbery. But Emilio's death had changed that. Secrecy had gone by the board. 'You may be sweating on revenge, Corbett, but for the rest of us it's strictly a cash transaction; and twenty-odd thousand quid split six ways is chicken feed. But Mrs Everard, now — she's quite an investment. Properly handled, she represents a tidy sum in ransom.'

'I should have been told,' Corbett

protested, twisting his scraggy neck against the heat. The faint breeze had died, and the ground shimmered under the haze. 'It was agreed we should hold her and the kid for a while, just to make Everard sweat. But there was no talk of ransom.'

'There is now. Any objection?'

Corbett knew that the question was academic, that any objection he might voice would influence Rossiter not at all. But he had none. If they wanted to squeeze Everard harder, that was fine with him.

'But why bring them here?' he asked, puzzled.

'Because Everard hasn't the kind of dough we're after. Her father has; he's one of the richest men in Spain.' Rossiter lit a cigarette. The sweat from his fingers left a damp stain on the paper. 'And we didn't bring them both. The kid's in England. Your friend Tasker's got him.'

The small spark of charity left in Corbett's heart revolted at this separation of mother and child. He had no enmity against Juanita Everard; on the one occasion they had met he had even liked her. But revulsion was swamped by the satisfying thought of what this would do to Everard. The screws were tight indeed.

'Fair enough,' he said. 'So what now?'

'We bury your mistake and clear out. After that, God knows! Even if we knew what Emilio had arranged we couldn't use it. Or would you care to explain to his Spanish friends why he is no longer with us?' He did not wait for an answer, but turned to the tall man who had stood silent beside them while they talked. 'Come on, Al. Let's get digging.'

Albemarle Johnson had enormous hands, and a weatherbeaten face with a deep scar running diagonally across the chin. His sad grey eyes and near-bald head made him look older than his thirty-seven years.

'What with?' he asked.

'Hands, man. What else is there?'

They dug only a shallow grave. The sandy soil was dry and soft on top, but hard underneath. Corbett watched them as they scrabbled at it with their fingers, and retched as they rolled the corpse into it and he saw again the mangled, lolling head. But he continued to watch; it seemed incumbent on him to do so. Only when they started to stamp down the soil, with the dead Emilio apparently resilient in protest, did he turn away.

'Scatter the dirt, Al,' Rossiter said. He stood up, arching his back, the sweat pouring from his face. 'No mound. The last thing we want is to make it look like a grave.'

The tall man made no answer. He had stopped stamping, and was staring across at the foothills.

'Looks like we got an audience,' he said. There was a soft West country burr to his voice. 'I thought them was bushes, but they ain't. Them's goats.'

The others followed his gaze, screwing up their eyes against the sun.

'Goats it is,' Rossiter agreed. 'And presumably a goatherd. I can't pick him out, but he'll be there somewhere. If he saw the plane he's going to be unpleasantly curious about this.' He nodded at the grave and scrambled up the bank. 'We'll move before he rounds up his pals for an exhumation. You take the Seat, Al, with Mrs Everard and Connie. The Corbetts can come with me in the Simca.'

'But the goatherd!' Corbett protested. 'Don't we do anything about him?'

'Such as what? Murder? You think that's the answer to everything, eh?' Corbett flushed under the sneer. 'Well, you certainly look the part. Anyone seeing you right now would take you for a bloody butcher.'

It was the first time since Emilio's death that Corbett had thought to examine himself, and he flinched at what he saw. The grey trousers, the fawn canvas shoes, were plentifully bespattered with blood. There was blood on his linen jacket, on his socks, on the cuffs of his shirt.

He shivered. 'I'll change,' he said. 'Can you give me a minute?'

It was not until they had left the airstrip and were some way down the track that he remembered his stick. He had dropped it in the river bed after the killing, and presumably it was still there. Could it be traced to him? His stomach heaved at the thought. But he did not mention the stick to Rossiter. The prospect of Rossiter's anger was too unnerving.

Out on the main road they headed west, the Simca leading. Eve sat alone in the back. Emilio's blood was on her too, brown spots staining the blue dress; but she seemed as indifferent to them as to the rest of her dishevelled appearance. Dazed and shocked, she stared ahead at the road, her body erect and swaying with the movement of the car. Rossiter had nodded to her curtly as he took the wheel, and then ignored her. Corbett turned to her once or twice as they went, hoping to catch a glimpse of acknowledgment, even though in anger or contempt, in the wide blue eyes. But there was only that blank stare. It was as though neither of the men existed.

The frown on Rossiter's face dissuaded Corbett from conversation. It was not until they had travelled some miles that he ventured to ask where they were going.

'Guadix,' Rossiter said curtly.

'Guadix! But that — '

'I know, I know. Guadix is — was Emilio's home town. It also happens to be the home of the man who introduced me to him.' The horn blared angrily as Rossiter pulled out to overtake. 'He must have similar contacts. Whether he's willing to play ball again is another matter.'

'Why shouldn't he? He gets paid, doesn't he?'

'Oh, yes, he gets paid. And the cunning old bastard will know we're in a jam, and fix the price accordingly. However, that's your worry. You got us into this mess, and you can damned well pay for it.' Rossiter's stubby fingers thumped the wheel as he waited for the expected protest. None came. 'My worry is more basic. Luis will pretend to accept whatever cock-and-bull story we care to feed him about Emilio, but he won't believe it. He'll know one of us killed him. He'll know, too, that when Emilio's friends start asking questions it's Luis who will have to find the answers. He may not fancy the risk. Not at any price.' They were travelling fast, but for a brief moment he took his eyes from the road to glare at his companion. 'If you're a praying man, Corbett, you'd better get cracking. Without Luis we're sunk.'

★ ★ ★

In the back of the Seat Juanita sat with the man they called Connie, a wiry, ferret-faced little Liverpudlian who breathed heavily through his mouth and smelt of onions and stale beer. Despite his lack of size he managed to occupy most of the seat, pinning her into a corner. She knew this was deliberate; with every left-hand bend in the road he leaned against her, to push himself away with a hot hand on her thigh. But so long as he did not actively molest her she was too shocked and troubled in her mind to protest at such minor intimacies.

It was not for herself she was afraid, but for her husband and Tommy. What would John be thinking, what would he do? Above all, what had happened to Tommy? Time and again — at the cottage, and later in the aeroplane — she had pleaded with the men to tell her, and they had replied with evasions and threats. Tommy was safe and presumably well, they told her, and he was likely to stay that way for as long as she co-operated. Otherwise — well, accidents happen, and a four-month-old baby is more susceptible to them than most. Only the big man, the one who was driving now, had seemed sympathetic. But even he had been evasive. 'Like the guv'nor said, Miss, it all depends on you,' he had said, in his soft voice. 'And your dad, of course.' After a pause he had added, with doubt in his sad grey eyes, 'He'll pay the money, won't he?'

'I don't know,' she told him. 'I hope so.'

To avoid Connie's heavy breathing she kept her head turned to the window. At first the terrain was meaningless to her. But presently they passed through a village and she saw the signpost to Guadix and Granada, and realized they were on the Murcia road; as a child she had travelled it many times on visits to her grandmother. It gave her some slight comfort to know that they were headed west. West meant Cordoba and home

— and security. Or did it? How much would these men demand for her ransom? She knew that her father was rich — but was he rich enough? What if he could not pay the price they asked?

The thought made her sick — not only with fear, but with frustration. It was frightening to be so alone, so helpless. And as the miles passed her frustration turned gradually to anger — so that when Connie's hand was again hot on her thigh and she felt his fingers squeeze the flesh she turned on him furiously.

'Bestia!' She tore his hand away. 'Don't touch me!' And then, because the sight of this thin, ferret face so close to hers had become unbearably hateful, she slapped it.

Connie was too startled to be angry. He stared at her openmouthed, displaying sharp, pointed teeth. Then his face twisted in a grin, and he said, 'We got a right one 'ere, Al. Reg'lar little spitfire.'

Without turning. Al said, 'You do like she says, mate. Leave her alone.'

Connie ignored him. Turning on the seat to face her, he grabbed her suddenly, pinioning her arms. To Juanita he seemed all bone and muscle, making her struggles ineffective; and the more she struggled the wider grew the grin on Connie's face. He was in no hurry to complete the embrace; the feel of her soft body turning and twisting in his arms was delightfully tantalizing. But he had reckoned without Al. Half-turning in his seat, Al swung his long arm in a wide arc, to clout Connie hard on the ear with the back of an enormous hand.

'I said leave her alone.' The soft voice had hardened. 'You do — '

He did not complete the sentence. With a jarring thud that sent Connie and Juanita sprawling the Seat bounced into a pothole, and came out with front wheels juddering frantically. Too late Al took both hands to the wheel, braking hard. The pothole was succeeded by others, so that within a few yards the car was out of control. Bouncing and bucking, it left the road, slithered down the crumbling verge, and turned over on its side in the cactus hedge.

# 8

Colin Alexander de Roget Sievewright, 5th Baron Dunmour, paused from wiping the perspiration from his face and well-muscled limbs to gape incredulously at his visitor. The gape revealed excellent teeth.

'You've done *what*?'

'I've killed a man,' John Everard repeated. Even to himself it sounded incredible. In emphasis he added, 'It's true. I hit him, and he just died on me.'

'The devil he did!' And then, because he was a practical person and not given to histrionics, Colin resumed his towelling. 'From the look of you it took place in a swamp. Care to tell me about it?'

Seated on the jumping horse in the Vauxhall Gymnasium, with the mud still on his shoes and the creases gone from his trousers and his collar soggy from the rain, Everard told him. The telling seemed to ease a little of the burden, but it also brought home to him how heavy the burden was.

'You're sure he's dead?' Colin asked. He had changed and was ready to leave by the time Everard had finished. 'It wasn't just a faint, or a shamming act?'

'Quite sure.'

'H'm! And this chap Tasker, the owner of the cottage. How does he tie up with Laroche?'

Everard shrugged. 'I don't know. I never got around to that.'

Colin pulled thoughtfully at his dimpled chin. He had a square face, bronzed and heavily freckled, with blond hair cut short and ice-blue eyes.

'It's murky, isn't it? Talk about a bum steer!' He had only a faint North American accent. 'You haven't been home, I suppose?'

No, Everard said, he had not been home; he had hitch-hiked direct to London. But he had telephoned Mrs Chater to tell her what had happened. She had been deeply shocked (he could not be sure whether it was the murder itself or the situation in which it had placed him which shocked her the most), but had promised not to tell the police of his call. He had been about to ring off when she had remembered a note that had been pushed through the letter-box that evening. At his request she had opened and read it to him. It was a ransom demand for Tommy.

'Ah! Now we're coming to it,' Colin said, with some satisfaction. 'How much?'

'Five thousand.'

'Phew! And Juanita?'

'It didn't mention her. Just Tommy, and how the money was to be paid.' Everard slid dejectedly from the horse. 'That's what gets me, Colin. It bears out what Laroche said — that Juanita had gone off to Spain with the others. But why, man? Why?'

'Because she couldn't help herself. That's why. Don't you see, Mr Everard? They — '

'The name's John,' Everard said. And felt awkward in saying it.

'O.K. John. But don't you see? They took her to Spain because they want her old man to cough up the ransom. You're not in a high enough income bracket, apparently. Five thousand from you for Tommy — and the Lord knows what for Juanita from her father. It tallies, doesn't it?'

Everard shook his head. Colin had never seen his back so bent or his face so tired.

'Perhaps. Although the way Laroche put it, she went of her own accord. There was no mention of ransom. And then there's that damned note they found in the car — and the lies she told. And why would she take a suitcase unless — '

Colin banged a massive fist on the leather cover of the horse.

'Come off it, man. Granted there's a lot needs explaining. But you can't seriously believe that a girl like Juanita would willingly take part in a sordid robbery, and then abandon her infant to go jaunting off to Spain with the thieves afterwards? Laroche — ' He shrugged. 'Well, that's possible, I suppose, however unlikely. But the rest — oh, it's preposterous.'

'I know. But — '

'There's no 'but' about it. It just isn't on, and you know it. Or you would if these damned 'ifs' and 'buts' hadn't obscured your judgment.' He put a friendly and comforting hand on the other's arm. The two were about the same height and build, with Colin slightly broader across the shoulders and slimmer round the waist. 'You look about all in. Come back to my place for a meal and a clean-up. We can discuss it there.' He hesitated. 'Sure you don't want to go to the police? About Laroche, I mean.'

'I can't,' Everard said. 'Not yet.'

He started to protest that he would not involve the other, but Colin cut him short. His offer of help had not been idly given. Maybe it wouldn't amount to much, he said, but he'd be glad to do what he could.

Driving to Colin's flat in Putney, Everard wondered why he had chosen this cheerful adventurer for a confidant. They had little in common. Colin Sievewright was the younger by eleven years, and possessed of no ambition for power or position or wealth. At eighteen he had left his home in Canada to roam the world, coming to rest (but only temporarily, Everard suspected) as instructor to, and part owner of, the Vauxhall Gymnasium. His unexpected elevation to the peerage, occasioned by the death of a cousin he had never met, had delighted him — as the unexpected usually did. But it had not changed his way of life. He remained as improvident, as gay, and as forthright as before.

Perhaps, Everard reflected, there had been no choice. Juanita had said he had no friends; and until Colin Sievewright had telephoned his offer of help he had believed that to be true. He had not hitherto thought of Colin as a friend. But marriage to a young wife had imbued him with a desire to match her youth, and since the honeymoon he had been a regular visitor to the gymnasium. There Colin was the master and he the pupil, so that his natural instinct to dominate, to command, was missing from their relationship. It made, if not for close friendship, at least for an easy companionship.

'Presuming we've guessed right, would

your father-in-law be prepared to fork out a large sum as ransom?' Colin asked, as they waited at traffic lights.

'I imagine so. He's rich as Croesus, and Juanita is his only child.'

'And Tommy? What do we do about him? Will you pay?'

'How can I?' Everard was grateful for the 'we'. 'I don't carry that kind of money in my current account. It would mean an overdraft, and with things as they are that wouldn't be easy to arrange.'

Colin's flat was on the first floor of an old house near the river. The large, high-ceilinged rooms had been furnished in stages, as funds permitted, from second-hand dealers, and the result was a catholic mixture of antique and modern. The carpets were worn but of good quality, the curtains faded. That the flat was untidy went unnoticed by Everard. He was only humbly grateful for its sanctuary. And humility was for him a new experience.

'I suppose you realize you're making yourself an accessory after murder,' he said.

'All I realize right now is that I'm hungry,' Colin told him, making for the kitchen. 'The bathroom's in there. When you're ready, come and prick the bangers while I peel the mashed.'

They talked as they cooked and as they ate. Colin ate most of the sausages, and with gusto; it was his boast that no aristocrat had a more plebeian taste in food. To please him Everard tried to simulate hunger, but it was a very pale hunger — particularly since he did not like sausages. Colin did his best to cheer him by dwelling on the less depressing aspects of the affair, but he found them few in number.

'Laroche's death was pure accident,' he declared. 'There was no intent to kill. I suppose the police might claim it was manslaughter if they're out to crowd you, but they couldn't stretch it to murder. Frankly, I think you'd have been wiser to confront them on the spot and explain.'

'Maybe. But I couldn't take the risk. I had to be free.'

That was something that Colin could understand. But, as he pointed out, there would be little freedom in England for a man wanted by the police; and without freedom what chance had Everard of finding his son? 'If you take my advice you'll hop over to Spain and leave Tommy to me and the police. You'll be more use there than here, if only to hold your wife's hand when the brutes release her.'

Everard nodded glumly.

'Perhaps. But let's be realistic. With the police almost certainly watching the ports, how do I get out of the country? Anyway, we don't know for sure that Juanita's in Spain.'

'She must be. Everything points to it. And what do you lose if she isn't? As for how — ' Colin grinned. 'I might be able to help there. We get all sorts down at the gym.' He scraped the last film of potato from his plate, transferred it to his fork, and sucked the fork clean. 'It'll cost money, of course.'

'What sort of money?'

'I've never had occasion to ask. A few hundred, at a guess. Any good?' Everard shook his head. 'Damn! And I'm skint as usual. Well, maybe I can blackmail some

130

of my customers. As I said, we get all sorts.'

'You can add me to the collection now.' There was no trace of a smile on Everard's face as he rose from the table and went to the window. 'Thanks, Colin; but it's a dead horse, and we both know it.' He peered down through a gap in the curtains. A few cars, Colin's Austin among them, were parked in the street below, but there was no sign of the police. By now they would be checking on his known acquaintances. Sooner or later they would get around to Colin. 'There may be a few quid at the house, but — No! Wait a minute!'

'Something come up?'

'The works! There's always a thousand or so in the office safe. I have the keys, and the police won't be watching the place at night. Why should they?' At the prospect of action Everard felt better. 'Lend me your car, Colin, will you? I can be there and back in a couple of hours.' He smiled grimly. 'I'll leave a note to explain where the money's gone. I don't want to be branded a thief as well as a murderer.'

Colin was against the proposal, and said so. 'Isn't there a night watchman? He'll ring the police if he sees you. Let me go.'

Everard shook his head.

'Fawsey — he's the night watchman — he won't have heard about Laroche as yet. It's only a few hours since it happened. I'll tell him I'm collecting the suitcase I keep at the office for emergency business trips. He may think it odd, but he won't try to stop me. He'd stop you.'

Colin grinned. 'I'd like to see him try. But have it your way. You go steal your money, and I'll smoke out the necessary contacts.' He took a bunch of keys from his pocket and threw them to Everard. 'Don't wait up for me if I'm out when you return. This mob may take some finding. They're not exactly home birds.'

As he followed Everard down to the car he wondered whether he would be as phlegmatic were he in the other's position. How did one choose between wife and son without tearing the guts out of one's heart? Or had the decision been reached less easily than it appeared? With John Everard it was hard to tell.

'Good luck,' he said cheerfully. 'And take it easy. Take all night if necessary.'

Everard put the car into gear and steered away from the kerb. Despite his impatience he had every intention of taking it easy; this was no time to tangle with traffic police. He was aware of gratitude to Colin, and wondered vaguely if he had been niggardly in expressing it; but he was unused to depending on others, and it was a relief to be once more making his own decisions, directing his own course. From the moment Laroche had said that Juanita was in Spain he had known, subconsciously if not consciously, that that was where he must go. Only the lack of means and his fear for Tommy had made him hesitate.

Absorbed in thought, he did not notice the blue saloon that followed him down the road and into Putney High Street.

# 9

Apart from an agonized exclamation of angry incredulity as he watched in his mirror the Seat bounce its way off the road, Rossiter had spoken not one unnecessary word. He had turned the Simca and driven back, to haul the shaken occupants from the overturned car. Now, with chattering, gesticulating Spaniards surrounding him and yet more cars pulling to a halt, his self-control suddenly broke.

'No!' he shouted, the muscles in his thick neck expanding. 'We don't need your blasted help. Leave us alone! Clear out, the lot of you!'

Momentarily his audience was silent; if they did not understand the words his attitude made their meaning clear. Then the chattering recommenced. A thin man in a grey linen suit stood with two suitcases he had taken from the wrecked Seat; Rossiter snatched them from him and shouldered his way through the crowd to the Simca, with Constant Smith in his wake. Albemarle Johnson, blood pouring from a cut cheek, was already on the front seat; Corbett and the two women sat in the back. Still cursing, Rossiter threw the cases into the boot, brushed aside the spectators peering in through the windows, and snapped open the off-side door.

'In you get.' He gave Connie a shove in the back. 'Let's scram before the bloody cops arrive.'

Three of them in the front was a squash. It took two attempts to close the door. Sweat trickling down his face, Rossiter put the car into reverse and backed across the road, scattering the crowd. Then, one hand on the horn, he steered a brisk course through the untidily parked cars and set off once more for Guadix.

Not until they had travelled several kilometres did he speak again.

'What happened, Al? And don't give me bloody potholes. I know better than that.'

Between the two of them Connie wriggled uneasily and looked at Al. He had emerged from the accident unscathed. Now he didn't feel so good. The guv'nor, as he had cause to know, was tough. He might look and talk like a gentleman, but when the chips were down he could be unpleasantly basic.

Al felt the wriggle and interpreted the look. He disliked Connie. But despite his profession he was essentially a peace-loving man, and he said, 'We hit that first hole a bit hard. Mrs Everard screamed, and I turned to see what was up.' He dabbed at his cheek with a stained handkerchief. 'I thought Connie here might be up to his tricks.'

'And was he?' There was real menace in Rossiter's voice. He was in no mood for leniency. Emilio's death — and now this. A first-class job carefully planned and neatly sewn up, and put in jeopardy because two of his so-called colleagues couldn't keep their blasted passions under control.

'I wouldn't know, guv'nor. That was when we hit the second hole.'

Connie said quickly, 'Honest, I never touched her. I mean — well, I just sort of fell against her when the car bounced. I didn't reckon to — '

'Shut up!' Rossiter glanced quickly over his shoulder. Juanita sat in the far corner, her eyes closed. A dark bruise on her forehead was the only sign of injury, but he knew she was both dazed and shocked. He decided to postpone further inquiry. 'I'll deal with you later.'

'But I didn't do nothing! You — '

'I said shut up.'

Wedged between her husband and Juanita, Eve listened distantly to the quarrel, relieved not to be involved. The accident had jolted her back to full awareness, and when Andrew climbed into the car to sit beside her she had tried to edge away from him, repelled by the pressure of his bony rump on her plump flesh. But there was no room for movement, and she had to accept the contact. Now, as the road slid away under her, she began to examine her emotions more closely. There had been no love in her feeling for Emilio (she had never loved anyone, not even Andrew), only a desperate desire. And desire, it seemed, had died with its object; certainly she felt none for Emilio now. Even his death had begun to seem less fearful, less important. It was the manner of it that repelled her.

She shuddered at the memory. That, she thought, would never fade.

Andrew felt the shudder. Glad of an opportunity to break the silence between them, he said hoarsely, 'Are you all right?'

'Yes.'

She spoke curtly. But at least she had answered him. He left it at that.

Out of the corners of her eyes Eve watched him. His lean face, still red from the Alicante sun, wore its normal bleak expression, and she wondered how the memory of Emilio's death affected him. Horror, remorse, fear of the conse-quences — was he experiencing any of these? Or was he perhaps indifferent to what he had done? They had been married twelve years, but beyond his jealousy and his bitter hatred of John Everard she knew little of what went on in his mind. In their brief moments of passion, long since past, he had said that he loved her, that his jealousy was an expression of his love. She had told him that it was pride, not love, and that it could only widen the rift between them; but never in her wildest thoughts had she anticipated it might drive him to murder. That it had done so made her see him afresh. In some perverted way it gave him stature, made a man out of what she had thought to be less than half a man; so that to the revulsion she felt at the killing was added a certain respect, compounded of curiosity and fear and even reluctant admiration.

Rossiter swung the car out to overtake, and she swayed against Juanita. Righting herself, she muttered an apology. Juanita did not answer; her eyes were still closed, and Eve wondered whether she was asleep. The girl puzzled her. Before the accident Rossiter had been telling Andrew about the robbery; and although Eve had not been listening, from snatches of their conversation she had got the impression that Juanita had been a willing participant. Yet the girl's attitude, the way the men treated her, did not bear out that impression. And was it likely that any woman — and the Johnson man had referred to her as Mrs Everard — would help to rob her husband's firm? And what was she doing in Spain? Emilio had said there would be a woman on the plane, but he had not said who or why. And no-one else had bothered to tell her anything.

The square was more crowded than before when they drove into Guadix, the people seemingly more curious. To all except Juanita it was a relief to leave the tightly packed car; clothes had stuck to hot flesh, and they plucked them away, flexing arms and legs to let the air circulate. Only Juanita stayed in the car. Her dark eyes were open now, watching them. But she did not speak.

Mopping his forehead, Rossiter said, 'Al, you stay here with the Corbetts. Find a bar if you must, but don't leave the square. We may have to skip in a hurry.' He opened the car door. 'Out, please, Mrs Everard. You're coming with me.'

She sat up slowly, her eyes dazed as from sleep. 'Where are you taking me?'

'It doesn't matter where. Get out.'

They went up past the cathedral, its walls red in the late afternoon sun. The cobbled street was narrow and uneven, flanked by small shuttered houses, the occasional open doorway giving a glimpse of a dark interior. Rossiter held Juanita's arm, helping her up the hill; she was unsteady on her feet in the high heels, and sometimes she stumbled. Connie walked behind, admiring the slim figure in the gay summer frock, his eyes hot.

Luis Moreno's house was near the top. Luis was old and big and stooping, with a fierce white moustache and a wrinkled, leathery face. Dressed in blue canvas jacket and bulging knee breeches, he stood in the doorway and eyed his visitors through eyes that were almost lost behind furiously bushy brows.

'Buenos tardes, Señor Rossiter. Señorita.' He gave Juanita a courtly bow. 'Adelante, adelante! Is cooler inside.'

He stood aside for them to enter. The room was large and low-ceilinged, with white-washed walls and a tiled floor and a large hazelwood table, scrubbed white, in the centre. In one corner a grandfather clock wheezed noisily, a low, brass-bound chest stood in another. The floor was covered with esparto-grass mats; grey fox skins hung on the walls, together with faded oleographs and an ivory crucifix. The small windows were grey with dust, and when the door was closed it shut out most of the light.

There were two other people in the room. The man was young and strikingly good-looking, with liquid eyes and long lashes and smooth olive skin. Luis introduced him as Pablo, his grandson. The woman was older. At a sharp word from Luis she disappeared down steps at the rear of the room, to return with glasses and a bottle of wine. She put them on the table, and vanished once more down the steps.

'Is this the woman?' Luis asked. And then, more sharply, 'Dónde está Emilio?'

'Dead,' Rossiter said. There could be no other reason for Emilio's absence. 'Morte. An accident.'

To Luis and his kind 'accident' had a

sinister meaning. The bushy eyebrows lifted.

'How — accident?'

'No es importante.' Rossiter had decided against embroidery. Luis' guess could be no more ugly than the truth. 'He's dead, and that puts me in a spot. I need somewhere for the woman to stay.'

Luis turned his attention to the wine, pouring it slowly to occupy time. Pablo said, his voice thin and reedy, 'Emilio had many friends, Señor. They will not like that he is dead.'

'Nobody likes it,' Rossiter told him, controlling his temper.

Speaking slowly, uncertain of their English, he elaborated his needs. Emilio was to have arranged a place for them to stay until the ransom had been paid and the woman could be released. His death had left them stranded. Now, too, they were six instead of the expected four. Luis, he knew, did not handle such matters personally; he was the go-between, the fixer. Time was short. What could he fix now?

'Six people.' Luis shook his head. 'Is

difficult, Señor. Where can one hide six people? In the Barrio, perhaps. But — '

'Not the Barrio. It may be the back of beyond, but it's not for us. Come again.'

The two Spaniards conferred. To Rossiter and Connie their conversation was unintelligible, but Juanita listened attentively. She was more awake now, had even bothered to replace the loose strands of hair. Watching her, Rossiter saw that she was frowning, and wondered if he had been wise to bring her to the house. Yet the alternative had been to leave her with Al and the Corbetts; and with disasters accumulating so rapidly he no longer trusted anyone. Besides, the letter had still to be written.

Presently Pablo went out. Luis said, 'There is a place, Señor. And a man — Manuel Aralar, a gypsy — who may help. Pablo has gone to find him.' He poured more wine. 'Entretanto, we wait.'

They waited, sipping the rough wine, and listening to Luis extolling Emilio's virtues and speculating on the effect the news of his tragic death would have on his friends. Rossiter knew what he was at.

The greater the danger the higher the price, and Luis meant him to know that the danger was immense. But at least there had been no definite refusal, and he began to plan the letter he must write. How much should he ask? Five million pesetas? Thirty thousand pounds would not break a man of Don Carlos's reputed wealth. But could he raise the money quickly? With things as they were, time could be both dangerous and expensive.

He took paper and envelope from his pocket and began to write.

Manuel Aralar was picturesque. Six feet tall, dressed in jacket and trousers several sizes too small, his coal black hair stood out in tousled tufts from a head that looked as though it had been severely hammered. His face was sallow, and adorned with long side whiskers and a heavy moustache. But it was the eyes that held Rossiter's attention. They were wild and glittering, like those of an animal at bay. Yet despite the man's appearance Rossiter was relieved that it was Manuel and not Pablo who was to be their escort. Eve Corbett could never have resisted

Pablo's good looks.

He did not want another murder on his hands.

Pablo did the talking. There was a cave village in the mountains, about twenty kilometres distant, which was now deserted. Manuel would take them there, would see that they were provided with bedding and provisions, would find them a woman to do the cooking. But it would be expensive. The track to the village was laborious, and everything would have to be transported by mule or donkey. 'And then there are Emilio's friends, Señor,' Pablo continued. 'They will be suspicious, you understand, when he does not arrive. They will wish to know — '

'All right, all right. I get the message. How much?'

Rossiter's bluntness took the Spaniards aback. Luis Moreno shook his head in grave disapproval. Pablo fluttered his long lashes and once more went into conference with Manuel.

'There are so many difficulties, Señor,' he said eventually. 'Many dangers. And with six people — '

'How much?' Rossiter demanded.

'Thirty thousand pesetas,' Pablo said. And added hastily, 'Cada dia.'

Rossiter did a quick calculation. One hundred and eighty pounds a day was twice the sum agreed with Emilio. But now there were six of them, and Emilio was to have had a share of the profits. From the wary look on their faces he knew that he was expected to bargain. But they would be bargaining from strength, and knew it. And he was impatient to complete the deal.

'All right,' he said. 'Tell Manuel to fix it. Why is the village deserted?'

'The villagers said there were ghosts,' Pablo told him. Both he and Manuel looked disappointed. Rossiter suspected that, from his ready acceptance, they were wondering whether they had set the price too low. 'But they were foolish, ignorant people, Señor. Is nothing.'

'Ghosts won't bother me,' Rossiter said.

They bothered Connie. Connie was superstitious, and a haunted cave in a deserted mountain village was an awesome prospect. But he uttered no protest.

147

It would, he knew, be futile.

Rossiter finished the letter and passed it to the girl. She read it, flinching a little at its contents. Then she looked at him.

'You would do this?' she asked. There was scorn rather than fear in her voice.

'Perhaps.' He knew that he would not. But there had to be a threat. 'It is up to you to persuade your father not to put me to the test.'

She stared at him. 'How can I do that?'

'Add a postscript. Tell him we mean business. When he sees your handwriting he'll know this isn't a hoax.' Her steady gaze angered him. 'Go on, write. We haven't got all night.'

She shook her head. 'My father will not read the letter. He is blind.'

Rossiter swore. Was the girl lying, or was this yet another malicious quirk of Fate?

He turned to Luis. 'Do you know a Don Carlos de Sagrera? Of Cordoba?'

'Por cierto, Señor.' Interest quickened on the weathered face. 'Everyone in Andalusia knows Don Carlos. Is a man very rich, Señor. Many lands, many — '

'Is he blind?' Rossiter asked.

'Si, Señor. An accident. He fell from his horse five — six years ago.' Luis fingered the white moustache, his eyes intent on the girl. 'Don Carlos is perhaps the father of the Señorita?'

Rossiter nodded. To Juanita he said, 'It makes no difference. Put something that will convince him it comes from you. In English, please, so that I can read it.'

She took her time over the postscript. Rossiter scanned it carefully. He said, 'Who is this Acci you mention?'

'She is accionista — a shareholder — in one of my father's companies. Señora Orzan — a very wealthy lady. As a child I always called her Acci. My father will remember.'

Rossiter grunted, reading the note again. Her easy explanation made him suspicious. Yet there was nothing here that could possibly help to trace them.

'You know this Señora Orzan?' he asked Luis.

'No, Señor. She is perhaps of Cordoba, Señorita?'

'Of Sevilla,' Juanita told him.

Rossiter hesitated. Then he sealed the envelope, addressed it, and handed it to Luis.

'I want that delivered tomorrow,' he said. 'Anonymously, you understand. Por mano. You can arrange that?'

'Si, Señor. A mano. Anónimo.' Luis read the address, looked pensively at Juanita, and pocketed the envelope 'Shall be done, Señor Rossiter. Do not worry.'

It seemed to Rossiter that for the next few days he was likely to do little else.

# 10

Everard had intended to leave the car outside the works so as to avoid attracting attention. But this seemed to savour too much of stealth, and he drove boldly in through the gap by the new buildings and parked the car in front of the office block. As he fumbled with his keys Fawsey came hurrying across the yard to challenge him.

'Oh! It's you, Mr Everard.' Fawsey was fat and getting old, and suspected he was not far from the managing director's axe. For that reason he both feared and fawned on him. 'Anything wrong, sir? Can I help?'

If Everard's explanation for his presence sounded implausible, Fawsey gave no hint of it. He said smoothly, 'Very good, sir. Oh! The office telephone rang a few minutes ago. Would that be someone for you, perhaps?'

Everard was puzzled. Only Colin knew where he was, and Colin would have no cause to ring him.

'Must have been a wrong number,' he said.

'Yes, sir. Er — any news of Mrs Everard and the boy?'

'None, I'm afraid. Well, I'll collect what I need and be off. I'm late already.' He did not invent a reason for his lateness. That would be out of character. 'Good night, Fawsey.'

'Good night, sir.'

He let himself into the office block and went directly to the safe, switching on lights as he went to avoid any appearance of stealth. As he bent to the lock he wondered what Fawsey would think should he chance to look through the window. The man must know that Juanita had been involved in the robbery. The fleeting thought came to him that he might be losing Fawsey his job, but it did not deter him. If necessary Fawsey could be compensated.

There were close on two thousand pounds in the safe. Everard took half, and packed it away in the suitcase containing the change of clothing he kept at the office. Then he sat down and wrote a short note, explaining what he had done but making no mention of Spain. He had stooped to put the note in the open safe when there came the sound of a soft footfall behind him. Turning quickly, he saw a tall figure, the face masked, tiptoeing towards him. The man was only a few feet away, and as Everard turned he leapt forward, a heavy desk ruler in his upraised hand. There was no time for Everard to avoid him. Too late he put up an arm to ward off the blow. The ruler cracked down on the back of his neck, and with a groan he slumped to the floor.

Some time later he drifted back to consciousness to find himself lying by the safe, his wrists and ankles tied. His head ached abominably, and he felt sick. Dimly to his ears came the sound of a voice; but it was not until his senses were fully awake that he realized the voice was speaking into the telephone. Rolling on to his side, Everard peered under a chair at a pair of trousered legs. The rest of the body was obscured by the chair seat.

'The woman's right, Sergeant,' the

voice said. 'I saw the lights myself as I was passing. That's what brought me in.' There was a pause. 'Yes, that's what I said; I found him robbing the safe. He must have knocked out the night watchman; the old man's in a bad way.' Another pause. 'No, he had a key. I know it sounds daft, but he looks like John Everard — you know, the chap whose wife is missing. But whoever he is he won't escape. I've got him tied up. Only hurry, please. I can't wait long, I'm hours late already.'

There came the sound of the receiver being replaced on its cradle, of crêpe soles on the floor. Everard breathed a sigh of relief as he realized that the footsteps were going away from him, and as the door closed he began the struggle to free himself. His wrists were tied with his handkerchief, and less securely than his ankles, but he was sweating profusely by the time he had managed to free them. That was some ten minutes later, and he wondered what was keeping the police. The local station was less than three miles away; they should have arrived by now had the sergeant acted promptly. But it was his good fortune that they had not, and he started on the rope round his ankles, his fingers so tired from the tussle with the handkerchief that they seemed all thumbs, his ears alert for the sound of a car drawing up in the yard. The safe was still open, and as he undid the last knot and scrambled to his feet he saw that the rest of the money had been taken. But his suitcase was where he had left it, apparently untouched. He grabbed it and made for the door, switching off lights as he went.

The Austin had not been moved. There was no sign of his assailant; having helped himself to the rest of the money, no doubt the man had decided that it would be wiser to leave before the police arrived. No sign of Fawsey either. But Everard did not stay to search for him. If Fawsey needed attention he must get it from the police.

Cars were moving on the main road as he bumped down the track from the works, and as each pair of headlights neared the junction he expected them to swing towards him, cutting off his retreat. None did. Nevertheless it was not until he had gone some way on the road to London that he allowed himself to relax and ponder on what had happened. His head still ached, but his mind was clear enough to realize that his assailant had not been the chance passer-by he had represented himself to be on the telephone. The mask denied that.

So who was he?

Colin was waiting for him at the flat. 'Thank the Lord you're back,' he said. 'What happened?'

'How did you know something happened?'

'Never mind that now. Tell me.'

Everard told him. 'I sweated blood to get free before the police arrived,' he said. 'Even now I can't understand how I managed it. They had bags of time. Something must have delayed them. And thank Heavens it did!'

'It didn't.' Colin's freckled face was one enormous grin. 'That was me. On the phone, I mean.'

'You?' Everard stared at him in disbelief.

'None other.' He took a pipe from his pocket and started to fill it. 'When you left here I noticed a car pull out from the kerb and follow. It turned into the High Street after you, and I had the nasty feeling that you were being tailed. If I'd been mobile I'd have played safe and tagged on behind; as it was, all I could do was give you time to reach the office and then ring you. No-one answered the first time. The second, I got your stockinged friend. At least, I suppose it was him.'

'It was,' Everard said. 'What made him think you were the police?'

'Because that's what I told him. It shook me when a stranger answered the phone. I thought it must be someone connected with the firm, so I said the first thing that came into my head — that I was the local sergeant, and that a woman had rung to say the lights were on in the office, and was anything wrong.'

'There bloody well was,' Everard said ruefully, tenderly fingering the back of his neck. 'Did you know he was a phoney?'

'Yes. He said he was just about to ring the police himself, and I dare say that was true. But when he told me you'd slugged the night watchman I knew he was lying. You're not that desperate. Or I hope not.' Colin struck a match, started to light his pipe, and then paused. 'Hey! How about that? Fawsey, I mean. The poor devil may need help. I'd better give the police a ring.'

Everard frowned. 'Is that wise? They might trace the call.'

From the look on Colin's face he realized that he must have sounded callous in his objection. Well, perhaps he was. But this was a question of priorities, and at that moment his freedom came first.

'I'll use the call-box down the road,' Colin said.

He was not absent long. 'Any luck with the contacts?' Everard asked, when he returned. 'Or didn't you get around to that?'

Colin shook his head. 'Too busy figuring how to dig you out. Even if I could find a car to take me I didn't know where the damned place was, or how to get in, or where to look for you when I was in. But I'd have had a go if you hadn't turned up within a reasonable time. The only joy was that, from what this comedian said on the phone, tying you up seemed to have satisfied his belligerency. Temporarily, anyway. I hoped you might free yourself, or that Fawsey would do it for you if he wasn't too badly dented.' He coughed as he inadvertently swallowed a mouthful of smoke. He was a wet smoker. 'Any idea who your visitor might be?'

Everard shrugged. 'If Tasker's name in this business isn't a coincidence, then I'd say it was him. Or one of his mates.'

'He sure must hate your guts.'

'He must, mustn't he? But I may be wrong, of course — in which case your guess is as good as mine.'

'H'm! Well, whoever he was, we'll have to move you out in the morning. If he's all set to get you locked up — as from tonight's performance one imagines he is — he won't accept defeat easily. Tonight's episode can't make the morning papers — it's three o'clock now — but when there's no news of your arrest in the mid-day editions he's going to start thinking. And this flat is where his thoughts will lead him.'

That possibility had not occurred to Everard. 'Where do I go?' he asked, dismayed.

Colin patted his arm. 'Leave that to me. I'll fix it.'

So much for independence, Everard reflected, as he went wearily to bed. It was Colin's quick thinking which had saved him from arrest that night, it was Colin who would hide him on the morrow and arrange his escape to Spain. Without Colin he would have been lost. There was also the unhappy probability that, in addition to murder, he was now wanted for robbery and assault; his written apology for borrowing the money had been tucked into one of the bundles of notes the thief had stolen. Unless Fawsey could identify his assailant (which was unlikely) the assumption would be that it was he, John Everard, who had knocked him down and cleaned out the safe.

But it was neither of these unpleasant reflections, nor the image of the dead Laroche, nor jealousy, nor the nagging dread of what might be happening to Juanita and Tommy, that kept him awake. It was the sudden impact on his tired mind of a problem which had not hitherto vexed it. Nor Colin's either, he supposed. Yet at that moment it seemed the most urgent problem of all.

He had told no-one he would be at the flat. He had not known he would be going there, or even where it was. So how had his assailant managed to pick up the trail? And if the man's fore-knowledge of his movements was so uncannily accurate, what chance had he of leaving the flat undetected on the morrow?

# 11

Juanita lay on her back on the truckle bed, hands clasped behind her head, and stared at the smooth rock above. It was cool inside the cave, and dark; there were no windows, and the only light came filtering in through the high entrance of the outer chamber. Once there had been a door between the two chambers, with white-wash on the walls and rough tiles on the floor. Now the walls were moist and crumbling and the white-wash showed only in patches, and the door was an old blanket, supplied under protest by Manuel Aralar. Manuel had also provided esparto-grass mats to cover some of the gaps in the tiles. A small alcove housed a tin bowl and an earthenware pitcher, and on a ledge cut from the rock wall stood a mirror encased in a large and ornate gilt frame. Apart from the two truckle beds there was no other furniture.

Eve came in from the outer chamber,

slipped on the damp steps, and stood for a moment to accustom her eyes to the gloom. The blood-stained blue dress had been exchanged for a green one, high waisted, and with a tight, low-cut bodice and a flaring skirt. Connie had whistled when he saw it. Andrew had frowned, but made no comment.

'Don't you want any breakfast?' she asked. Juanita did not answer, and she went over to the empty bed and sat down. 'Not that I can recommend it. Stale rolls and Tulipan and black coffee. Or the woman said it was coffee.' She bent to take off her shoes and massage her ankles. 'Lord, but my feet ache! They're still raw.'

They had left the car at the foot of the mountains. Pablo had said there would be donkeys for the women, but the decrepit animals Manuel had produced had been sufficient to carry only the baggage. They also looked mangy and flea-ridden, so that, although Eve had protested vociferously when told that she and Juanita would have to walk, it had been more on principle than in anger. She had not known then what the walk would entail.

But Juanita had said nothing, and Eve found that bewildering. It was unnatural in a woman — and particularly a woman of Juanita Everard's gentle upbringing — to accept with such silent stoicism the trials and indignities which the men had heaped on her. If I were in her place, thought Eve, I would just about tear my hair out. Theirs too if I got the chance.

The trek to the caves had called for all the strength and endurance the women could muster. It was a long, rugged journey, with the evening sun hot on their tired bodies and the inevitable flies swarming round their faces. Except in a few places the climb had not at first been particularly steep; but once they had cleared the olives and the scrub the track had deteriorated into a deep gully littered with boulders, down which a stiff wind had blown, flinging the red-grey dust into eyes and nose and mouth. When they emerged from the gully on to the face of the mountain, with only a few patches of blue gorse and white poppies to relieve the monotony of rock and shale, the going had been even tougher. Manuel, and his two friends with the donkeys, wore rope-soled *alpargatas* and moved easily and quickly; but the rest of the party had reached their destination in varying stages of exhaustion. Corbett's leg had failed him on the climb out of the gully, and one of the donkeys had had to be unloaded for him to ride. Even the tough Rossiter and the long-striding Johnson had shown signs of distress. But it was the women who suffered most. To Eve it was as though every bone in her body had been jarred and battered. Her feet were raw and inflamed, and towards the end she had scarcely the strength left to brush the flies from her face. It seemed to her incredible that the fragile Juanita, despite her obvious exhaustion, could endure the journey without complaint or protest.

Recalling the journey now, she said, 'Mountaineering is not for me. I don't think my feet will ever be the same again.' She prodded tenderly at a broken blister, and sighed. 'Wouldn't it be heavenly to lie in a hot bath and soak for hours?' There was no reply from the other bed, and after a pause she asked, with some diffidence, 'Is there anything you need? Apart from hot water, I mean. That's out. It seems there's little enough of the cold variety.'

Juanita's feet were sore also. She had suffered the pain and discomfort in silence because it had seemed important that the men should not subdue her spirit; to plead or protest would have given them moral as well as physical ascendancy over her. Yet the journey had been agony, and only a fierce pride had enabled her to endure it. Even after a night on the truckle bed her body still ached, her limbs were stiff and heavy. She wanted neither breakfast nor conversation; she wanted only to rest. Yet she was also curious. Why should this woman, the wife of her husband's enemy, of the man who was presumably responsible for her present predicament, seek now to be friendly?

She said coldly, 'All I want from you and your unpleasant friends, Mrs Corbett, is my freedom. And I understand that will be expensive.'

Eve flushed. 'You hate me, don't you?' she said.

''Despise' would be more correct.' Juanita paused. 'I understood it was you and your husband who hated me. Isn't that why I am here? And the money, of course. It is more satisfactory, no doubt, if one can make one's hatred pay.'

The contempt in her voice stung Eve to a hot retort. Her friendly overture had been a half-hearted attempt to assuage the sense of guilt she felt towards the other. Nothing that had happened to Juanita had been her responsibility, yet the guilt had persisted. Now, temporarily at least, it vanished.

'We don't hate you, Mrs Everard. But we have good reason to hate your husband. It was he who sacked Andrew — and after thirty years with the firm.'

'No doubt he had a reason.'

'Oh, yes, he had a reason. He was a new broom, and he wanted to show his strength.' Eve wondered if her angry defence was for her husband or for herself. She had never thought to defend Andrew before. 'He knew that his changes would be unpopular, so he invented charges of inefficiency and negligence — even dishonesty — against anyone with enough influence to be difficult. Men like my husband, and Tom Manning, and — ' She paused. 'Did you know Mr Manning committed suicide?'

'Yes. I am sorry.'

'I doubt if your husband is.' Now that defence was turning to attack Eve was beginning to enjoy herself. 'Mrs Manning was left without a penny, but your husband did nothing to help her. Not a damned thing.'

There was silence, broken only by the sound of men's voices in the outer chamber. Then Juanita said quietly, with biting sarcasm, 'And the money you get for my ransom will of course be given to the widow. How noble of you!'

'Perhaps,' Eve retorted. 'I wouldn't know. Bringing you to Spain wasn't my husband's idea; Rossiter did that without consulting him. All Andrew wanted — '

She stopped, aware that she was

becoming indiscreet. This was a conversation neither Andrew nor Rossiter would approve.

'He wanted what?' asked Juanita.

Eve swung her legs on to the bed and lay back. 'I don't wish to discuss it any further,' she said, with a weak attempt at hauteur.

In the outer chamber Connie and Al were playing cards, with Connie chattering incessantly, his more obscene comments quickly hushed by his companion. Eve supposed they were there as gaolers, as Rossiter had been during the night. In a sense she too was a gaoler; why else would Rossiter have put her in a room with the girl instead of with her husband? But she had not protested. Neither, so far as she knew, had Andrew. Emilio's death was still too fresh in their minds for them to be alone together.

Juanita did not press for an answer. What Andrew Corbett had wanted was not important. It was what had happened, what was going to happen, that mattered — and presently she said, the anger and the coldness gone from her voice, 'One thing you can tell me, perhaps. Where is my son? What have they done with him?'

'I don't know,' Eve told her. 'I'm sorry, but that's the truth. I just don't know.'

They spent most of the morning in the cave — Eve, because she could avoid the issue with Andrew, Juanita because she was too weary, too sad, to move. Had she been right, she wondered unhappily, to obey her captors so docilely? When the car had overturned, and she had found herself surrounded by those sympathetic Spanish faces, she had been tempted to ask their help. But, dazed as she was, she had remembered what Rossiter had said. Tommy was their hostage, his fate lay in her hands; only when the ransom had been paid and they were back in England would he be released. He had not put into words what would happen if they were baulked in any way; but Connie had drawn a significant hand across his throat, and Rossiter had said grimly, 'Well, that's one way of putting it.' She had known he could be bluffing, but she had not dared to call his bluff. She could not gamble

170

with Tommy as the stake.

It was the flies that eventually drove them out. As the morning sun climbed into the sky they came swarming into the cave, to maintain an incessant buzzing on the walls and over the limp figures on the beds. Eve was the first to move. Pawing frantically at the insistent horde round her face, she slipped on her shoes and hobbled stiffly out, ignoring Connie's wolf whistle. As she emerged from the gloom the heat seemed to pour over her, and she paused, blinking at the strong light.

'Look at them legs, wack,' Connie said.

Eve moved away from the entrance. She had no objection to displaying her figure. But not to men like Connie.

The village bore little resemblance to the Barrio at Guadix. There were no tall pinnacles, no ravines, no smooth glaciers of lava-like rock. The caves had been cut from a shallow escarpment, a tenement block of single-storeyed dwellings lacking the air of permanence that managed to pervade the Barrio. No bricks and mortar had been used to bolster a crumbling face, no lime plaster to stop a vein of sand; there had been no attempt to arch the ceilings, to smooth the walls or erect chimneys. According to Pablo the village had been empty for little more than a year, yet already some of the caves had fallen in; others, their outer walls crumbling, looked likely to collapse with the first heavy fall of rain. Only two appeared reasonably safe for habitation; the one occupied by the two women and their guards, and another taken over by the men. At the far end of the village a third cave had been appropriated by Manuel as a storeroom, although the woman cooked in the open. She was there now, crouched by the brazier. The crushed olive stones she used as fuel gave out a bitter, yet not unpleasant, smell.

Andrew and Rossiter sat in the shade of the escarpment, with the boulder-strewn mountainside rising steeply behind them. They sat apart, not talking. Andrew was staring moodily up at the sky, watching a falcon as it glided lazily in an ever-tightening circle. Rossiter whittled aimlessly at a sliver of wood. The frown that had settled almost permanently on his face since his return to Spain was there now. He had taken off his shirt, and his stomach bulged whitely above the top of his shorts.

Eve walked slowly towards them up the rough track that had once been the village street. Juanita's scornful comment about the destination of the ransom money had given her food for thought.

Andrew watched her as she came up to them. He had a tired, defeated look. His shoulders drooped dejectedly, and she could see his long fingers beating a nervous, rapid tattoo on the palms of his hands. She had a sudden feeling of compassion for him, and gave him a brief smile. But it was Rossiter she had come to talk to. She said briskly, 'I've been thinking, Mr Rossiter. This money you're getting from the girl's father — what happens to it? Have you discussed that with Andrew?'

'That's my business,' he said, still whittling. 'I've discussed it with no-one.

But you'll get your whack.'

'I should hope so!' She flapped irritably at the flies that had followed her down the track. 'After that nightmare of a journey last night — and sleeping in a filthy cave — and the food! Ugh!' A fly landed on her lip, and she spat it away. 'Well, all I can say is, it had better be generous. I'm not going through all this for peanuts.'

'You're not, eh?' He looked at her then. She could not see his eyes behind the dark glasses, but the line of his mouth under the dark moustache, the anger in his voice, made her vaguely nervous. 'That filthy cave, Mrs Corbett, is costing us more than six times as much as your fancy rooms at the Carlton or the Alhambra Palace. But don't blame me if it isn't to your liking. If you and your husband between you hadn't managed to dispose of Emilio we wouldn't be here.' He jabbed the knife viciously into the shale. Once he had sympathized with the woman, admired her for her objectivity, her directness. Now he could think only of the

174

misfortune she had brought him. 'Now get the hell out of here, will you, before I lose my temper? Why I had to get involved with a bloody nympho and a crazy killer I'm damned if I know. But never again. No more bloody amateurs for me.'

Andrew Corbett jerked his tired back erect. He said bitterly, 'Abuse comes easily to you, doesn't it, Rossiter? But you're not entirely blameless for what's happened. Had you stuck to the original plan — kept Mrs Everard in England — '

He stopped as a large stone came rattling down the mountain to land at his side. Rossiter got to his feet and looked up. High above, picking their way between the boulders, three men were coming down towards them.

'We've got visitors,' he said. And swore. 'Pablo and a couple of strangers.'

They were not strangers to Eve. Furious at Rossiter's scathing attack and at the mildness of her husband's rebuke, yet frightened too at the viciousness of Rossiter's tone, she had hesitated, uncertain whether to counter-attack or beat an undignified retreat.

'They're Emilio's friends,' she said; anger gone, one fear replaced by another. 'The two he met in the bar at Guadix.'

Corbett stood up, leaning against the rock face for support, his face grey under the tan. Farther down the track Juanita emerged from the cave, shielded her eyes against the sun, and stood staring up at the mountain. Rossiter shouted for Al and Connie and waited, hands dug into the pockets of his shorts.

The visitors were in no hurry. They came down slowly, their eyes watchful. Eve thought again how handsome Pablo was, how villainous his companions. She wondered why Manuel was not with them. Lucia, the woman who cooked their breakfast, had told her he would come soon.

A few yards above the waiting trio Pablo halted, putting out a detaining arm to his companions.

'Bueños dias, Señora — Señores,' he said, in his reedy voice. He looked across at Juanita, at Al and Connie emerging from the cave, and smiled. He had beautiful teeth. 'You are comfortable, si?'

'We're not here for comfort,' Rossiter growled. 'What do you want?'

'For myself — nothing, Señor. But Federo and Antonio here, they are sad. Emilio Ginachero was their friend. They wish to know what will be done for his family.' Pablo shook his dark head. 'Emilio had big family, Señor.'

'I bet he had,' Rossiter said. 'And all dependent on him, no doubt.'

'Si, Señor.' Pablo looked grateful for this ready acceptance of the point he wished to make. 'Many cousins, many brothers and sisters. And his mother is a widow. Without Emilio they will starve.'

'And they expect me to provide for them, eh?' Rossiter nodded. 'Very well. They can have what I agreed to pay Emilio. Forty thousand pesetas — when I get it.'

Emilio was to have had nearly twice that sum. But his death had already proved expensive, and Rossiter saw no reason to be generous. This was hush money. Emilio's family, if he had one, would probably never receive a peseta of it. The men would carve it up between them.

Pablo conferred with his companions. The conference was short, and ended in an explosive epithet from the squat Antonio that needed no translation for his listeners below.

'They say it is not enough, Señor.' Pablo's tone was grave — hypocritically so, Rossiter suspected. 'They say — '

'I don't give a damn what they say. It's all they're getting.'

Federo muttered something to Antonio, and again there was a conference. The lightweight suits they had worn in the Guadix bar had been replaced by jeans and loose-fitting jerseys, the flat caps by berets. Eve wondered if they always dressed alike. She wondered too if Federo did not understand at least some English. His sharp button eyes had watched Rossiter closely as he talked, had seemed to grow angry at his refusal.

'Perdóneme, Señor Rossiter, but I think you do not understand,' Pablo said slowly. 'You see, we have found Emilio.'

Eve put a hand to her mouth to stifle a

scream. Her husband leaned more heavily against the rock and swallowed hard, the Adam's apple prominent in his long neck. Even Rossiter looked worried.

'The devil you have!' he said.

'Si, Señor. Emilio has told Federo where the airplane is to land, and this morning we go to see. Is just curiosity, you understand; we do not look for Emilio. But then we meet *el cabrero* — the goatherd, Señor — and he tells us he has seen men digging.' Pablo blinked his long lashes at them. 'Is not a very deep grave, Señor.'

'No.' Rossiter spoke abstractedly. He was thinking ahead. 'We had no tools. But we did what we could.'

'Si. But his friends, Señor — they wish to give him a proper funeral. That will be expensive.'

'Of course,' Rossiter said tartly.

'And then there are the authorities, Señor. If there is a funeral they will wish to know why.' Pablo's dark eyes lifted to gaze across the distant vega. 'It will not be good for you, Señor Rossiter, that the

179

police should interest themselves in Emilio. But with money much may be done. That is why my friends say that forty thousand pesetas is not enough. They do not wish to see you in trouble with the police, Señor, and they say — '

'Very kind of them. But you can cut the patter, Pablo. How much?'

Softly, as though the sum were too sacred to be spoken aloud, Pablo said, 'Doscientos mil duros, Señor. One million pesetas.'

Rossiter stared at him. He guessed that Pablo had spoken first in Spanish for the benefit of his accomplices. But — one million pesetas! Six thousand quid! They must be off their heads to think he would pay that sort of money.

'Don't be a bloody fool,' he said curtly. 'I'll make it a hundred thousand, and that's final. And in case your friends should think of throwing a spanner in the works, tell them they don't get a bean until the ransom has been paid. Not one single bloody peseta.'

Antonio broke into a torrent of rasping Spanish. Pushing Pablo aside, he took a

180

step forward, his good eye glaring balefully down at Rossiter. Pablo frowned, and caught his arm to pull him back.

'Is a small sum to hide a murder, Señor,' he said.

Only when the word was actually spoken did Eve realize that she had known from the beginning that this was why the men had come. Andrew had known it too, she thought. And Rossiter. But that did not make the moment less tense.

Rossiter scratched thoughtfully at the dark hairs on his chest. He did not seem perturbed.

'Emilio's death was an accident,' he said calmly. 'And you can cut out the blackmail, Pablo. I don't frighten easily.'

'A strange accident, Señor Rossiter, that can do so much hurt to a man's head.'

'All right, so it was strange.' As with Luis Moreno before, Rossiter did not try to invent an explanation. 'That doesn't make it murder, and you can't prove it does.' He took a handkerchief from his pocket and mopped his forehead. 'Now beat it, will you? I've had enough of this party. Your friends will get their whack when I get mine. But a hundred thousand only — which is a darned sight more than they deserve.'

He was turning away when Pablo said, 'There was a stick by the grave, Señor. A stick with blood on the handle. My friends here, they say it is Señor Corbett's stick. They say he has it when he comes to Guadix with Emilio.'

Rossiter stopped abruptly. He was facing Eve, and she could see the heavy sweat on his white face.

'Beat it,' he said again. He said it with difficulty, as though at that moment words were hard to come by.

'Si, Señor.' There was a hint of laughter in Pablo's voice, an exultant look in his eyes. 'But we come back. Mañana, eh? Mañana por la mañana.'

Corbett watched the men turn and start to climb the mountain. Then he left the support of the rock and limped across to Rossiter.

'I'm sorry,' he said. 'I didn't realize I'd left the damned thing until it was too late to go back. But is it important? I mean — well, they didn't need the stick to know it was murder.'

Slowly Rossiter raised his fist. He had the look of a man about to commit unbridled violence. Then he gritted his teeth, slapped the fist into the palm of his other hand, and strode off down the track.

# 12

As the aircraft swept down the wide Andalusian plain, with the snow-capped Sierra Morena to the north and the strange, pagoda-like peaks of the Sierra Yequas away to the south, Everard had kept his eyes fixed on the ground below, trying to pick out the de Sagrera estancia. But somewhere it had been lost to him in a sea of olives. Now, directly ahead, lay the airport, and beyond that Seville itself and the wide, slow waters of the Guadalquivir, with the high tower of La Giralda and the soaring cathedral dancing like giants in the shimmering haze that lay over the city. He was never happy in the air, but the sinking sensation that attacked his stomach as they came in to land was not caused solely by the descent. He was unhappily aware that this might prove to have been a wasted journey, that Laroche might have lied when he said that Juanita was in Spain.

He took a taxi from the airport. The estancia lay east of the city, out towards Cordoba, and as he travelled the familiar road he reflected on the journey, deliberately shutting his mind to contemplation of what might lie ahead. To anticipate might be to dull his judgment, his clarity of thought, when they were most needed.

They had left the flat early on the Sunday morning. He had slept little, and his head still ached abominably, but he was restless on the journey to the coast; the cars behind had seemed to be in menacing pursuit, their occupants bent on his arrest or destruction. He watched them through the rear window, willing them to drop farther behind or sweep aloofly past. Neither eventuality gave him relief. There were always other cars.

They reached the coast without incident. Everard had expected his departure from England to be wrapped in secrecy, and was surprised by its apparent normality. The *Giraffe*, a smart, forty-foot cabin cruiser, lay at anchor in the harbour. They were taken out to her in a dinghy, and as he climbed aboard Everard received yet another surprise. The skipper was not the bearded, piratical figure of his imagination, but a slim, fresh-faced woman in tailored slacks and a suntop, her blonde hair tied in a silk scarf.

'Colin has told me all about you,' she said. 'Glad to have you aboard, Mr Everard. I hope we bring you luck.' She had a cultured voice with a mid-European accent that he could not place. He never learned her name.

Colin had gone ashore an hour later, briefed with what information Everard could supply and bent on effecting Tommy's release, with or without the help of the police. The fine morning worsened to a wet, squally afternoon, and Everard spent most of it in the neat little cabin, talking to the woman or watching the other craft in the harbour. He was too tense to sleep, although occasionally he dozed. Towards evening his passport and papers had arrived, apparently authenticated, together with French and Spanish currency. Their possession made him feel slightly more secure.

They had crossed to France that night, and early the next morning he had flown to Madrid and on to Seville. The journey had gone so smoothly that he had almost begun to disassociate it from its purpose, so great was the contrast. Only when the large wrought-iron gates of the estancia clanged behind him did he fully appreciate the connection.

The de Sagrera estancia stood in the midst of orange groves and myrtles, with the Sierra Morena for backdrop. A dozen or more buildings, a chapel among them, were clustered round the main building, giving the place a feudal appearance. The house itself was typical of the older estancias, a square white building round a tiled patio, with a double-tiered colonnade on all four sides, and high arched entrances at back and front. In the centre of the patio a fountain played, flanked by young palms. There were geraniums in niches in the walls, and tall cages in which canaries and linnets vied with the chirruping of hidden crickets.

Ramon Perez emerged from the patio as Everard was paying off the taxi. Ramon was Don Carlos's secretary; a plump, grave young man, impeccably groomed and darkly handsome.

'Señor Everard!' There was surprise and delight in his greeting. 'The Saints be praised that you are here! Since last night I have been trying to telephone you. I spoke with your housekeeper, but she said you had not been home, that she did not know where you were. I have been frantic with worry.'

Everard wasted no time in preliminaries. 'Juanita,' he said. 'You have heard?'

Ramon nodded energetically. 'A note came yesterday. A man gave it to one of the workers and told him to bring it to the house.' He sighed. 'Is a pity they did not hold the man. Some say they have seen him before, in Cordoba. They are looking for him now, but I do not think they will find him.'

'What was in the note?'

'They are demanding ransom, Señor. Five million pesetas — and by tomorrow.'

To Everard the information brought relief as well as pain. At least he had been right to come to Spain.

'And Don Carlos?' he asked. 'He has agreed to pay?'

'Madre de Dios, but he cannot!' There were tears in the young man's eyes. 'That is the terrible thing. He is ill, Señor Everard; an *ataque fulminante*, the doctors say. It arrived as I was reading the note to him. He was seated in his chair, and suddenly he gave a strange little cry and collapsed. He has not moved or spoken since.' He dabbed at his eyes with a handkerchief. 'Forgive me, Señor, but I am much distressed. Don Carlos has been good to me. The doctors say he will recover. But I ask myself — when? And how well?'

To Everard this was the crowning disaster. It had never occurred to him that if Juanita were held to ransom the money might not be available. Don Carlos was a rich man, and devoted to his daughter; and five million pesetas, large as the sum was, would be well within his means. But if he had suffered a stroke . . .

'Who signs the cheques on his behalf?' he asked. 'You? His solicitor?'

Ramon shook his head. 'He signs

everything himself. And it is a good signature. I guide his hand to the place where he must write, but that is all.'

So even that faint hope was out. 'I had better see him,' Everard said.

'Si. But he will not know you.'

If the exterior of the house was Spanish, the interior owed much to Moorish influence. The rooms were vast, with wide windows and polished marble floors and massive doors that clanged; the ceilings were of cedar, the curtains of damask or velvet. Rich oriental rugs covered the floors, and everywhere there were Greek sculptures and pottery, Egyptian ornaments, oriental bronzes. But the pictures adorning the walls were all by Spanish painters, some of them little known outside their own country. Zurbarán, Leal, Francisco Pachecho, Herrera el Viego — Everard had heard their names, but he did not recognize their art. His knowledge of painters was confined to a popular few. As he followed Ramon Perez through the rooms and up the broad marble staircase he was in no frame of mind to appreciate pictures.

Vaguely he recognized a Murillo and the fantastic, clownish work of Joán Miró. The rest were as strangers.

Don Carlos lay in a massive fourposter, his eyes closed. He was only a few years older than Everard, yet the latter always thought of him as old; his frailty, the waxen skin, the slow, precise voice, the thin grey hair — all gave the impression of age. Now he looked older still — as near to death as living man can be.

'All day he has been like that,' Ramon said, the tears starting anew.

Everard grunted. He could not share the other's grief. There had been neither friendship nor liking between himself and Don Carlos. All his concern was for Juanita.

'Don Carlos.' He bent over the bed, his voice urgent. 'This is John Everard. Juanita is in danger, she needs your help.' There was no movement from the sick man, the parchment-like eyelids stayed closed. 'Don Carlos! Can you hear me?'

'It is no use, Señor,' Ramon said. 'Believe me, I have tried many times.'

Reluctantly Everard turned from the

bed. 'Show me the note,' he said gruffly.

Ramon fetched it. Everard was filled with an unholy rage as he read it. It was not the size of the ransom that appalled him, but the threat which followed — that if the money were not paid at the stipulated time Juanita would be sold into a Moorish brothel. 'She would fetch a good price,' the note ran. 'If we have to cut our losses it would be a more profitable solution than murder. And after my somewhat uncouth companions have done with her I doubt if she would protest.' It went on to warn against invoking the aid of the police, since murder might then be forced on her captors. She would hamper their escape, yet be too dangerous a witness to leave behind.

'The bastards!' he raged. 'The filthy bastards!'

'You think they would do that?' Ramon asked anxiously.

Everard did not answer. He was reading Juanita's pathetic little postscript. 'Please act quickly, father,' she had written, in her rather cramped style. 'If you have not the money perhaps Acci will help. But please, please hurry!'

The wording of the appeal puzzled him. Surely she could not have doubted her father's ability or willingness to pay?

'Who is this Acci she mentions?' he asked.

'I do not know,' Ramon said. 'It is a strange name. I have not heard it before. Neither has Señor Gonzales, the attorney.'

'It must be a nickname. Is there anyone it might fit?' And as Ramon gaped at him, 'Think, man, think!'

But thought brought Ramon no solution. Everard glared angrily at the man on the bed, cursing his frailty.

'Her Aunt Soledad,' he said. 'Have you tried her?'

'She is in America.'

'Damn! Well, there must be someone. Don Carlos has friends, hasn't he? Rich friends? Can't Gonzales tackle them?'

'He will do his best, Señor. But five million pesetas is a large sum to find in so short a time.'

They went down to the patio. In the

shade of the high walls it was pleasantly cool, and as they sipped their Amontillado Everard read and reread the ugly note, seeking some hint that the threats would not be implemented, some guidance as to what he must do.

Ramon said, 'I did not go to the police because of what is written there. I asked Señor Gonzales, and he said to wait. But if you think — '

'No. Not yet. Not until we have exhausted every possible alternative.'

'But what alternatives are there?'

'I don't know,' Everard said impatiently. He tapped the note with the back of his hand. 'Do you know this place where we have to hand over the money?'

'No. But I have looked at the map. It should not be difficult to find.'

The hours that followed seemed interminable to both men. They could only wait, hoping against hope that Gonzales would be successful, that if he could not find the whole sum demanded by the kidnappers he would raise at least enough to satisfy their greed. They talked little — Ramon because he had neither comfort nor advice to offer, Everard because he was sunk in an apathy of despair. Rejecting the uncertainty of the future, his tired mind turned presently, in a welter of self-pity, to the sorrows of the past, so that he found himself wondering why he should care so desperately about his wife's fate. She had left him for a despicable creature like Laroche, she had involved herself with a bunch of criminals who were apparently set on wrecking his life; because of her he had committed murder. He owed her nothing. And if by some miracle she were free — what then? She could not go back to Laroche. Laroche was dead.

He shuddered at the memory of how Laroche had died, clenching his fist. The crackle of the note in his hand recalled him to his senses, and he drove the rebel thoughts away, hating himself that he had given them harbour. This was no time for jealousy or self-pity or despair. No matter what Juanita had done, what she might or might not do in the future, he loved her. And because he loved her he must fight for her. He had no choice.

When Señor Gonzales eventually arrived he brought with him little more than a quarter of the ransom demanded. Don Carlos, he explained, was not a man with many friends, and the few who might have helped him now were away. 'At this time of the year people go to the sea or the mountains, where it is cooler,' he said. 'Give me more time, Señor Everard, and I will find you more money. But in one day — ' He shrugged. 'Is impossible.'

The money was in notes of varying denominations, many of them small. Piled high on the wrought-iron table, it looked an impressive amount. Everard said doubtfully, 'We couldn't bluff them, I suppose. Pretend it is more than it is. They're English, remember, not Spanish. This would look a fortune to them, and it would take a hell of a lot of counting.'

Gonzales shook his head. 'It would be safer to inform the police. Even if the whole sum were available I would still advise it. Such men cannot be trusted.'

Everard knew he was right. He did not need the lawyer to remind him of the dread pervading all kidnappings — that even when the ransom had been paid the kidnappers might find it more expedient to destroy their captive rather than release her. If it were paid only in part anger might be an additional spur to expediency. Yet he was reluctant to agree.

'It's not only Juanita we have to consider,' he explained. 'There's Tommy. You've read the note, you know what it says. The threats may be idle, but I can't risk calling their bluff. Not until all else fails.'

Gonzales said bleakly, 'I think it has failed already, Señor.'

Ramon's plump face puckered in a frown. 'There is something I do not understand,' he said. 'You say that in England they ask ransom for Tommy also. But if you had paid it they would have had no — no — ' He turned to Gonzales. 'Que es rehén en inglés?'

'Hostage,' the lawyer told him.

'Si. Hostage. They would have no hostage to force you to obey their instructions.'

Everard shrugged. He did not understand it either. 'They may have meant to hold him until Juanita's ransom had also been paid,' he said bitterly. 'How can one tell?'

'Exactly, Señor,' Gonzales said. 'With men like these nothing is certain. Believe me, the police are the ones to deal with them.'

'Perhaps. But I'm going to talk to them first.' He began to stow the money back into the suitcase. 'Fourteen hundred thousand pesetas is a long way short of five million, but it's still a tidy sum; and if I can persuade them that it's all we can raise, maybe they'll take it. It's worth trying, anyway. And no tricks,' he said, looking hard at Gonzales. 'No police lurking round the corner. That will give me no chance at all. They'll have provided against that sort of contingency.'

Gonzales shrugged. 'No tricks, Señor.'

It was midnight when the lawyer left. As they watched his car drive away Everard said, 'It's easy for Gonzales to be so smug about the police. It's not his family that's in danger.'

'That is unfair, Señor,' Ramon protested. He had an expressionless face that belied his intelligence. 'He is most concerned.'

Everard was not listening. 'Acci,' he said. 'Acci. It's an odd name. Does it sound Spanish to you?'

'No, Señor. Latin, perhaps. But not Spanish.'

'Latin, eh? Could be. But who — ' He caught his breath. 'No, dammit! Not who — where! Don't you see, Ramon? It isn't a person, it's a place. The place where they're holding her. She dared not give the Spanish name, so she used the Roman. It would mean nothing to those bastards, but to a scholar like her father — ' He started to run. 'Come on. If there's an answer we'll find it in the library.'

It did not take them long. From Gasset's *Spain under the Romans* Ramon read the passage aloud in halting English. 'Acci, the original Roman and Iberian name for Guadix, changed to Wadi Ash by the Arabs when the site was moved a few miles to the south east. It was here that — '

'Guadix,' Everard said. 'Where's that?'

'About sixty kilometres east from Granada.'

'Is it a big town?'

Ramon shrugged. 'About twenty thousand persons. It is a dry, dusty place. Tourists visit it to see the cave dwellers.'

It took time for Everard to realize that this apparently vital piece of information was not in fact as valuable as it at first appeared. To search so big a town in the few hours left to them would take a whole regiment of police. It was not even certain that Juanita was there. She had named Guadix because that she could do without arousing her captors' suspicions. But she could as well be in one of the surrounding villages.

'We're back where we started,' he said, pacing up and down the marble floor in a fury of indecision. 'Gonzales is right; we need the police. And yet — ' He paused to glare at a Leal portrait of a de Sagrera ancestor. 'Hell, no! I can't risk it.'

'You will still meet these men, then?' Ramon asked.

'Yes.' He sighed. 'If I fail, at least the police will know where to start looking for her. I suppose that's something.'

'It could be more, Señor.' There was an eager look on Ramon's plump face. 'Wait, please. I have something to show you.'

He went quickly from the room, to reappear a minute later with a small black box which he handed to Everard.

'What is it?' Everard asked, examining it.

'A radio transmitter. When the foresters go up the mountains in winter they take one with them. Sometimes they are lost, sometimes they are trapped by the snow. With this we can find them.' He pressed a switch. 'Now it gives out a signal. You cannot hear it, of course. For that you need a receiver.'

While admitting the possibilities, Everard could not see its present use. 'It's at the wrong end,' he said. 'Juanita should have it, not us.'

'Si, Señor.' Ramon was quivering with excitement. 'But suppose the men take it to her, eh? And they will if you hide this little box in their car when you meet them. If they take you with them it will be easy. If they do not — ' His voice sank a little lower in the scale. 'Well, then it may be difficult. But not, perhaps, impossible?'

Everard's body tensed. 'What's the effective range?'

'Twenty — perhaps thirty kilometres. Enough, I think. We have cars fitted with receivers. In the morning I will take one to Guadix, and when the men come I pick up the signal from the transmitter.' He hunched his shoulders, spreading his hands in a semitic gesture. 'So then I follow. Is easy.'

'Not easy,' Everard said, his voice hoarse. He was climbing out of the depths of despair. 'But it gives us a fighting chance!'

# 13

Insulated from the hot stone by a coarse mattress stuffed with dried maize leaves, Rossiter sat with his back to the cave wall and sweated. There was no shade. The sun was directly overhead, beating down on the dead village from a cloudless sky; when the air moved it moved sluggishly, bringing no relief. Only the flies moved with purpose. Attracted by the refuse which Manuel and his woman, regardless of hygiene, had scattered so liberally, they swarmed over the village in their thousands.

Rossiter had never known it so hot. His shirt was open; the damp stains under his armpits had spread to back and front, beads of sweat trickled down his face, soaking still further the matted hair on his chest. Occasionally he leaned to one side to pull the sticky shorts away from his buttocks, or flapped an angry arm at the hungry flies. Even his stomach was uncomfortable. Starch did not agree with him, and starch had figured largely in the diet which Lucia had provided. Rice and meat, rice and fish — and a particularly revolting mess which she called *migas*, a form of porridge cooked in olive oil and garlic. There would be rice again for lunch; Lucia was preparing it now. Rice and *bacalao* — dried codfish. Even from a distance of twenty yards he could smell it. The thought that he would shortly be expected to eat it caused his stomach to heave.

'Damn and blast the bloody heat!' He slapped furiously at a bare leg. The flies rose buzzing, only to settle again. The cloud of cigar smoke with which he surrounded himself formed no barrier to their attack. 'If I'm not baked alive I'll bloody well be eaten alive.'

Corbett and the women were in the cave. Thinking of them, envying them its comparative coolness, the sweat seemed to pour off him the faster. But he resisted the temptation to join them. Pablo had said he would be back *mañana*, and despite his apparent good humour Pablo had not been joking. He would come, all right; and when he came there could be trouble. Rossiter grinned wryly at the thought, and gripped the hot metal of the revolver beside him on the mattress. Trouble would at least break the monotony. It would break him too if he were not ready for it. That was why he must sit in the sun and watch. He could not delegate the task. Corbett was no longer reliable, and Al and Connie had been gone some time.

His ordeal seemed more bearable as he reflected on their mission.

He took the cigar from his mouth, waved away the smoke and the flies, and peered up at the mountain. For a few hundred feet it rose sharply, arid and boulder-strewn, devoid of vegetation; above that it split into what appeared to be a series of deep ravines, their entrances darkly sinister. It was down one of these he supposed that his visitors would come, although as yet there was no sign of them. Higher still — much higher — would be the snow line. From where he sat it was beyond his vision, but he knew that it was there.

He looked at his watch. One fifteen. Al and Connie should be there by now; they had left at eight, and even on Spanish roads a hundred and fifty kilometres could not take over five hours. Emilio and he had reconnoitred the place weeks ago. But Emilio was dead, and with Pablo on the warpath he could not go himself; he had had no choice but to send the others. Neither had been there before; but with a good map it should not be difficult to find, and they had left in good time. It was unfortunate he had had to send both men. But Al alone might not be smart enough to deal with some unexpected contingency, and Connie he could not trust. Not with five million pesetas.

Lucia left her cookpot and came striding towards him. She was a tall woman, her face and body brown and wrinkled as old leather, her coarse black hair tied in a gay *pañuelo*. As she squatted on her haunches before him he could see her long pendant breasts under the unbuttoned blouse. He understood little of her rapid Spanish, but gathered she was complaining of the lack of water;

Manuel was to have brought it, and Manuel had not come. Her body had a strong, earthy smell and her breath stank of garlic. There was nothing he could do about the water, and to escape her he got to his feet, stuck the revolver in his hip pocket, and moved away with a negative shake of the head.

And then he saw the men.

There were five of them now — the three from the previous day, and two newcomers. The latter were strikingly dissimilar; one small and delicately boned, thin lipped, and with enormous eyes that seemed almost to be bursting from their sockets; the other large and ponderous, with long sad moustaches adorning a blubber-mouth in a long yellow face. The small man wore jeans and *alpargatas*, and a loose jacket with no lapels. Blubber-mouth was dressed in open-necked shirt and breeches, with high leather boots on his feet and a red *faja* round his waist.

They came to stand where they had stood the day before, as though that slight elevation gave them a sense of mastery, of command. Pablo and the small man were smiling. The other three stared fiercely at Rossiter.

Lucia gave them one frightened look and hurried back to her cookpot. Rossiter tried not to show his anger. He said lightly, 'Quite an impressive deputation, Pablo. But it cuts no ice with me.'

The Spaniard's smile widened. He said, 'Your friends have gone for the money, Señor? Is not that so?' Rossiter nodded. 'Good. Then we wait.'

'Not here you don't.' There was no valid reason why they should not wait. But to Rossiter their presence formed a threat, and he did not like threats. 'You'll get your cut when I'm good and ready. That might be today, or it might be tomorrow.'

'One million pesetas?'

'A hundred thousand. And if you hang around long the price will go down, not up. So beat it.'

He waved his hands at them in a shooing motion. Blubber-mouth puffed out his cheeks and spat; the spittle sizzled on the hot stone, and vanished. Antonio lifted the eye patch, knuckled the empty socket beneath, and said in his harsh, rasping voice, 'Esperamos aqui.'

'Sí,' said Federo. 'Dígale, Pablo.'

Pablo shrugged. 'You hear, Señor? They say to wait. They fear that if we are not here when the money comes you may forget to pay us.' He spread his hands in an apologetic gesture. 'Is better that we stay.'

Rossiter knew they were mocking him, that they felt secure in their numbers. But it was neither their mockery, nor the thinly disguised threat, nor the blistering heat, that drove him to action. Corbett and the women had come out from the cave and were listening. He had to demonstrate his authority. Particularly to Corbett.

The revolver was heavy on his hip. He took it from his pocket and held it loosely, slapping the barrel against his thigh.

'I said to get, didn't I?' He knew he was acting foolishly, but he could not stop now. 'So get. Now — before I'm tempted to use this.'

Antonio and Blubber-mouth took a

step back, turning as though to leave. But not the others. Federo spoke sharply, tugging at Antonio's arm, delivering what was obviously a blistering homily.

Pablo said quietly, 'I think you will not use it, Señor. We stay.'

Rossiter brought the gun up quickly and fired. He was a good shot. The bullet ricocheted off a stone near Antonio's feet, and whined away up the mountain. Antonio and the small man had been about to sit down. Now they sprang up.

'I shan't miss next time,' Rossiter said grimly. 'Get going.'

They went without a word, fear on the faces of some, anger on others. As he watched them climb Corbett said, 'Was that wise? They may return with reinforcements, and you can't shoot them all.'

Angry with himself, with Pablo and his crew, but above all with Corbett, Rossiter rounded on him.

'Don't you tell me what is wise or unwise.' He stuck the gun in his pocket and mopped his brow. 'Wisdom went out of this business the day you joined it.'

Still smarting from his bitter invective

of the previous day, Eve plucked up courage to speak. Yet it was more to denigrate Rossiter than to champion her husband.

'They were doing no harm,' she said, hesitant in her temerity. 'And haven't we enough enemies without creating more? If I may say so, Mr Rossiter, I think you — '

He never learned what she thought. From high on the mountain came a shout, and they looked up, startled. The five Spaniards stood in a bunch, gesticulating wildly. But it was not the Spaniards who held their attention. Its progress marked by a cloud of dust and debris, an enormous boulder was thundering down the slope towards them, seeming to grow rapidly in size as it came.

There was little time in which to act. Eve screamed and ran for the cave. At the entrance she tripped and fell. Still screaming, she scrabbled at the hard, dusty ground, trying desperately to crawl farther under its shelter. Rossiter grabbed Juanita by the wrist and half-threw, half-dragged her to one side. But Corbett seemed frozen into inactivity. Only at the last moment did he move. Hampered by his twisted leg, he took one awkward, tortured stride and flung himself to the ground.

In a shower of dust and shale and flying stones the boulder leapt in the air and crashed down on the roof of the cave. Crouched over Juanita in an instinctive but futile gesture of protection, it seemed to Rossiter that the whole mountain was crumbling about them. Something hit him a heavy blow on the side, and with a sharp cry of pain he collapsed on top of the girl. He felt no movement beneath him. As he shut his eyes against the dust and shielded his head with his hands from the cascade of flying debris he wondered dully if she were dead.

Was this the end of the road?

# 14

It was just after one o'clock when Everard drove through Antequera and took the Granada road. Because of his impatience he had driven fast from the estancia; now, with only twenty kilometres to do and nearly an hour in which to do them, he slowed. It was essential to obey the instructions exactly if he hoped to gain the kidnappers' confidence. Both Juanita's and Tommy's safety might depend on it.

He pulled into a lay-by to smoke a cigarette, and sat drumming on the steering wheel with nervous fingers.

Two o'clock, the note had said, and only Don Carlos or his emissary alone in the car. From there, provided the money was right and the men who would meet him were satisfied that he had not been followed, he would be taken to where Juanita was held. Both would be confined for sufficient time to allow their captors to make good their escape, after which the police would be informed of their whereabouts. Everard had thought it strange that the men should take both money and bearer. Why not the money alone? He could only assume that they feared to leave the bearer behind lest he should put the police on their trail before their arrangements were complete.

His own arrangements were necessarily elastic, depending as they must on what happened at the meeting. If the men accepted the money, then presumably they would take him with them. But what if they did not? Would he have the opportunity to plant the transmitter in the car? By now Ramon and one of his men would be in the Guadix area with two receivers, hoping to pick up the kidnappers' car and, by cross bearings, to pinpoint the locality of their hide-out; although even if they succeeded they were not to call in the police without instruction from him. And if the men take you with them? Ramon had asked. What then? Then, Everard had told him, there would be no need for the police. It would mean that the kidnappers had accepted the money and would in due course release both Juanita and himself. And that was the way he hoped it would be. It would mean safety for Tommy as well as for Juanita. Ramon had protested that he was taking unnecessary risks. Why not inform the police as soon as the hide-out had been located? he had wanted to know. They need not interfere, but at least they would be in a position to act quickly should the need arise. Everard's answer to that had been that they *would* interfere; however co-operative, it was unlikely that they would allow a gang of criminals to escape unhindered when they had them cold. Nor had he agreed to Ramon's suggestion that he should go armed to the meeting. The men would most certainly search him, and to be found with a gun would be to deny the part he was trying to play. There was another reason for his refusal. He could not forget that he had killed a man, that he was wanted for murder. He did not fancy another killing on his conscience, however despicable the crime that provoked it.

A quarter to two. As he put the car into gear he recalled his rebel thoughts of the previous night, and again he felt ashamed. No matter what Juanita's relationship with the dead Laroche had been, it was not important now. It had been important once — perhaps, at some time in the future, it would be important again — but not now. All that mattered now was that she and Tommy should be free.

He reached the secondary road indicated in the note, and turned down it. Vast groves of olives stretched away into the distance on either side, to thin and give place to vines as the road climbed into the hills. Then the vines disappeared also, and there was only scrub and a few stunted trees. Presently he came to a disused stone barn, with only the high walls standing, and forked left up a rough track that followed the contour of the mountain, to rise steeply until it vanished behind a rocky spur.

It was beyond that spur that the men would be waiting.

★　★　★

'That'll be him, wack,' Connie said, climbing down from the buttress. 'Don't look like the old boy, though.'

'It don't have to be,' Al said. 'Not so long as he's brought the cash.'

They were not beyond the spur. They were concealed behind the high walls of the old barn, waiting for their man to pass. Only now, when they were certain that the stranger was alone and that no other car was shadowing him, did they drive out on to the mountain track and follow the billowing dust cloud up to the spur.

Everard had left the car. Bag in hand, he watched as they dismounted from the Simca and came towards him.

'And who might you be, wack?' Connie asked.

Everard explained. Connie said, 'Oh, aye? How come you knew we was in Spain?'

'Laroche told me.' He decided not to add to that simple statement.

Connie scowled. 'He did, did he? Bloody scouse!' But Laroche had been part of Corbett's outfit, not Rossiter's. To

Connie he was only a name. Pointing to the bag, he said, 'That the money?'

'Yes.'

To Everard the meeting seemed wholly unreal. The men were not what he had expected. The short one, the one who did all the talking, had a sharp, ferrety look; with his Liverpool accent Everard would have guessed him to be a petty dock thief or a small time trickster at worst. But the taller man could have been one of his own employees; a solid, dependable tradesman with a union card and a council house and a wife and children. Neither looked like a desperate criminal.

Taking heart from their mild appearance, he said, 'How is my wife? Is she all right?'

'She's all right,' Al said.

'And the boy? My son?'

'We don't know nothing about him,' Connie said. 'Put the bag down, wack, and get into the back of the Simca while we have a decko at the lolly. All there, is it?'

'Not quite,' Everard admitted. 'The note you sent Don Carlos caused him to have a stroke. He's completely helpless — can't speak, can't move. We've raised what we could without him, but you didn't give us much time.'

Connie frowned. Rossiter had not allowed for this.

'How much?' he demanded. He was suddenly suspicious, and ran his hands down Everard's body, seeking a weapon. Everard submitted to the search without protest. He had no fear that they would find the transmitter. It was concealed in one of the high boots he was wearing, cunningly adapted by the de Sagrera shoemaker.

'I don't know,' he said. 'We didn't count it.'

'Oh, aye? Then we'll count it for you.'

He put down the bag and walked across to the Simca. It took only a few seconds to hide the transmitter under the seat. Thankful that at least that part of his mission had been successfully accomplished, he watched the men as, squatting on their haunches, they emptied the suitcase on to the ground and then stacked the notes back into it. The tall man was still stacking when Connie rose and came over to the car.

'You're bloody short,' he said angrily. 'It ain't even half there. What's the big idea? You trying to be smart?'

Hastily Everard denied the accusation. In his anxiety to placate he even apologized for the shortage; nor did it seem incongruous that he should do so. But Connie was not impressed with his explanation, and Everard said desperately, 'Good God, man, haven't you got enough? It may be weeks before the old man recovers, and where else can I raise that sort of money?'

'That's your worry,' Connie told him. 'But the guv'nor ain't going to like this. He ain't going to like it at all.'

'Let me talk to him, then. Take me with you. I'll submit to any restrictions you wish. You've nothing to fear from me, that I swear. All I want is to get my wife and son back. I'm not interested in the money, or revenge.'

'No dice, wack. You ain't going no place with us. Best thing you can do is nip back to the old boy's estancia and wait till you hear from the guv'nor. And while you're waiting you try digging up some more lolly. I reckon you're going to need it if you want your missus back intacta like.'

Al Johnson had replaced the last of the notes in the case. He came across to the car and threw it on to the seat beside Everard. Connie said, 'Keep an eye on him, Al. I got a job to do.'

He disappeared round the back of the car. Everard thought to see sympathy in the tall man's eyes, and he said earnestly, 'Can't you make him change his mind? Believe me, I'm not out to cause trouble. All I want is to see for myself that she's all right.'

Albemarle shook his head. The cut on his cheek was deep and had not healed properly. It looked raw and inflamed.

'Sorry, mate. But you don't have to worry none. Like I said, your missus is O.K.'

'Not worry, eh?' Everard's tone was bitter. 'Thanks a lot!'

His helplessness made him angry. He wanted to hit out at the man, to batter him and his accomplice into submission. It did not matter that there were two of them, that they might be armed; at that moment it was action he wanted, so that even physical pain would have been preferable to this tame acceptance of defeat. Only the knowledge that the use of force could avail him nothing, that it might injure Juanita, restrained him.

Connie returned to the car. He said briskly, 'Right. Out you get, wack. And don't forget what I said. Get cracking with that lolly.'

He watched them drive away. They drove fast, the dust billowing behind them. A cloth had been tied over the Simca's number plate, but so far as Everard was concerned it was an unnecessary precaution. He had no intention of calling the police. Not yet. He had to make his own moves first.

The tyres of his car had been slashed. He would have driven it on the rims, but when he tried the starter the engine failed to respond.

He started to walk the long, dusty miles to the main road.

# 15

'In the early hours of yesterday morning thieves broke into the premises of Messrs Anstey and Rylance (Contractors) Ltd, near Tonbridge, and stole an estimated seventeen hundred pounds from the office safe. Neither doors nor safe had been forced, which suggests that the thieves possessed keys. The night watch-man, Mr Jack Fawsey, was found unconscious in the yard some hours later, and is now in Pembury Hospital suffering from severe head injuries. His condition is said to be serious.

'This is the second robbery sustained by the firm in four days. Last Friday bandits carried out a daring raid inside the premises, hi-jacking the wages van as it arrived and escaping with twenty-three thousand pounds after wounding the gateman. The car used in the raid, a black Jaguar, belonged to the firm's managing director, Mr John Everard, and was being driven by his wife. Mrs Everard, whose father is a wealthy Spanish landowner, has since disappeared. The police believe that the thieves forced her to take part in the raid, and may have kidnapped her and her infant son, who was with her at the time.

'The police are anxious to contact Mr Everard, who also has disappeared. They believe he may be able to further their inquiries into the death of a young actor, Peter Laroche, whose body was found in a cottage at Melwich, in West Sussex, late on Saturday evening.'

Colin Sievewright put down the paper, refilled his coffee cup, and reflected that the Press were apparently using the rather insignificant theft of seventeen hundred pounds as a peg on which to hang a rehash of the more succulent news of the Everards' disappearance and their implied connection with murder and large scale robbery. But it was not the journalism which concerned him. This was Tuesday morning — and it was Monday's paper he was reading. Everard's assailant must have read it too, and have wondered why there was no mention of Everard's name in connection with the theft from the safe. The man had left the office under the impression that the police were already on their way to effect Everard's arrest, and his only possible conclusion must have been that his victim had somehow managed to free himself and escape before they arrived. Why, then, had he not taken further action? Was he no longer interested? Did he consider that revenge (if revenge was, as Everard seemed to think, the motive) was now adequate?

Colin took another look at the street below. It was only seven-thirty, and traffic was light. Most of the parked cars he recognized as regulars, but as always there were a few he had not seen there before. Did one of these hold Everard's unknown assailant? Or was today to prove as uneventful as the day before? So far, apart from a telephone call to Mrs Chater requesting her to hand the ransom note for Tommy to the police, he had done little to fulfil his promise to Everard that he would concern himself with the child's rescue. But what else could he do? He had banked on John's assailant coming to him. Without that lead he was helpless.

He went down the steps to the street, whistling loudly to ensure that his departure should not go unnoticed, casting an eye over the parked cars in an effort to memorize the unfamiliar before climbing into the Austin. As he drove slowly to join the heavier traffic on the main road he watched the rear mirror hopefully. At the far end of the street a blue Cortina, not one of the regulars, was moving in his wake, and he slowed to a crawl, waiting to see which way it would turn. Then the traffic piled up behind him and he lost it. He watched for it all the way to Vauxhall, but without success.

That Tuesday morning was much as other mornings at the gymnasium. The hours between eight and ten were always busy; after that business slackened until the lunch hour. It was not until ten-fifteen that he handed over to his two assistants (two were more than enough, but they allowed him greater freedom) and went out for his morning coffee — to see the blue Cortina parked at the end of the street.

He knew that it was not necessarily the same car; the other had never been close enough for him to read the number. But the man at the wheel was obviously waiting for someone or something, as perhaps he had waited the previous day. To Colin the inference was clear. The man had decided that Everard was not at the flat, that he was in hiding elsewhere, and that Colin would lead him there. That he had not needed to stick close to the Austin that morning indicated that he had known where Colin was going.

He must have followed us to the flat from here Saturday evening, Colin thought ruefully. We should have been more careful. But how the devil could he have known in advance that John would make for the gym?

He was tempted to walk down the street to take a close look at the man. Instead he went as usual to the café. The Cortina was still there on his return, and he hurried to the small room he used as an office and reached for the telephone.

'Dusty?' There was an answering grunt from the other end of the line. 'I think we're in business. How soon can you make it to the gym?'

'Not the flat, like you said?' Dusty Cope had a voice like a corncrake with a sore throat.

'No. I was wrong. Can you pick up Ed on the way?'

'Sure. Be with you in ten — fifteen minutes.'

'Fine. And Dusty — park the car round the back, and use the iron staircase up to the gallery. I don't want our inquisitive friend to see you.'

The gymnasium was almost empty. An elderly businessman sculled laboriously; Mike, the permanent assistant, was sparring with a well-muscled schoolboy. Harry, the part-timer, had already left. Colin changed quickly, collected an empty suitcase and the mud-stained raincoat Everard had left there on the Saturday and, after a word with Mike, mounted to the gallery at the far end of the gymnasium to wait for Ed and Dusty.

They were not long in coming. Dusty

was an ex-cruiserweight, overweight now at forty-five, but still strong and solid. Ed Ballantyne was bigger and younger. He had been a postman until winning a handsome sum on the pools. Now he and Dusty were partners in the betting shop which Colin frequented.

Colin took him to a window overlooking the street and pointed out the Cortina. Dusty said, 'How do we work it, Baron? Like you said? Me with you in the Austin, and Ed following in the Morris?'

'I think so.' The partners were the only ones of his friends who insisted on using his title. Colin had tried without avail to stop them — until he realized that they got a kick out of it. 'Come on. Let's get started before he grows impatient and quits.'

Ed went back down the outer staircase, Colin and Dusty to the floor of the gymnasium. Colin had chosen Dusty to accompany him because he was about John Everard's height and build; in Everard's raincoat, and with the collar turned up, there was every likelihood that from a distance he would be mistaken for

Everard. Particularly as it was Everard the watcher would be expecting to see.

Colin went first. Carrying the suitcase, he stepped across the pavement, deposited the suitcase in the boot of the Austin, and took a quick glance up and down the street. The Cortina had not moved. He got into the driving seat, opened the nearside door, and beckoned. Head down, Dusty hurried out from the gymnasium. As the car door slammed shut Colin grinned happily. Adventure had been scarce in London.

'Now for it,' he said, letting out the clutch. 'Let's hope I haven't guessed wrong; I'd hate for this to be a flop.' A few minutes later, as they turned into the Vauxhall Bridge Road, he let out a gleeful whoop. 'It worked, Dusty. He's bought it.'

'The more fool him,' Dusty croaked.

They took the Maidstone road. Colin kept to a reasonable speed; to loiter might make the man suspicious, to hurry might be to lose him. But he did not worry unduly when the traffic hid the Cortina from view. If by misfortune their pursuer should lose them he would obviously stick to the main road, would catch up with them eventually. It was when they branched off that care would be needed. He must be given no opportunity to take a wrong turning.

They were some miles past Maidstone when Dusty said, 'Take it easy, Baron. We turn left about three miles on. Is he still with us?'

Colin looked in the mirror, and slowed.

'Not at the moment. But I saw him this side of Maidstone. He can't be far behind.'

A mile later there was still no sign of the Cortina. Worried, Colin braked the Austin to a crawl, changing down as they rounded the next bend.

'Maybe he's lost interest,' Dusty said glumly. 'It's a long way to come.'

Colin swore. 'Stop being cheerful, and think. Can we give this turning a miss? Carry on until he catches up, and then double back?'

'I wouldn't know, Baron. This is the way we always come.'

Still in low gear, Colin kept the Austin going. To stop might lead to complications if their pursuer came on them unexpectedly, and he began to wish that they had chanced their arm in London. It had been Dusty's idea that they should make use of the cottage, at present unoccupied, which he and Ed had bought earlier that summer. It had seemed a good idea at the time. It did not look so good now.

Dusty turned in his seat and looked back. 'We're not exactly popular,' he said. 'They're queuing behind.'

Colin grunted. The queue was obscuring his rear vision; the Cortina might be there, several cars behind, and he would not know it. They were approaching a lay-by, and he decided to take a chance. He drew off the road, waited until the following cars (the Cortina not among them) accelerated past, took a quick glance at the empty road, and drove on.

He was changing up to third when Dusty said, 'Here he comes! Better step on it, Baron.'

He stepped on it, letting the revs climb furiously before changing into top, anxious that their pursuer should not come up on them so quickly that he would realize they had been waiting for him. It had been a mistake for Dusty to watch the road through the rear window. The gap between the two cars had been too great for the man to have seen his face clearly, but the action might have made him suspicious. It was essential he should believe they had no idea they were being tailed.

'There's the turning,' Dusty said. 'Opposite the farm.'

The Cortina was about three hundred yards distant as Colin slowed and spun the wheel. The secondary road was straight. As he drove down it he kept his eyes on the mirror, praying that the Cortina would not sweep on down the main road. He breathed a sigh of relief when he saw it turn and follow.

'How far now?' he asked, accelerating.

'Not far. I'll tell you when to turn.'

Colin took another look in the mirror. The Cortina was dropping back, the driver obviously concerned lest he should appear to be following. He was more conspicuous now. Colin grunted in relief and started to whistle. It did not worry him that there was no sign of Ed. Ed had been a refinement, not a necessity.

'There's the cross-road,' Dusty said. 'We turn right.'

The lane was narrow, twisting awkwardly between high hedges. From necessity Colin slowed. They could not know if the Cortina was following, but it had been in sight when they turned.

As they rounded a bend Dusty said, with no trace of excitement in his gravelly voice, 'This is it, Baron. Stop here.'

Colin halted the car in the middle of the lane and got out. Dusty got out too, took off the raincoat, and threw it on to the front seat. Under his direction they ran back down the lane, making for a gap in the hedge. But the Cortina had closed with them quicker than they expected. They were still some yards from the gap when it came slowly round the bend and stopped with a jerk that made the body lift. As they ran towards it Colin could see the man's face, pock-marked and bespectacled and with a small goatee beard, staring at them through the windscreen. But only for a moment. As he reached for the wing mirror the engine revved briskly, there came the sound of tyres biting sharply into the gravel, and the Cortina moved away from them, swinging crazily from verge to verge as it reversed down the lane.

Colin spurted. 'Come on, Dusty!' he yelled. 'Don't let the bastard get away.'

Dusty slowed, dragging his big feet. 'He's hooked, Baron,' he said, panting. He was less fit than Colin; on leaving the ring he had happily cut exercise to a minimum. 'There's Ed.'

The driver of the Cortina had also seen Ed's Morris. It was in the middle of the lane, some thirty yards behind him, and there was no way past. At first he did not appear to realize its significance; he pressed frantically on the horn, still reversing, expecting the newcomer to do the same. Only when his rear bumper smacked into the Morris did he recognize the trap and seek another way of escape. It was too late. As he scrambled out on to the road and started to run Ed was waiting for him. And against the muscular Ed he had no chance at all.

'Take him to the cottage, Ed,' Colin said. Ed had one arm hooked round the man's neck, holding it high and tight so that his captive had to stand on tiptoe to breathe. 'Dusty and I will see to the cars. We can't leave them here.'

The man glared at him, his eyes bulbous and bloodshot behind the spectacles. His pock-marked face was red — perhaps from rage, perhaps from near-suffocation. There were flecks of froth at the corners of his mouth.

'Don't lose him,' Colin said, as Ed dragged the man away. 'He's not much to look at, but he's all we've got.'

The cottage was some yards down the lane: a wooden box of red brick and grey slate standing in a wilderness of weed and tall grasses, with wire to separate it from the surrounding field and a wide iron gate to provide an entrance. Colin and Dusty parked the three cars among the weeds, tucking them close to the hedge to screen them from passers-by, and then joined Ed and his captive at the cottage door.

'Open up, Dusty,' Ed said. He had a round, well-scrubbed, pink and white face, with a small mouth and innocent, baby blue eyes. 'Don't keep the gentleman waiting.'

The rooms were small, but there were electricity and water and a few pieces of furniture. Ed and Dusty were in the process of 'doing the place up', and spent occasional week-ends there for that purpose. But neither quite knew why they had bought it. They did not like the isolation of the country.

They sat the man down on a chair and stood round him.

'Introductions first,' Colin said. 'I'm Colin Sievewright.' It was information he suspected the other already knew. 'These gentlemen are my friends. Who are you?'

The man did not answer. He looked more angry than frightened. His tie and collar were awry, the hair on his balding head was rumpled. Colin put his age in the early fifties.

'Speak up,' Ed said. 'No call to be shy.'

The man licked the froth from his lips and glared at them. Dusty leaned forward, removed the spectacles, and slapped him across the cheek. It was a stinging blow that left its mark and echoed loudly in the small bare room. The man winced.

'Answer his Lordship when he speaks to you,' Dusty said.

Colin frowned. If the man was what he supposed him to be he deserved no sympathy. But, except as a form of exercise, Colin disliked violence.

'He'll have a driving licence on him,' he said. 'We can get his name from that.'

They had to hold him while they searched him. He seemed to resent this intrusion on his person even more than the hi-jacking, and swore vociferously as he struggled.

'What dreadful language!' Ed said, genuinely pained. He was a strict Methodist.

'Cyril George Tasker,' Colin read from the licence, and nodded to himself. From what Everard had said it had to be Tasker or Corbett. 'All right, Cyril George, let's get down to business. Where is Tommy Everard?'

'I don't know what the hell you're talking about,' Tasker said. He straightened his tie and smoothed his scanty hair. The anger was still there in his voice, but it sounded less spontaneous; Colin suspected that anger was inherent in the man. His face had a drawn look, with deep vertical lines; the corners of his mouth turned down. 'Stop this bloody horse-play and give me back my licence. I'm getting out.'

As he started to rise from the chair Ed pushed him back.

'Why the hurry?' Ed asked. 'You've only just arrived.'

'Don't try to come the innocent,' Colin said. 'We know damned well that you're gunning for John Everard. You were in on the wages snatch and his wife's disappearance, and you kidnapped young Tommy. Well, we want Tommy back. Where is he?'

Tasker shrugged. 'You're talking bloody nonsense.'

'Am I? Then why did you follow Everard to the works Saturday night?' The look on Tasker's face told Colin that he had guessed correctly. 'And if you weren't out for revenge why did you clobber him and then tell the police where to find him? That wasn't exactly friendly, was it?'

Tasker shrugged again. 'Would you be interested to know what went wrong — why Everard isn't in custody?'

'You're doing the talking,' Tasker said, with a show of scornful indifference. 'I can't stop you. Not with your musclemen around.'

'True. Well, it wasn't the police you spoke to on the phone that night, it was me. So you can see why bluff will get you nowhere. I recognize the voice.'

The lie worked. Tasker said hoarsely, 'So what? Why shouldn't I inform the police? He's wanted for murder, isn't he?'

'Officially, perhaps — although in fact it was an accident. But, like I said — don't try to kid us, Tasker. It wasn't right-minded citizenship that prompted you to follow Everard. It didn't bring you here today either, did it? You thought Everard was with me, and you wanted to know where I was taking him so that you could turn informer again. Or had you some other nasty little trick in mind?' Colin frowned. 'You really hate his guts, don't you?'

'Yes, damn you, I do!' Tasker was

240

shouting, all restraint gone. 'And why wouldn't I? The bastard murdered my son!'

Colin stared at him. 'You mean — Laroche was your son?'

'Yes.'

'Oh! Well, I'm sorry. But if you play rough games you must expect someone to get hurt. And it wasn't your son's death that sparked you off; you were involved long before that. However, all this is beside the point. It's Tommy who interests us right now. So suppose you tell us where he is?'

'Suppose nothing,' Tasker snapped. 'Find out.'

'I'm trying to. Is Mrs Everard in Spain?'

Tasker's reply was so crude that Ed Ballantyne nearly choked on the gum he was chewing. But it was not the man's language that worried Colin. What did he do if Tasker refused to talk? Use violence? Or would threats do the trick? It would depend on whether fear was stronger than rancour.

If Colin had doubts, Dusty had none.

Clenching his fists, he stepped forward.

'You pick him up, Ed,' he said, staring hungrily down at the seated man. 'I'll knock him down. Fair do's?'

'Fair do's,' Ed agreed. He too disapproved of violence in general. But here it seemed that violence was justified. He lifted the struggling, cursing Tasker under the armpits, kicked away the chair, and gripped him by neck and beard.

'Not too hard the first time, Dusty,' Colin said, accepting the inevitable. 'He may be stubborn. We don't want an anticlimax.'

Dusty's fist sank solidly into the man's stomach, so that the oaths were suddenly stifled. He doubled up, reeled a few erratic steps as Ed released him, and leant against the wall — still bent, still holding his stomach.

They watched him, waiting while he regained his breath. As he slowly straightened Dusty said cheerfully, 'Stick him up again, Ed. He's tougher than I thought; they used to go down with that one. Or am I losing my touch?'

Tasker cried out hoarsely as Ed

grabbed him. Colin said, 'Hold it a moment. Maybe he'd prefer to talk.'

Ed righted the fallen chair with a deft foot, dumped his captive on it with a jarring thud, and flicked the balding head with his forefinger. Tasker flinched. But his eyes were full of venom as he said, between gasps, 'You'll pay for this, damn you!'

Dusty said, 'You frighten us, Cyril George. You really do.'

'Where is Tommy Everard?' asked Colin.

'I don't know. And I damned well wouldn't tell you if I did.'

Ed shot out a hand and hoisted him up, clutching him by the throat so that he nearly choked.

'Try to improve on that last dig, Dusty,' he said. 'It wasn't really you. And what's wrong with the chin?'

'We don't want him unconscious, do we?' Dusty asked. 'He can't talk then. No, the stomach's the place. It hurts, but it doesn't show.' He considered the gasping Tasker. 'I was a mite high the last time, I think; not right in the pit. That's what comes of being out of practice. Rusty Dusty, eh?' He laughed hoarsely at his own joke, and carefully folded the fingers of his right hand into the palm. 'Let's see how we go this time.'

He hit Tasker so hard and so fast that the breath whistled from the man's gaping mouth, and he jack-knifed and fell, his legs threshing feebly. To Colin it sounded as though he were fighting a losing battle to regain his breath, and he wondered uneasily if they had gone too far. He had hated every moment of the performance. But Tommy was too important to be squeamish, and if a man like Tasker answered to anything it would be to violence.

When the threshing legs stilled and straightened Ed bent and lifted the limp body. He had to hold him in the chair. Mind and body were no longer co-ordinated in Tasker. Tears streamed from his eyes, the slack mouth was working like a fish out of water. His arms hung limp.

He's breaking, Colin thought. One little push, and he'll talk. He said loudly,

244

'That was more like the old self, Dusty. Try again when he's got his breath back. It could be third time lucky.'

His friends eyed him doubtfully. Colin winked at them to signify that he was bluffing, and Ed smiled back, relieved. Even Dusty looked more cheerful; there was no pleasure in hitting a defenceless man. As Ed jerked back the sagging head he took off his jacket, laid it carefully on the floor, and rolled up his sleeves.

'It's coming back,' he said. He felt his biceps, clenching and unclenching his fists. Through misty, tear-filled eyes Tasker watched him. 'Right. And hang on to him a fraction longer, Ed. He's riding the punch.'

As the man felt Ed's hands reaching for his armpits he screamed, jerking his body forward.

'No!' The word came out shrill and strained, as though its utterance was unbearably painful. 'That's enough! I'll talk, damn you, I'll talk!' He shuddered, the tears rolling unchecked down his pitted cheeks. 'I've had all I can take.'

Ed released him, the motion of his jaws

slowing with the cessation of strain. Dusty grinned, and started to roll down his sleeves. Colin knew they were as relieved as he.

'Good,' he said briskly, trying to sound tough. 'Let's start again, shall we? Where is Tommy Everard?'

★ ★ ★

As they turned on to the London road Ed said thoughtfully, still chewing, 'What do we do with the kid when we pick him up? You want Dusty and me to be nursemaids?'

'And feed him on fish and chips and gum?' Colin laughed. 'Not on your nelly. We'll hand him over to the housekeeper.'

'And the young couple?'

'The police can deal with them.'

They had had to prise the information out of Tasker, item by item. At times his reluctance to talk had overcome his fear, and it had needed Dusty's fist, poised threateningly, to persuade him to continue. But eventually they had got what they needed. Tommy had been lodged with Corbett's niece in Clapham, and for a consideration she and her husband had agreed to look after the child. 'Nobody's going to hurt him,' Tasker had said sullenly, replacing the spectacles Dusty had thoughtfully removed. 'It's Everard we're after, not the kid.' 'And money,' Colin had pointed out. 'You're greedy, Cyril George; you want revenge *and* affluence. But it looks like you're losing out on both. Your son's dead, and if you made anything out of the robbery you won't be able to spend it in gaol.' Tasker had started to swear, protesting that he had taken no part in the robbery, working himself into a rage that ended in unspecified threats of reprisal — until Dusty had grabbed him by the beard and jerked his head back, choking him into silence.

They had left him in the cottage with Dusty, roping his wrists and ankles to make Dusty's vigil less onerous. 'Take your time, Baron,' Dusty had said, with a hoarse chuckle. 'Cyril George and me's going to have a nice, cosy chat. I guess he's got plenty to tell me. You know what a chatterbox he is.'

The house was an old, three-storeyed building of greying brick, gaunt and square, standing alone in a narrow unkempt garden amid a welter of new houses. It was obviously the sole relic of a bygone age, and Colin wondered idly how it had managed to escape the fate of its fellows. According to Tasker the couple occupied the basement flat, and they went down the worn steps and rang the bell, listening impatiently for the sound of movement or voices within the house.

'I don't like old houses,' Ed said, eyeing with disfavour the peeling paintwork. 'Not in London. They always look like they're waiting to die.'

'This one probably is,' Colin said. He rang again. 'Come on, Mrs Price. Let's be seeing you.'

No-one answered the ring. 'She could be out,' Ed said. He tried to peer through the area window, but dirty lace curtains obstructed his view. 'Or maybe her husband don't like her opening the door to strangers.'

'Maybe. Let's take a look round the back.'

On the long grass that had once been a lawn an elderly woman was removing washing from a line. She looked up at their approach, her mouth stuffed with pegs.

'We're looking for Mr and Mrs Price,' Colin told her. 'I believe they occupy the basement flat, but they seem to be out.'

The woman nodded, took the pegs from her mouth, and placed them in her apron pocket.

'Went out this morning,' she said. 'About ten o'clock. A gentleman called for them in a car.'

'Any idea when they'll be back?'

She shook her head. 'They took a suitcase, if that's any help.'

Colin frowned. A suitcase indicated an overnight stay, perhaps longer. How long could they hold Tasker?

'They took the child with them, I suppose?' he said.

The woman paused in the act of unpegging the final garment to look at him in astonishment.

'You don't think they'd leave it behind, do you?'

'No. No, of course not.' He realized she was becoming suspicious, and to ask the questions he wanted to ask would increase her suspicion. A pity she was not the kind to offer gratuitous information. 'Well, I'm sorry to have missed them. I'm not often in this neighbourhood. They're a nice young couple, don't you think?'

'I've only been here three weeks,' she said, bending to tuck the last garment into a plastic bowl. 'I don't see much of them, but they seem pleasant enough. And the child is reasonably quiet, thank goodness.'

It was an opening of sorts. He said briskly, 'I'm glad to hear it. I was afraid he might be fretful. He's not their own child, you see; they're looking after him for a friend of mine who's in hospital. But I expect you knew that.'

'No,' she said. 'They didn't say.'

She picked up the bowl of washing, bade them a curt goodday, and started to walk back to the house. Irritated by her lack of interest and his own ill luck, Colin followed. He said bluntly, 'In that case, weren't you surprised when the child appeared out of the blue on Friday? Or was it Saturday?'

That stopped her.

'Out of the blue?' The suspicion was back in her eyes. 'I don't know what you're after, young man, but it seems to me you don't know the Prices as well as you say you do. Nor the child neither. They've only the one, and he was here when I moved in and he's been here ever since.' She looked from one to the other of the two men, a sour expression on her face. 'I think you'd better go before I call the police.'

# 16

Ramon was waiting at the junction of the main road with that which led up the hill to Gaudix. Small villas with green- or blue-tiled roofs lined the road, and beyond them the cathedral glowed redly in the evening sun. A bevy of children surrounded the car. When he saw Everard alight from the taxi Ramon shooed them away.

'They did not take you, then?' he said. His plump face was damp with sweat. As he stood by the car his fingers drummed unceasingly on the bonnet. It seemed that the hours of waiting had greatly taxed his nerves.

Briefly Everard told him what had happened. He too was feeling the strain. The long trek back to the main road, with the hot sun directly overhead and gusts of wind enveloping him in sudden clouds of dust that choked his lungs and filled his eyes and nostrils, had been the more exhausting because he was too distraught to walk. He had run most of the way. Once on the main road he had thought himself lucky to hitch an almost immediate lift with some American tourists. But luck had seemed less kind as the journey progressed. He grew so impatient of the frequent stops for photographs or to admire the view that by the time they reached Granada the flesh round his fingernails was bleeding.

Fortune had smiled again in Granada. He had had no difficulty in hiring a taxi. The promise of a fat tip had spurred the driver to cover the miles to Guadix in near-record time.

'Did you pick them up?' he asked anxiously.

Yes, Ramon said, he had picked them up. They had passed him two hours previously. But they had driven on down the main road, not forking right for Guadix as he had expected. Unfortunately other cars had gone by at the same time, so that he had been unable to determine which carried the transmitter. He had memorized one number. There had not been time to note the rest.

To Everard exact identification seemed unimportant. It was the car's destination, not the car itself, that mattered; and with bearings from the two receivers they should be able to fix that. But when he mentioned this to the secretary the drumming fingers quickened.

'I am sorry, Señor. Unfortunately there has been an accident. It is not Eduardo's fault, you understand; the other car was going too fast. They have taken Eduardo to hospital. He is not badly hurt, but — '

'The receiver, man! The receiver!' Everard thumped the car wing. 'Where is it?'

'In Jaen, Señor.' Ramon's tone was humbly apologetic.

Jaen. Vaguely Everard remembered the town. It lay on the road to Madrid, north of Granada — which put the receiver some sixty miles away from where it could be of use. He swore volubly. Then, catching sight of the young secretary's unhappy expression, he smiled wanly.

'Not your fault, Ramon,' he said. 'It's just one of those things. Are you still getting a signal?'

'Si, Señor. But it is very faint.'

'Then we'll move on east until it's stronger.' Everard turned to pay off the taxi. 'With a little luck we can still locate the bastards.'

Ramon's plump face paled.

'But, Señor, there may be many of them. Would it not be safer for the police — '

'I said locate them, man, not tackle them. Once we've done that you can come back for the police while I stay to keep an eye on them. I'm not having a horde of eager, clumsy policemen stampeding the bastards into action. Not unless I'm there to protect Juanita.'

He did not say how he intended to protect her. He did not know. He only knew that he had to be with her if he could.

Everard drove, with Ramon at the receiver. He drove fast, so that soon they had left the cork trees and the mulberries behind and were running down a narrow, arid plain, with the Sierra de Baza to the south and low, undulating hills to the north. It was a desolate area, with almost no vegetation or human habitation to break the monotony. But Everard welcomed it. This was the kind of country in which guilty men might choose to hide.

They had gone some twenty kilometres when Ramon said eagerly, 'The signals are stronger, Señor. Much stronger. But the direction is changing. It is more to the south.'

'Good.' Everard eased his foot on the accelerator. 'They'll be over in the foothills. Keep listening. I want to know when to turn off.'

'It is not as accurate as that,' Ramon said doubtfully. 'There will be many tracks. How do we know which to choose?'

'We'll know.' He felt suddenly full of confidence. 'Look out for tyre marks.'

They found the track some five kilometres farther on. The tyre marks were fresh, and had been made by a car coming from the west. Everard stopped to examine them. To his untrained eye they looked remarkably similar to those left by the kidnappers' car near Antequera.

'Do you know this part?' he asked.

'No, Señor.'

Everard followed the track with his eyes. It was ill-defined, but it appeared to lead through a distant olive grove to a sharp spur in the foothills. The mountains towered above it, the lower slopes covered with scrub and ridges of esparto grass, and above that the bare rock.

'Right. Let's go,' he said.

Controlling his excitement, he drove slowly. A rasping wind was blowing, so that the heavy dust raised by the car was whisked instantly away. Fervently Everard prayed that it would not attract the kidnappers' attention. At the far end of the olive grove the track disappeared; but the tyre marks continued, and Everard followed them, bumping over the uneven ground, his eyes searching the mountainside for a sign of life.

'The signals are very strong,' Ramon said. In the excitement of the chase his nervousness had gone, he no longer thought of the police. 'Beyond — how do you say? La estribación?' Everard shook his head. 'No matter. Perhaps they are there, behind the mountain foot. Should we not stop, Señor?'

Everard had the same idea. The men might well be behind the spur, which ran almost parallel to the road and offered concealment. Some fifty yards from it he stopped the car and got out. As he started to walk away Ramon said quietly, 'You had better take this, Señor.'

'This' was a Beretta two-five automatic.

'It is not very powerful,' Ramon apologized. 'But perhaps the men will not know that.' He hesitated. 'Is it not better that I come with you? Or do you wish me to fetch the police?'

'Come with me,' Everard said, guessing that to be the hoped-for answer. 'Let's first make sure they are here.'

The men were not, but the car was — tucked away behind a buttress, with only its boot showing as they rounded the spur. They approached it cautiously, uncertain what to expect. No-one challenged them. At Everard's suggestion Ramon immobilized the car and removed the transmitter, and they followed the line of the spur up a gully that ran deep into the foothills, and down which the wind blew fitfully. The going grew rougher as they went, and when eventually they climbed out of the gully and began to pick their way up the boulder-strewn slope, their feet slipping on the loose shale and the wind flinging dust into their faces, both men were panting heavily.

When they came to an escarpment, small but sheer, Everard paused.

'We're wrong,' he said. 'Juanita could never have climbed that. They must have gone some other way. But which?'

Ramon leaned against the rock, grateful for the respite, and mopped his face. He was beginning to regret his eagerness. But he had no suggestion to offer, and Everard turned to scan the face of the mountain. A grey hare sprinted across their tracks, and he watched it go bounding away to the west. As it neared an enormous dumbbell-shaped boulder it stopped suddenly, sat motionless for a moment with ears pricked, and then turned and scampered directly down the slope.

Everard did not follow its progress. He

was watching the boulder.

'Ramon! Look!' He gripped the secretary's arm. 'What do you make of that?'

Ramon's dark eyes followed the pointing finger. In the curve of the dumbbell a snake-like object had appeared. It moved slightly from side to side, was still, and then moved again.

'It looks like an arm,' he said, screwing up his eyes against the westering sun.

'It damned well *is* an arm. If I'm not mistaken there's a head too. Come on!'

It did not take them long to reach the boulder. As they neared it, treading circumspectly, they saw the man more clearly. He half-sat, half-lay against the far side of the boulder, one arm slung over it for support, his head resting on his shoulder.

'That's one of them!' Everard's mouth was dry and full of dust, and the words came out in a hoarse squawk. 'I recognize the ginger mop.'

Either the words carried, or the shale slipping away under their feet alerted their quarry. He struggled into a more upright position and turned his head.

Surprise and alarm were writ large on his ferrety face, but he made no attempt to escape.

'Well, well!' Exultant at this unexpected encounter, Everard sounded almost genial. 'Someone has been handing you the hiding you deserve, eh? Did your big friend get greedy?'

Connie scowled. His left eye was black and swollen, his lips bruised. From the corner of his mouth a trickle of blood had dried and caked.

'How did you get here?' he asked thickly.

'That's our business.' Everard's voice hardened. He leaned forward to clutch Connie by the shoulder. 'What's your name, rat?'

'Smith,' Connie said promptly. It was such an obvious alias for situations such as this that he was never believed.

Everard was no exception. 'Smith will do for now,' he said. 'Where's my wife?'

'Find out, wack.' Connie probed tenderly at his swollen mouth. 'You've got this far on your own. Just keep going. You don't need me.'

The grip on his collar tightened 'Get smart with me, Smith, and you'll learn what a real hiding is like.' Everard shook him violently. 'Now talk. I'm not giving you another chance. Where's my wife?'

'Up there.' Connie was no coward, but he knew when to surrender. 'And stop choking me.'

'On your feet, then, and show us.' Everard started to drag him up, blind to the pain in the little man's eyes. Only when Connie screamed did he pause.

'My ankle!' Connie gasped, clutching at him for support. 'I reckon it's broke. Put me down, for Gawd's sake!'

Everard put him down, none too gently, and turned to scan the long crest of the sierra. The sun was low in the sky, the shadows deep; if they were to locate the kidnappers and bring in the police before dark — and he knew now that there was no alternative to the police — there was no time to be lost. But 'up there' was vast, and the man's directions, even if not purposefully misleading, might be difficult to follow in such a featureless area.

'You're coming with us,' he said. 'If you can't walk we'll damned well carry you. And heaven help you if you try any tricks.' He stooped to catch Connie by the shoulder. 'Come on, Ramon. Up with him.'

It was a difficult and tiring climb for all of them. Although the evening sun was losing the fierce heat of the day, Ramon was soon once more perspiring freely; he disliked physical exercise, and as Don Carlos's secretary he was seldom called on to practise it. But he did not complain. Connie accepted the journey philosophically. His bearers handled him roughly, indifferent to his discomfort, intent only on reaching their destination as quickly as possible; occasionally he gave a gasp of pained protest, but otherwise he was silent except to point the direction. He saw no need to explain that it was Pablo and his friends, not Albemarle Johnson, who were responsible for his injuries. They had surprised the two of them on their way up the mountain and had demanded their million pesetas; and when this demand was refused they had taken the money by force. All of it. In the preceding fight Connie had fallen and damaged his ankle, and Al, too bruised and exhausted to carry him, had gone on alone to break the news to Rossiter. Picturing Rossiter's reaction, it was a mission Connie had not envied him.

As the village came into sight he pictured it again, even more vividly. To arrive in his present company would not exactly endear him to the angry Rossiter, and he said nervously, 'They're up there. Put me down, wack, will you?' With an attempt at humour he added, 'The guv'nor's fussy about the company we keep.'

They put him down, glad to be rid of their burden, and squatted on the ground to regain their breath and take stock. The village was some fifty yards away, sloping upward along the line of the escarpment. To Everard it looked both uninhabitable and uninhabited; an untidy row of broken rock and rubble, amid which the mouths of the few caves still standing yawned darkly. The one sign of human life was the still smouldering brazier at the far end of the track.

Ramon flexed his aching shoulders and massaged the muscles of his arms.

'Is very quiet,' he whispered. 'Do you think they have gone?'

It was certainly quiet. The only sound was the evening call of the cicadas, harsh and unpleasant. It had been with them throughout their journey up the mountain, but until now it had not impinged so insistently on their ears.

'How many of them are there?' Everard asked Connie.

Connie did not answer at once. He had crawled to lean against a rock, and was gazing in perplexity at the seemingly deserted village.

'Three,' he said, as though talking to himself. 'But where did all them stones come from? They wasn't there this morning.'

Keyed up as he was, and with his objective so close, Everard could not bear to wait the hours that it would take for Ramon to fetch the police. Three was less than he had expected. Taken by surprise

— and why not, with no-one on guard? — Ramon and he could tackle them unaided. The men might be armed, but so was he. And his gun would be ready.

'What do we do, Señor?' asked Ramon.

'I'm going in,' Everard said. 'We've a good chance. Coming?' Ramon nodded, and he took the gun from his pocket and looked at Connie. 'One squawk from you, Smith, and you get the first bullet. Understand?'

'Oh, aye,' Connie said. 'I understand.'

They walked slowly up to the village, Everard leading. As they reached the start of the rough track that formed the village street Everard paused. He could see the full length of it now; but there was still no sign of life, and he went on, picking his way over the loose stones, with the plump secretary breathing heavily at his back. At the mouth of each cave he looked quickly into the dark interior, fearing an ambush. No-one challenged them, no dim figure moved in the shadows. And finally they came to the end of the escarpment, with the sheer wall of the mountain barring further progress, and looked at each other in unhappy defeat.

'We're too late,' Everard said, slipping the gun into his pocket. His boots felt as though they were made of solid lead, and he slumped wearily on to a rock, to sit with his head propped between his hands. 'They've gone. God knows where or why — but they've gone.'

'Perhaps the man lied,' Ramon suggested. 'Perhaps this is the wrong place.'

'Perhaps,' Everard agreed listlessly. 'If it is I'll break his neck. But I think they were here. There's the brazier — and that blanket.' He pointed to where a coarse grey blanket had been flung over a pile of rock and stone that spread across the track. 'It looks like they left in a hurry.' He forced his tired body to its feet, pressing the palms of his hands against his sides. 'We'd better search the caves properly before we tackle Smith.'

There were only a few caves still standing, and some of these looked near to collapse. Everard took the first, Ramon the second. As he waited for his eyes to become accustomed to the gloom Everard welcomed its dank coolness. Even when he could see that the cave was empty he stayed there, leaning heavily against the wall. Victory had seemed so near that his disappointment was the greater. The fight had temporarily gone out of him.

He was still there when he heard Ramon cry out.

Ramon stood in the entrance to the next cave. The shadows were longer now, stretching across the track. But even in the shadows Everard could see the horror on the young secretary's face. His dark eyes were wide, his mouth slack.

'What is it, Ramon?' His tiredness was forgotten. 'What happened?'

'In there, Señor,' Ramon's voice was little more than a whisper. 'A man. I — I think he is dead.'

For a moment Everard stared at him. Then he hurried into the cave. His eyes were better attuned to the dark now, but at first he saw only a vague mass in the centre of the floor. It was not until he moved closer that he distinguished the man, and it needed no second look to know that the man was dead. He lay on his back with his eyes closed, and when Everard knelt beside him he saw the blood and the ugly wounds in his chest. Gingerly he touched an arm. The flesh felt chill, and unpleasantly sticky. He guessed that the man had been dead for some hours.

He took a quick look round the cave, noting the suitcase and the scattered clothing and the empty bottles, and went out into the open, glad to be away from death.

'Do you know him, Señor?' Ramon asked breathlessly.

Everard shook his head. The dead man was not important. Presumably he was one of the kidnappers, and Everard could feel no sorrow at his death. But where were the others? Where was Juanita? It was that thought that troubled him. If these men were capable of murder . . .

'The man Smith,' Ramon said. 'He will know.'

Everard nodded. He strode off down the track, deliberately shutting his mind to the thoughts that ravaged it. His fists were clenched, and he muttered to himself. As he passed the blanket he kicked at it savagely; the folds tangled round his foot, and he heaved it free. Smith still sat against the rock, watching them. Smith could not tell them where the men had gone, but he must know something of their plans. And if he were reluctant to talk . . .

Everard's fists tightened. In the mood that was on him it would be a pleasure to deal with the little man's reluctance.

'Señor! Señor Everard!'

He heard the words vaguely, but he did not stop. Only when Ramon called him again did he realize the urgency in the other's voice and turn back. Ramon stood near the blanket. He was gazing in horrid fascination at the heap of fallen rock from which Everard had kicked it.

'Look, Señor.'

Everard looked. At that moment it seemed to him that all life had stopped — not just for the dead, but for the living too. The ground rocked under his feet, and he clutched at his throat as nausea rose from his stomach to choke him. Blinking his eyes to clear the smarting tears, he looked again. And suddenly inertia was gone, and he threw himself on his knees and with savage fury attacked the tumbled pile — from under which, torn and bruised and stained with blood and dirt, projected a woman's legs.

★ ★ ★

From down the mountainside Connie watched them travel the length of the village street; and with each unchallenged step he grew more puzzled, more alarmed. Where were Rossiter and the others? Where was Al, who a little over an hour before had left him to get help? Had they abandoned him? Had Al's news panicked Rossiter into vacating the village, fearing that Pablo and his friends, having got possession of the money, might try to take the woman also to hold her to fresh ransom? It was a frightening thought. Yet if Rossiter had decided to run, surely he would have gone down the mountain, not up? He would have made for the car, picking up Connie en route. And that he had not done, or Connie (or his captors) would have seen them. So where were they? What had happened?

Everard and his companion were on their way back now. As they disappeared into the caves Connie considered the possibility of escape, quickly to reject it. With his damaged ankle he would not get far; even should he manage to elude his present captors, the prospect of spending a night alone on the mountain, at the mercy of men like Pablo and his friends and the ghosts which had driven the villagers from their caves, was too terrifying to contemplate. Even a Spanish prison seemed preferable.

The two men left the caves and came striding down the track towards him. He heard Ramon cry out, saw Everard turn and go back, to pause for a moment before both men fell on their knees and began to scrabble furiously at the heap of fallen rock which half-blocked the village street. It was that heap of rock which had puzzled him earlier. It had not been there when he and Al had left that morning.

For a while he watched them. Then curiosity overcame him, and on hands and knees he started to crawl slowly up the slope. As he came nearer he realized what had happened, that one of the caves had collapsed; he got to his feet and, gritting his teeth against the pain, hobbled clumsily up the track. This was the cave the women had used. Had they, together with Rossiter and Corbett, been inside it at the time? Yet it must have happened before Al left him; the sound of such a heavy fall would travel far, and he had not heard it. So — where was Al?

And then he saw the woman's legs, and the green dress, and he slithered to the ground and turned his head away.

'It's — it's Mrs Corbett,' he said weakly. And he remembered how he had joked about her legs to Al.

If Everard heard he took no notice. But Ramon did. Staggering under a load of rock, he heaved it on to the track.

'Quien?' he gasped.

'Mrs Corbett,' Connie told him. 'Her husband was working with the guv'nor.'

'You are sure?'

'Of course I'm sure. I seen her wearing that dress this morning.'

'Señor!' Ramon bent to tug at Everard's shoulder. 'You heard, Señor? This is not the Señora. It is another woman.'

Everard straightened his back and looked at him. His face was grey with dust, his hands torn and bleeding.

'I know,' he said flatly.

He had known from the beginning. But the knowledge had brought him little comfort. There would have been others in the cave with this unknown woman when it collapsed, and among them Juanita. Somewhere underneath that grey sepulchre of mountain rock her poor mangled body would be lying. Reason told him she could not be alive, yet he disregarded it. Only when he had found her would he cease his labours.

Ramon did not understand, but Connie did. Searching the face of the tumbled rock, he said with a shudder, 'His missus'll be under that lot. They kept her in there.'

Ramon crossed himself, the tears starting from his eyes, and bent once more to the task.

The light was fading by the time they had uncovered Eve Corbett. She lay on

274

her side, her right leg broken at knee and thigh and twisted grotesquely. But it was the sight of her face that caused Ramon to turn away and vomit. Her head had been crushed into a bloody mess of flesh and bone and tangled hair.

'Oh, Gawd!' Connie exclaimed.

The thought came to Everard that Juanita might look like that when they found her. He said hoarsely, 'We'll have to move her. Take her feet, Ramon.'

They moved her farther down the track and covered her with the blanket. The feel of the cold, dead flesh in his hands made Ramon want to vomit anew, and he kept his eyes averted from the lolling, mangled head. Despite his bleeding hands and aching muscles, it was with relief that he returned to labouring in the cave.

They worked in silence, their mouths too dry for unnecessary speech. As they tunnelled deep into the cave the darkness closed in on them, and more than once they were hit by falling rock. They could not move the enormous boulder that had caused the roof to collapse, and they worked round it, one on either side.

Beyond it the rock fall grew less, and presently they came to the inner cave and found it clear. And empty. As they groped their way along the walls they found only the two truckle beds, and the suitcases, and everything covered with a thick layer of dust. But no more.

They peered at each other in the darkness, breathing hard. Ramon said hoarsely, 'She is not here, Señor. Is all right. She is not here.'

Everard's emotions were too deep, too overpowering for speech. He felt for Ramon's arm and gripped it, and then turned and went unsteadily from the cave.

Connie still sat near the entrance. 'If you can't lick them, join them' — and he had done what he could to help; not from humanitarian motives, but to curry what favour he could. His friends had abandoned him. It remained to be seen what his enemies would do.

'She ain't in there, then?' he asked.

'No-one's in there,' Everard said, and flopped wearily down. He felt utterly exhausted, drained of all energy. For the moment he was incapable of further thought or action. It was Ramon who put the obvious question.

'But where is she? What has happened to her?'

'The wops,' Connie said. 'They'll have taken her.' Remembering that his captors knew nothing of Pablo and his friends, he explained briefly. 'They must have taken Corbett and the guv'nor too. They ain't here. But it beats me what happened to Al.'

Everard shook his head. The fate of Albemarle Johnson did not concern him. Vaguely he recognized the name of Corbett and its significance, but they slid from his mind immediately. He could think only of Juanita. He had come so far and fought so hard — to find that she had exchanged one set of kidnappers for another. It was all to be done again.

'The dead man!' Ramon said suddenly. 'We have forgotten him.'

'Dead man?' Connie stared at him through the twilight. 'What dead man?'

'In the cave. Back there.' Ramon pointed. 'He has been shot, I think.'

Painfully Connie scrambled to his feet. The wops had carried no guns. But the guv'nor had one. So who . . .

He began to hobble up the track. Everard did not stir. The identity of the dead man was unimportant; if he did not belong to one gang of villains he belonged to the other, and his death was well warranted. But Ramon remembered that the little man was one of the kidnappers; he must not be allowed to escape into the darkness.

He rose wearily, stumbling over the scattered rock. He had taken only a few paces when Connie said sharply, 'Sh! Listen!'

Ramon listened. From somewhere up the mountain came the rattle of stones descending, bouncing and bumping over the hard ground. Then the noise ceased, to start again a few seconds later — and louder. It was an eerie sound. Connie thought of the villagers' ghosts, and moved closer to the secretary.

Ramon had a more practical mind. He said quietly, 'Someone is coming down the mountain.'

# 17

It seemed to Rossiter that he had been shifting rock for hours. Hours since the thunderous roar of the shattered cave had rumbled into silence and he had rolled clear of the girl and staggered to his feet, wincing at the pain in his side — to see Andrew Corbett tearing savagely at the tumbled pile of rock and stone, the blood flowing freely from a cut on his forehead and mingling with his tears. Rossiter had thought him mad. Only when he had realized that Eve was missing had he gone to help.

He sat up now, spitting the dust and dirt from his mouth, gritting his teeth against the pain that seemed to flush his body as he straightened his back. Perspiration poured down his face, forming tiny rivulets in the grime. His hands were cut and bleeding, the nails torn; there was blood on his arms, blood on his knees and legs. But these he could fight against. It was that stabbing, searing pain in his side which defeated him.

'It's no use,' he said hoarsely. 'No bloody use. I'm beat.'

If Juanita heard she did not answer, and he turned his head wearily to look at her. She was still tearing away at the rock, her slim hands as bloody as his, the long nails broken and torn. Torn too was her dress; there were rents where she had knelt on it, or caught it on a jagged edge. Her hair had long since come loose, and hung about her face and shoulders in a wild tangle. Occasionally she paused to throw it back. But she was seldom still for long. When Rossiter had staggered away from her after the rock fall he had feared that she too was dead; her closed eyes had looked like empty sockets in the dusty pallor of her face, and in his clumsiness he could not find her heart. It was with enormous relief that he had suddenly found her working beside him, her tears mingling with the sweat.

'Stop it!' Rossiter said. 'You're killing yourself to no purpose. She's dead.'

She looked at him then, brushing the

hair away from her mouth. Her lips were red where she had bitten them.

'But we — we cannot leave her like this.' Her voice was a mere whisper. She glanced down at the dead woman's legs, uncovered now, and burst into a fresh paroxysm of tears. Rossiter marvelled that she had any left to shed. 'Madre mia, but how terrible!'

'Terrible, yes. But tears won't help.' He tried to stand, but the pain was too acute. 'Can you find a blanket? I don't think I can make it. We'll cover her up until the others return. They'll do the rest.'

'You are hurt?' She blinked at him, her long lashes grey with dust.

'A rock caught me on the side. It's gone stiff on me. I'll be all right presently.'

He watched her walk wearily down the track and disappear into a cave. Then he turned to look at Corbett. Propped on one elbow, Corbett lay on his side, tossing a stone into the air and catching it. Occasionally his eyes strayed to his dead wife's legs, and the stone fell unheeded while he stared glassily, shaking his head as though denying what he saw. Once he had put out a tentative hand to touch her. But the contact was never made. The hand started to shake and was slowly withdrawn. After an interval of tracing idle patterns in the dust he found another stone to toss.

He had been that way for some time now. It had happened suddenly. At one moment he had been working furiously beside them, heedless of the heat and the pain and the immensity of the task; and then he had stopped. Rossiter had thought it was because he had finally realized that his wife was dead, that their struggle was as pointless as it was monumental. That was until he had seen Corbett's eyes. The past week had impressed on Rossiter the man's mental instability. Now, it seemed, instability had developed into madness — temporary if not permanent.

Juanita returned with the blanket, dragging her feet. He watched her cover the dead woman's legs and then, crossing herself, kneel to whisper a prayer. Corbett let the stone drop and watched her too. It seemed to Rossiter that a gleam of understanding showed in his eyes, and he said gruffly, 'I'm sorry, Corbett. But it's all we can do now. Later — ' He paused. 'Anyway, I'm sorry. Damned sorry.'

The blood on Corbett's forehead had caked with the grime, the lines on his thin face were etched sharply in dust and dirt. At the sound of Rossiter's voice he looked up, cocking his head to one side like a blind man seeking direction. His mouth was slack, the lower lip quivering.

'Sorry?' he muttered. 'Sorry?' For a brief moment a look came into his eyes that was something more than madness, a look that caused Rossiter to shiver in the heat. Then the eyes glazed over, and his head drooped. 'Sorry? Yes, of course.'

He leaned over to adjust the blanket, tugging at a corner until the furrows were smoothed out. It was a simple, automatic gesture, with neither sentiment nor sorrow to it. He gave the blanket a final, approving pat, and then got awkwardly to his feet and limped away.

Juanita watched him go. 'Poor man,'

she said softly. 'Is he all right, do you think?'

'No,' Rossiter said. 'But there's nothing we can do to help him.'

'But that cut on his forehead. If it is not cleaned it may turn septic.'

He was suddenly angry at her solicitude. Corbett was her enemy, it was Corbett who was primarily responsible for her present plight. Her sympathy was illogical.

'Let him be,' he said shortly. 'The poor devil has just seen his wife killed. You can't bandage him for that.' Slowly and painfully he pulled himself up, clutching at the rock for support. His back and shoulders were raw from the sun, his neck stiff. 'Let's get out of this bloody sun before we fry.'

The cave was only a few yards away, but to Rossiter it seemed a mile. Movement so intensified the pain in his side that he had to strangle a scream with every step. But he was grateful to the girl for not offering to help. He wanted no coals of fire.

There were no beds in the cave. He

lowered himself gingerly on to one of the coarse mattresses, and sighed with relief at the stillness and the shade. The girl stood watching him, and he said roughly, 'Better take the weight off your feet. It'll be some hours yet before they're back. Or are you contemplating escape? There's no-one to stop you. I couldn't, and I doubt if Corbett would even try.'

She shook her head. 'I had not thought,' she said.

'No? Well, take my advice and don't. You might run into Pablo and his friends. But suit yourself; it makes no odds to me. If your father intends to pay, then the money will be on its way by now. You can't stop it.'

'And if not?'

He stroked his moustache, scattering the dust, and looked at her thoughtfully.

'You read the letter, Mrs Everard.'

She shivered, blinking her eyes. 'But you could not do that. I know you could not.'

'Your optimism must be comforting.' He grimaced as he eased his body into a less painful position. 'But you're right, of course. I've no contacts in the white slave traffic. To be honest, I don't know what the hell I do with you if your father lets us down.'

'He won't,' she said. And then, after a pause, 'Why did you do this?'

He laughed. It was a dry sound, not entirely humorous.

'For the money, of course. What did you think? Early in life I developed a taste for luxury. Since I also have an adventurous spirit, crime was the obvious answer. I've found it a reasonably profitable profession to date.' Once more he shifted his position. It seemed that nowhere could his body be at ease. 'You haven't answered my question. Are you staying or going?'

'I will stay.' Better the devil she knew than those she did not. She had no doubt that the ransom would be paid; freedom was only a few short hours away. And there was Tommy to consider. Perhaps, when he had the money, he would tell her about Tommy.

'Right. Well, now that's settled, let's have a drink.' He nodded at the wall behind her. 'There's a bottle of wine over there.'

She fetched it, kneeling to give it to him and watching while he drank.

'Are you in much pain?' she asked.

'Enough. But don't worry, I'll survive. Cracked ribs don't kill.'

'I am sorry.' Neither of them noticed the ambiguity. 'I have not thanked you yet for protecting me. I might have been killed.' His side was bruised and swollen, and she frowned as she looked at it. 'Is there nothing I can do to ease the pain?'

What was it in women, he wondered irritably, that urged them either to seduce a man or minister to him? He had caused Juanita Everard only injury and suffering. In return she offered sympathy and gratitude.

'Nothing,' he told her. 'And spare me your thanks. My motives were entirely mercenary. You are an investment, Mrs Everard, and I like to protect my investments.' The sight of her kneeling beside him, with her sad eyes in the dirt-streaked face, angered him. He took another swig from the bottle and thrust it at her. 'Have a drink. You look as though you could use one.'

She took the bottle and stood up. But she did not drink. She said, 'You are a strange man. Why do you wish to seem more wicked than you are?'

'I don't. And stop analyzing me.'

She put down the bottle and wandered aimlessly round the cave, pausing in the entrance to examine herself. Lifting one slender leg and then the other, she frowned at the shredded stockings and the scars, then flounced out the torn dress and released it with a sigh. Her hands were still bleeding. She put a finger to her mouth and sucked.

'I look as bad as I feel,' she said. 'My father will be shocked.'

'You said he was blind.'

'Yes. But he will know. He uses his hands.'

He grunted. 'Well, I can't provide a new dress, but there's water and a towel over there.' He jerked a thumb behind him. 'A comb too if you can find it.'

She thanked him and disappeared behind his back, and he sought in the hip pocket of his shorts for his cigar case. The cigars were flattened and broken, but he found one with the leaf reasonably intact and lit it, grateful for its solace. As Connie would say, this was a right mess; Emilio and the Corbett woman dead, Corbett with his mind deranged, himself incapacitated, and a band of Spanish brigands lurking menacingly somewhere on the mountain. Only if driven to it, he suspected, would they resort to physical violence; that crashing boulder had not been meant to kill, or why had they shouted a warning? But they would demand their million pesetas, and it seemed inevitable now that he must pay it. And what then? Arrangements had been made to get himself and the money out of the country, but both mobility and time would be needed. That damned rock had checked his mobility; and time, with two corpses in his wake, might be more pressing than he had anticipated. Equally pressing was the problem of Andrew Corbett. In his present state Corbett would be a menace to their escape, whether they took him with them or left him behind. And if sanity returned? To abandon him would be to drive him to the police — if not out of revenge (and Corbett, as Rossiter had reason to know, was a fanatic for revenge), then from a wish to see his wife decently buried. Yet could he be persuaded to go with them, leaving her there on the mountain, that tumbled pile of rock her cenotaph?

He had almost finished his cigar when Juanita returned to stand beside him. Inconsequentially, he thought how young she looked. Her dark hair, combed but still loose, rippled about her shoulders. She had washed the blood and dirt from hands and face and legs, so that the bruise on her forehead showed the more clearly.

'Feeling better?' he asked.

'Yes.' In the last hour she had lost much of her fear of him. The sight of him lying at her feet added to her courage. 'Please! Tell me about Tommy. Where is he? Who is looking after him? I have to know, Mr Rossiter. Even when my father brings the money I will not go until you tell me.'

'You won't, eh? In that case I suggest you make yourself comfortable. You are in for quite a stay.' He looked at her mockingly. 'What kind of a fool do you think I am? I tell you, you tell your father, he tells the police, the police contact Scotland Yard — and, hey presto! Tommy is released, and I'm arrested. No, thank you. But not to worry. The kid is safe enough. If you and Don Carlos obey orders he'll stay that way.'

'But he is only a baby,' she protested. 'How can I be sure that they feed him properly, that — '

'You can't. So stop asking damn' fool questions and find out what Corbett is up to. I don't like this silence. I hope the idiot hasn't wandered off.'

It was warm in the cave, but outside the heat was intense. Shading her eyes against the sun, she looked to where they had laboured so desperately a little while before. Heat haze danced on the hot stones, so that at first she thought to see movement. But there was only the tumbled rock and the blanket and, farther up the track, the smoking embers of

Lucia's abandoned fire. She brushed away a cloud of flies and looked the other way. Some thirty yards distant, Corbett sat in the shade of a cave entrance, his back against the rock. His face was hidden from her; but the drooping shoulders, the thin legs outstretched in the dust, filled her with pity.

'What's he doing?' Rossiter asked, when she returned.

'Just sitting.' The flies had followed her into the cave, and she spat one from her mouth. 'He is playing with something, but I cannot see what it is.'

'Probably another stone.' He stubbed out the cigar and looked at his watch, and then remembered that it had been smashed in the rock fall. 'So long as he doesn't wander off he can amuse himself as he pleases, poor devil. Relax, Mrs Everard. There's still some time to go.'

At his insistence she sat uncomfortably on the other mattress, hunching her slim body, the torn dress pulled over her knees and her hands clasped round her legs. But she could not relax. The thought of

Tommy in alien, unfriendly hands tormented her, so that presently she renewed her pleading, begging for information. He gave her none. Tommy was his trump, his assurance against defeat. To alleviate her distress would be to weaken its effectiveness.

She was still pleading when the light from the entrance suddenly dimmed, and they looked up to see Corbett standing there. From somewhere he had found a length of rusted iron, and was using it as a prop. His right hand hung limp at his side.

'Come on in,' Rossiter said, screwing up his eyes to peer at the man's face. But Corbett was in silhouette, and he could not read his expression. 'You've been out in the sun too long, man. Have some wine. There's still a drop in the bottle.' Then he saw what was in the other's hand, and he raised his body awkwardly and sat up, heedless of the pain. 'Is that my revolver you've got there? I must have dropped it when — ' He paused. Unwise, perhaps, to mention when. 'Hand it over, will you? I'll need it if those wops return.'

Corbett limped farther into the cave, the iron ringing dully on the stone floor. Now he was only a few yards from Rossiter. Juanita saw his eyes, and shivered.

The gun was steady in his hand. But there was a quiver to his lip as he said, 'You killed her, Everard, damn you! You killed my wife. Now it's your turn.'

'Now wait a minute!' Rossiter was struggling to get to his feet; but his body had stiffened, and he could not move fast. 'I'm not Everard, and I didn't kill your wife. It was an accident — you know that. I'm sorry it happened — we all are — but it wasn't my fault. I didn't kill her, man. I tell you, I — '

The report was not loud, but it seemed to grow in volume as it echoed round the cave. As Juanita screamed it was followed by another, and then another. Rossiter was on one knee when the first bullet hit him. She saw the ugly red mark suddenly appear in his chest, saw the startled look in his brown eyes. Then he collapsed, his body jerking as the second and third bullets thudded home.

It jerked twice more before it was still.

As the sound of the shots died away Juanita scrambled to her feet and ran to kneel beside him. Rossiter's mouth was open — twisted in pain, fixed in death — with blood seeping lazily from one corner. His eyes stared back at her, sightless, and with tears flooding her own she turned away.

'Muerto! Muerto!' she muttered, repeating the word to convince herself. Then her voice rose hysterically, and she swivelled on her knees to look up at the silent figure standing over her. 'Oh, Madre mia! Es muerto!'

She blinked away her tears to see the still smoking barrel of the gun pointing at her throat.

# 18

Against the dark background of the mountain the newcomer was only a moving blur in the late twilight. He had no shape; they saw him, but they could not distinguish him. It was not until he had slid down on to the track and was coming towards them, his feet stumbling over the uneven ground, that Connie emitted a loud hiss and said, with obvious relief, 'It's Al.'

Everard had recovered from his stupor and joined the other two. He said sharply, 'Stop right there, you! And keep your hands down if you don't want a bullet in your guts.'

Al stopped. He stood with his arms loose by his sides, his shoulders drooping wearily; they could not distinguish his features, but in the gloom his bald head gleamed palely. If he recognized Everard's voice he gave no sign. He was the personification of dejection and defeat.

Connie said, 'This here's Mr Everard, Al. Remember? He — '

'Shut up!' Everard said. Suspicious of the tall man's inertia, he advanced cautiously towards him, the gun pointed at his stomach. 'Search him, Ramon. See if he has a gun.'

Ramon ran his hands inexpertly down the man's clothing. It was an exercise he had not previously performed.

'No gun, Señor.'

'Right. Where's your boss, you?'

'In there,' Al said, and pointed to the cave where Rossiter lay. 'He's dead.'

'Oh, Gawd!' Connie said, and collapsed on an adjacent boulder. 'Them bloody wops!'

Everard's tired brain wandered round the possibilities. The man in the cave had been dead for several hours, his body was stiff and cold. If Smith had told the truth about the Spaniards' attack — and the tall man's face was as marked as Smith's, he had certainly been in a fight — then Johnson was not the killer. And yet . . .

'Where's my wife?' he demanded, and

jabbed the automatic into Johnson's stomach.

'I don't know, mister.' Al did not budge. 'When I found the guv'nor's body, and seen Mrs Corbett under them rocks — ' He nodded towards the wrecked cave — 'I thought she'd be there too.'

'She isn't. Where have you been since?'

'Up the mountain,' Al said. He had thought he heard voices and, angry at what had been done in the village, he had gone to investigate, hoping to find Pablo and his friends and enact some sort of vengeance. But he had found no-one. Instead, he had lost his way.

'I'm glad your missus wasn't killed,' he said simply.

Connie saw his opportunity. Pablo was his only trump, and this was the time to use it. He said cautiously, 'I don't reckon much to her chances now. Not with them wops.'

He had braced himself against instant reaction, and he got it. Everard swung round sharply, gun in hand. 'What the devil do you mean by that?' he snapped.

'I mean they didn't take her and Corbett for ransom, Mr Everard. Not as I sees it. No-one ain't paying good money for Corbett.' Connie kept a watchful eye on the gun. 'I reckon they took 'em 'cos Corbett and your missus was witnesses to what they done here, and they don't want 'em squawking to the scoffers.'

Everard stared at him, cold fear clutching at his heart. Ramon gasped. He said, stammering a little, 'We must go to the police, Señor. And quickly. We cannot deal with these men ourselves.'

'Where do they come from?' Everard asked. 'Do either of you know?'

'Guadix,' Connie said promptly. He told of the visit to Luis' house, and the meeting with Pablo and Manuel. But this could be dangerous, and he added hastily, 'Of course, I wouldn't reckon to find the house meself. But the scoffers must know. Luis, his name is. Luis Moreno. Pablo's his grandson.'

Everard looked up at the mountain. There was a glow in the sky beyond; but the moon had not yet risen nor the stars come out, and he knew that to search for

Juanita unaided would be an impossible task. As Ramon had said, this was for the police. And the sooner they acted the greater the chance of finding her alive.

'We'll make for the car,' he said. 'It won't be easy in the dark, but there's no choice.'

'It will be easier with the moon,' Ramon said.

'We can't wait, man.' He was so desperate to be gone that already he had forgotten the two kidnappers. He was some yards down the track when Ramon called to him.

'But Señor! These men. What do we do with them?'

Everard swore and turned back. To Johnson he said, 'You come with us. If your friend can't walk he can stay here. The police will pick him up in the morning.' He waved the gun. 'Come on, move!'

It was for this that Connie had been scheming. Yet now that it had come he was suddenly afraid.

'You mean leave me here on me tod? With her?' His voice was bleak as he

300

pointed to the blanket. 'And the guv'nor up there in the cave? You ain't even going to bury 'em first?'

'They won't harm you,' Everard said, signalling to Johnson. 'And I couldn't care less if they did.'

Al was not a quick-thinking man, but for once he was gifted with inspiration.

'Couldn't we move him up the mountain a bit, mister?' he suggested. 'Some of them Spaniards might come back to hide the bodies. They wouldn't want to leave 'em around for the cops. If they was to find Connie here they'd do him.'

Connie gasped, shuddering at the awful picture.

Everard hesitated. Time was urgent, he had none to spare for moving the injured Smith to safety. The men were morally responsible for the danger that threatened his wife, and he owed them nothing. Yet Johnson was right; the Spaniards would almost certainly return to conceal their crime. And if they had murdered once . . .

'Move him yourself,' he said curtly,

impatient to be gone. No doubt they would make a run for it — or as near to a run as Smith could manage — but the police would pick them up eventually. Even if they made good their escape — well, much as he wished to see them punished for their crimes, compared with Juanita's life punishment was unimportant. 'I've no time. But don't waste your energy getting him down to the car. It's out of action.'

Connie watched the two men vanish down the track into the darkness. He said cheerfully, 'That was smart, Al. Bloody smart. On me tod I didn't fancy it, but I reckon we can make it together.'

'Make it where?' Al too was staring after the two men. Glad as he was of this chance of freedom, a small fraction of his mind regretted he had not gone with them. He had a deep anger against the men who had killed Rossiter.

'Over the mountain, of course. You heard what he said about the car. Besides, that's the way they'd expect us to go. There's villages the other side — I seen 'em on the map. We could hire a car.'

Johnson too had seen the map. 'It's a long way,' he said doubtfully. 'And you with a busted ankle.'

'Oh, aye, it's a long way. But we got all night. And me ankle's sprained, not busted.' He pulled himself to his feet and hobbled a few paces. The ankle was sore and swollen, and when he put his weight on it a shaft of pain shot up his leg. He swore, and sat down. 'It ain't all that good, but I'll make it. I got to.'

'We'd need money for a car.'

Connie put his hand in his pocket and pulled out two bundles of notes. 'I lifted 'em while we was counting,' he said, grinning to himself in the dark. 'I can be smart too.'

Al knew that had events gone according to plan Connie would have kept the money for himself. But he was too relieved to reproach him for his treachery.

They waited for the moon to come up. Connie spent the time putting a cold compress on his ankle, and bandaging it tightly with strips of material torn from the women's wardrobe. To Al, who had had an affection and admiration for

Rossiter he had felt for few others, it seemed important that he should perform some last rite for the dead man. Burial without implements in that hard ground was impossible, and might hinder the conviction of the murderers; and prayer was unfamiliar. But he remembered that Rossiter had once told him he had been brought up in the Catholic faith, and he covered the body with a blanket and shamefacedly put candles, taken from Manuel Aralar's meagre store, at head and feet. He was glad that Connie was too scared of the dead to see him. Connie would have ribbed him unmercifully.

They drank the last bottle of wine, and ate a meal of maize bread and raw ham and fruit; they had no haversack, but they took what they could in their pockets. Then they set out, heading south-east, hoping eventually to reach the secondary road that ran from Baza to the coast. Both of them knew that the journey was a gamble, that across unknown and harsh terrain they might land up anywhere or nowhere. But freedom was worth a gamble.

It was a cold night; clear and bright, and with a keen wind that cut through their thin clothing and whistled fiercely about their ears. Al fretted silently at the slowness of their progress, both from a sense of urgency and a desire to keep warm. Connie struggled manfully, but he was far from silent. The scree and shale provided treacherous footholds for his damaged leg; and each time he slipped, or came down too heavily on the sprained ankle, or knocked it against an unseen rock, the pain caused him to swear fluently and profanely. At first Al tried to help him over the more difficult stretches; but he was rewarded with more curses than thanks, and presently he left him to struggle on unaided, and concentrated on choosing the least arduous route.

Rossiter had said there would be snow at the top. It felt cold enough for snow, but they found none — although once they skirted a small tarn on which lumps of ice floated. There was no defined crest, only a long flat plateau across which the wind blew even more fiercely; they struck eastward along it, not too certain of their direction, but consoled to some extent by the knowledge that at least they were heading away from Guadix and the inevitable pursuit.

They stopped less often on the plateau than they had on the climb; there was no shelter and, tired and pain-racked though he was, Connie found the wind too keen to remain static for long. Half-way across they came to a small hut, with walls of unmortared stone and an earthen roof, and stayed there while Connie readjusted the bandage on his ankle. The longer rest brought stiffness but little warmth to their frozen limbs, and the resumption of their journey was an agony to both men.

They came at last to the far side of the plateau and began the descent. Here the terrain was different, broken by deep valleys and sheer precipices, and dotted with pinnacles of rock which to their tired eyes assumed strange, disturbing shapes in the moonlight. Avoiding the more broken ground, they started down the side of a narrow gully, keeping out of the shadows so that they might choose their path more easily. But the surface was treacherous. Al, who was leading, found himself slipping continuously on the loose gravel. It was after one such slip, and before he had fully recovered his balance, that Connie came sliding into him and sent them both sprawling.

Al picked himself up and looked anxiously at his companion. Connie sat nursing his ankle, shouting obscenities in a shrill voice, his face contorted in pain and anger and his teeth chattering.

'Hell, what a country!' He spat a mouthful of dust. 'If you're not bloody fried you're bloody frozen. And as for walking — ' He released his ankle and fell sideways. 'Jeepers! What was that?'

'That' was a sharp report and a sudden scattering of the gravel above them. Al had ducked to his knees at the sound. He was still crouching when there came a second report, followed by a loud cry from Connie. He ducked lower, searching frantically for cover. None offered, and he lay flat on his stomach and turned his head away and waited with thudding heart for the next bullet.

'He nicked my arm!' wailed Connie.

He too lay flat, his head close to Al, clutching the wounded arm. Al saw the stain spreading over the sleeve below his fingers. 'The bastard nicked my arm! Who the hell is he?'

'I don't know. But he ain't friendly, that's for sure.'

'That you, Everard?' The voice rang shrilly across the gully. 'Looking for your wife, eh? Well, she's here — right beside me.' There came the sound of a woman's scream. 'Hear that, Everard? Want to come and get her?'

'Gawd!' Connie said. 'That's Corbett, ain't it? So it was him took the woman, not the wops.'

'And it was him killed the guv'nor,' Al said grimly. 'Must have been.'

Still prone, they turned their heads to look. Across the gully the cliff rose sheer for some twenty-five feet, its summit broken by massive boulders. And on one of the boulders, sharp and clear in the moonlight, stood the figure of a man.

'How does he know Everard's looking for her?' whispered Al.

'He don't. He's a nut case, that's what.

Got Everard on the brain. I reckon seeing his missus killed shoved him over the edge.'

'I'd like to shove him over the edge, the bastard!' Al said, remembering Rossiter.

'Come on, Everard,' Corbett shouted. 'It's her or you. I'm giving you the choice. That's more than you gave me when you killed Eve.' There was a long pause. Corbett stooped on the boulder, peering down into the gully. 'Well? Are you coming? Or do I shoot her now, with you listening? Would you prefer that?'

Lifting his head, Al shouted hoarsely, 'It's not Everard, Corbett. It's us — Al and Connie.'

The answer came in the form of another bullet. It hit the ground some yards from the crouching pair. Connie said angrily, 'No use arguing with a nut case. Let's blow. If it's move and be shot or stay and be shot, then I'm moving.'

They began to wriggle down the slope on their stomachs. Another bullet whined over their heads, accompanied by an unintelligible shout from Corbett. The cliff on which he stood sheltered them from the wind, but both shale and gravel bit sharply into hands and knees. Johnson could hear Connie muttering behind him, and thought with some irritation that he would do better to save his breath; if Corbett was using Rossiter's Smith and Wesson (and what other gun could it be?) they had some way to go before they were out of range. It was with enormous relief that he felt the ground dip suddenly, and rolled over to find himself in a fold in the mountainside that effectively concealed him from the cliff top.

Connie came slithering after him. Al had a quick look at his arm. The bullet had done no more than crease the flesh; but it was bleeding freely, and he bandaged it roughly with his handkerchief. Corbett continued to shout at them, his taunts and threats interspersed with bullets which smacked into the ground around them.

'He's got too much bloody ammo,' Connie growled. 'Spraying it around like that, it's odds on his hitting one of us when we move. But we can't stay here.'

Al said slowly, 'When we move he'll kill

310

her. You heard what he said. It's her or us.'

'Her or Everard.'

'Same thing. He thinks we're Everard.'

'Well, we ain't.' Connie raised himself on one knee and peered cautiously up at the cliff. 'And it's time we was going, Corbett or no bloody Corbett. The girl ain't our responsibility, and we couldn't do nothing if she was. She'll have to take her chance, wack — same as we will when we crawl out of this ditch and the bastard starts shooting.'

'It was him killed the guv'nor,' Al said.

'So what?'

'So he ain't going to get away with it,' Al said firmly. 'And we ain't going to let him kill that girl, neither.'

Connie spat in disgust. 'You're as nuts as he is. How the hell can we stop him? Get anywhere near the bastard and he'll plug you.'

'Not if I take him from behind.' Al lifted his long body to peer over the edge of the trench. A bullet whistled past his head, and he ducked hastily. 'I'll try it, anyways. You stay here.'

'You bet I will. I'm no ruddy hero.'

'And keep him talking. If he yells at you, yell back. It don't matter what you say. He won't do nothing to the girl while he knows you're still here. It's Everard he wants, not his missus.'

Flat on his stomach, he wormed his way along the trench. From the far side of the gully the cliff had been in shadow, and he had hoped there might be a way up it. He was no stranger to rock climbing. But one look at the face as he neared it told him that, for a man without equipment, it was unclimbable — smooth, and almost completely sheer, with a slight overhang at the top. From here the trench sloped diagonally down the side of the mountain, and he climbed out and ran for the shelter of the cliff. Another shot rang out; but he guessed it was aimed at Connie, and began to work his way along the foot of the cliff, away from the gully, seeking a possible way of ascent. Rounding the most southerly point he felt the wind again, and could see the face of the cliff stretching away to the north-west, austere and precipitous in the moonlight. He almost abandoned the attempt then. He told himself that he was neither a superman nor a hero, and it seemed he would need to be both to succeed. I'll go another twenty yards, he thought. If no possible ascent offers by then I'll give up.

He had gone nearly the twenty yards when he spotted the chimney. He judged the cliff to be more than fifty feet high at this point, and clouds scudding across the moon gave a chiaroscuro effect to the rock surface, making it difficult to distinguish between concave and convex. But as far as he could see the chimney looked reasonably easy — a convenient width, and with adequate footholds. Rubbing his hands briskly together to restore the circulation, he began the ascent.

He was about half-way to the top when the mist descended. It came down suddenly, blanketing his vision and making the rock surface damp and treacherous. But he went on. It was as easy to go on as to return. And the mist gave him one advantage. Corbett might hear him coming, but he would not be able to see him.

And then, unexpectedly, the chimney finished. It opened out like a funnel, so that his legs could no longer span the gap. He descended until pressure on feet and back was firmer, lowered one foot to a narrow ledge on the near wall, and turned cautiously, his cold fingers searching for a hold in the slippery rock above. Then, slowly and laboriously, he began once more to climb.

It was hard going. The holds were few and precarious, and despite the cold and the damp his body was soon perspiring freely. But as the funnel opened the angle became less acute, and presently he was able to tilt his body forward and lean against the cliff face, with only a toe hold to support him. Welcoming the chance to rest, he cautiously lifted each hand in turn to blow on his numb fingers. He had heard no shots during the climb. There had been voices up top — Corbett, he supposed, talking to the girl — but no shouting, and he wondered what Connie was up to. He had counted on Connie to distract Corbett's attention. The chimney would be almost due west of the spot from where Corbett had been firing. If he were still there, watching the gully — and if the girl did not involuntarily give him warning — it should be possible to creep up on him through the mist and the dark and take him from behind.

It was as he started to move up again that the firing recommenced; two shots in rapid succession, followed some seconds later by a third. Al hesitated, puzzled. That last shot had sounded different; more muffled, perhaps more distant. Was Corbett on the move? Had he tired of waiting for the supposed Everard to come to him, and gone to hunt him down?

Then why the first two shots?

As a possible explanation occurred to him — that Corbett had shot the girl before leaving — he dug his fingers into the rock and heaved himself up, all caution gone. But the surface was smooth and slippery. His feet were searching for a purchase when another muffled shot rang out. Breathing hard, clinging to the cliff by fingers alone, he heard a shrill, choking scream, and out of the mist a body came tumbling down the funnel towards him. There was no way to avoid it. The force with which it hit him was not great. But it tore his fingers from their hold, and he found himself falling, his body ricocheting from side to side of the chimney as he hurtled down it to the ground.

# 19

Even in her fear Juanita found room to wonder how Andrew Corbett managed the climb. There was no path. They had to pick their way round boulders and enormous outcrops of rock, and the loose shale made uneasy footholds for a man with a twisted leg and only a piece of iron, heavy and unwieldy, for support. In the other hand he carried the revolver. He made her go in front, snapping directions at her, although one way was as good as another so long as it was up. Once, when he slipped and fell, she was tempted to run — anywhere, so long as it was away from him. She knew he could never catch her. But she had gone no more than a few yards when a bullet flattened itself against a rock to her right, and she stopped.

'You do that again,' he said angrily, jabbing the gun barrel into her side as he came up to her, 'and I don't wait for your husband. I'll get him later.'

The wild look on his face, the way his finger fondled the trigger as he lifted the gun, left her in no doubt of his meaning. But she was puzzled by this reference to John. He had called Rossiter Everard when he shot him; how could he now think that Everard was alive? Somewhat fearfully, she put this question to him later when they rested. He looked at her vaguely, his eyes screwed tight as though he were trying to remember, a hand against his forehead. Then he sighed, abandoning the effort.

'He'll come,' he said. 'He's looking for you. We may have to wait, but he'll come. They told me.'

'Who told you?' she asked, emboldened by this new, apparent calm.

He shook his head. 'He doesn't know I'm here. He thinks he got rid of us both — me and Eve. But we're going to surprise him.' The gun was by his side and he picked it up, to turn it over and over in his hands. Then he reached for his iron bar and dragged himself to his feet. 'Come on. We're not there yet.'

'Why not wait here?' she suggested.

The question angered him. The wild look came back to his eyes, and he shouted at her, telling her not to argue. 'And hurry,' he snapped. 'We haven't got all day. We must be ready when he comes.'

But John would not come, she thought sadly, as she started to climb. John was in England. How long would Corbett wait? And what would happen when the waiting was over?

It was some time before they rested again. She was weary and footsore and sick with fear, but he seemed possessed of some inner fire that put him beyond tiredness and physical disability. He kept telling her to hurry. She could hear the iron bar ringing on the ground behind her, and for most of the way he muttered to himself. Only occasional snatches made sense. Once he mentioned pictures — 'It's the pictures that are important. The other stuff doesn't matter' — and the names of John and his dead wife constantly recurred. He never spoke of Rossiter. It seemed that Rossiter had become inextricably merged in his mind with John, the personification of his hatred.

Not until he shot the defenceless Rossiter had she realized the depth of his madness. She had thought before, when he sat in the sun and played with his stones, that his mind was too sick with grief to cope, that it had managed temporarily to retire from reality. But the senseless killing, the look in his eyes as he gazed down at the dead man, had told her that this was no transient derangement. That was when she had first known fear. She had thought that he meant to kill her too. The smoking gun barrel at her throat, the acrid smell of cordite, had stifled the outcry that the murder had spontaneously evoked. Crouched on the floor of the cave, she had stared up at him, frozen into silence and near immobility. Even when a slight movement of her hand behind her had caused her to touch the dead flesh of the man on the mattress, and she had felt the stickiness of blood on her fingers, she had not cried out or shifted her position. Face to face with death, she had been filled with a passionate longing for life.

When at last he had lowered the revolver and told her to get up she had found herself unable to move. He had had to drag her to her feet. She had waited against the wall of the cave, watching him search Rossiter's suitcase. It was ammunition he was seeking; he took nothing else. When he had found it they had started to climb the mountain.

It was late afternoon when he told her they had arrived, that this was where they would wait. She could see no reason for his choice, and he offered none. It was a bleak and desolate spot at the far side of the summit, on the edge of a cliff that dropped sheer some thirty feet. All around were the mountains. It was wild-looking country, with no sign of habitation or people. They could stay there for days, she thought, and no-one would find them.

If he would wait that long.

As afternoon faded into evening and evening to chilly night they sat on the cliff top and waited. For long spells Corbett was silent, and when he spoke it was usually to utter bitter tirades against her husband. Once she ventured a mild defence on John's behalf; but argument angered him, and from then on she accepted his vindictive condemnation in silence. Sometimes his mind wandered so far that he mistook her for his wife, calling her Eve, alternately pleading for her affection or rebuking her for unfaithfulness with someone he called Emilio. But he did not molest her. He sat perched on a large boulder, apparently impervious to the bitter wind, with the revolver in his lap and herself crouched at his feet, seeking what shelter she could. In one of the silences she tried to plead with him, offering money, immunity, anything he wished if he would let her go. He did not answer. Only when she continued to plead did he tell her sternly to hold her tongue.

'But why are we waiting?' she asked tearfully. 'My husband will not come, he is in England. Even if he were not he would not find us here.'

He picked up the revolver and smoothed

the barrel lovingly with his fingers.

'He'll come,' he said. 'Keep quiet. I want to listen.'

As the cold took possession of her body her brain too became numb. She no longer listened to his snatches of talk. It was as though she were in a trance; she heard his voice, but the words had no meaning for her. Occasionally her mind drifted back to the past, and she was at home in England with Tommy and John, serene and secure and happy. But not for long; the fantasy would fade, and she was back in the dread present. She knew that when Corbett's patience gave out she would die. She was the bait; when the quarry failed to appear — as it must — he would take the only revenge left to his crazed mind, and kill her. And what then? What would happen to Tommy? And John? John would never know the truth now. He might not even learn of her death. A body could lie hidden for months in that desolate place, so that when eventually it was discovered it would be unrecognizable. John would remember her as the faithless wife who had left him for a younger man. And when Tommy grew up (if the men who held him allowed him to grow up) he would think of her that way too.

She did not hear the voices that Corbett heard. It was the sound of that first shot which whipped her into sudden awareness. Her head had been sunk on her breast, and as she lifted it the sharp twinge in her neck caused her to give a little whimper of pain. Corbett took no notice. He was on his feet now, staring down into the gully with his back to her, the moonlight glinting on the revolver in his hand. And then she too heard the voices, and knew that there were people down there; real people, not just the figments of Corbett's madness. But despite the little glow of hope that warmed her heart her body was too stiff and numb to take advantage of her captor's preoccupation. If she were to escape rescue must come to her. She could not run to meet it.

When he shouted her husband's name it startled her even more than the shot had done. She knew he was wrong, that this was all part of his crazy belief that John would come. Yet because she so desperately wanted to think him right she allowed herself the luxury of hope. She even cried out for help. Then a hoarse voice shouted back, and she sank once more into the apathy of despair. Johnson and Smith — the men who had been with Rossiter. There could be no help there. And now more than ever she needed help. These men would make no effort to rescue her; not with five million pesetas to share between them, and all to lose if their escape should be hindered. And when they went Corbett would believe that John was abandoning her.

There was no doubt in her mind what he would do then.

The voices went on, but she no longer listened. Each time Corbett fired she gave a slight shudder, as though the bullet had been meant for her. For now it was only a matter of time. The mist came down, soaking into the thin summer frock, adding dampness to the icy cold. Her limbs were so numb that when Corbett moved on the boulder above she did not feel the little shower of stones that fell on to her legs. Vaguely she thought that if the final bullet were delayed much longer it need never be fired. She would be dead from the cold.

From across the open plateau a voice came faintly through the mist, calling her name. She paid it no heed. If she thought at all it was to dismiss it as an illusion, another facet of the nightmare. Perhaps she too was close to madness now. But Corbett scrambled down from his boulder and limped to the far side of the spur, putting her between himself and the voice. Listlessly she watched him. He stood with his back to the cliff edge, the outline of his thin body blurred by the mist.

'Juanita!' It sounded like John's voice, and she stirred, lifting her head. 'Juanita! Where are you?'

She did not answer. It could not be John. John was in England. But Corbett had no doubt. From behind her he called shrilly, 'Over here, Everard. With me. Come and get her.'

There were other voices now, calling to

each other. Then the first voice came again, nearer this time, and her heart leapt as she heard it.

'You harm her, Corbett, and I'll kill you!'

Doubt vanished. Incredible as it seemed, that was John. 'John!' she cried, too faint for him to hear. 'John!' Painfully she moved her stiffened limbs, struggling to rise. She was on her knees when she heard Corbett laugh, and it was the laugh that stopped her. With dreadful clarity she realized what was about to happen. John would come running towards her out of the mist, his eyes only for her. He would not see the shadowy figure beyond. But Corbett would see him. It was for this he had been waiting. This would be the moment of vengeance

'Be careful, John!' Fear for him gave strength to her voice and movement to her limbs. She was on her feet now, stumbling towards him. 'He has a gun. He means to kill you.'

Her foot caught against a rock, and she fell. As she started to rise she heard the gun speak behind her, felt a searing pain in her shoulder. Shadowy figures formed in the mist. They were all around her, shouting. Again there came the sound of gunfire, and a shrill, agonized scream that echoed and died.

Someone was kneeling beside her, taking her into his arms.

'John!' she whispered. 'Oh, John!' And fainted.

# 20

It was as the aircraft crossed the French coast, and he saw the Channel below him and the hazy outline of England ahead, that Everard switched his thoughts from Juanita and Spain and considered the immediate future. The past four days had been too full for reflection or anticipation. At the back of his mind had been the constant fear of what might be happening to Tommy. But of the robbery and the dead Laroche he had thought scarcely at all.

He had to think of them now. Especially of Laroche.

He half-expected to find the police waiting for him at the airport. But no-one stopped him, no-one questioned him, and he took a taxi to a small residential hotel in Kensington and registered under an assumed name. Then he went out and bought an armful of newspapers. There was nothing in them relating either to himself or the robbery. I suppose we're old hat to the Press by now, he thought with relief. And until something breaks we're likely to stay that way.

He rang Colin at the flat. Colin was delighted to hear that Juanita was safe, but guarded in his talk. Everard guessed he was not alone.

'Where are you staying?' Colin asked. Everard told him. 'Right. Wait for me there. I'm on my way.'

'Have the police bothered you?'

'Never been near me.'

While he waited Everard considered telephoning Mrs Chater. She might have news for him; news of Tommy, perhaps. But reluctantly he abandoned the idea. He had to make the most of what little freedom remained to him, and the fewer people who knew of his return the better. Better for him and better for them.

'You look all in,' Colin said, when they met. 'Tough, was it?'

'Very,' Everard said. He led the way to a corner of the hotel lounge and ordered drinks. 'Any news of Tommy?'

'Of a sort. I'll tell you presently; it's a

long story, and unfortunately it's inconclusive. Right now I want to hear about Juanita.'

Everard's was a long story too. But impatient as he was for news — even indefinite news — of Tommy, he knew that he owed Colin much. Without Colin he would never have got to Juanita. Reluctantly he decided to satisfy his friend's curiosity before his own.

He was describing how he and Ramon had found their way down the mountain after searching the cave village when Colin said, 'Hold it a minute. There's a large gent in a soup and fish looming to port. He seems to be heading for us.'

Everard turned. Coming towards them was the tall, rather portly figure of Superintendent Morgan. His tailored dinner jacket had neatly rolled lapels; beneath it he wore a maroon cummerbund and bow tie. His massive chin and heavy jowls were newly shaved, his shirt would have done credit to a detergent advertisement. He looked more like a well-groomed man-about-town than a policeman.

'Good evening, Superintendent,' Everard said coldly. 'You don't waste much time. How did you find me?'

'Good evening, gentlemen.' Morgan gave a stiff little bow. He had recently taken to wearing a foundation garment to keep his expanding paunch in check, and bending troubled him. 'Lord Dunmour brought me, Mr Everard. No, my Lord, not intentionally — ' as Colin started to protest. 'But for the past two days we have been keeping an eye on you. Perhaps you can guess why. One of my men followed you here.' He paused, expecting some comment. None came. Colin had decided not to commit himself. 'I must apologize for the glad rags. I'm supposed to be dining with the Assistant Commissioner.'

'Don't let us keep you, then,' Everard said. 'Or do you intend to make an arrest here and now?'

Morgan frowned. But his voice was smoothly polite as he said, 'I imagine you two gentlemen have much to tell each other. Might I be allowed to eavesdrop?' He gazed round the room, which was slowly filling. 'Not quite the cosiest place for a chat, is it? Your room might be more suitable, Mr Everard.'

Without comment, Everard led the way upstairs. He did not want Morgan as an auditor, but he supposed he had no option. This was a command veiled as a request. Nor was he fooled by the superintendent's genial, almost apologetic manner. The bastard wanted his fun first — a cat-and-mouse game before making the kill.

Morgan refused the proffered drink. Choosing a straightbacked chair and hitching up his trousers, he said, 'Would you mind starting again at the beginning, sir? Just to put me in the picture.'

Tight-lipped, Everard obliged. He sat on the bed, with Colin on the only other chair. Out of consideration for Colin he made no mention of how he had left England, and the superintendent did not ask. Both Colin and Everard found that strange. He listened without comment until Everard told how he and Ramon had made their way to Guadix to seek the aid of the police. Then he said, 'A pity you didn't consult them earlier, Mr Everard. If you'd let the police handle this from the beginning you might have saved yourself and your family a deal of suffering.'

'I had no reason to believe in their infallibility,' Everard said curtly. Morgan's unexpectedly sudden arrival had unsettled him. Now he was regaining his composure and his assurance. There was nothing to be gained by currying favour with the man. Arrest was inevitable. What he said or did now could not alter that. 'Quite the reverse.'

Morgan shrugged. 'We don't claim infallibility. Only more and better resources. But I apologize for interrupting. Please continue.'

The police had located Pablo without difficulty. They had found him in his customary bar, and he had admitted wresting the money from Smith and Johnson. But he had insisted, with a great show of moral rectitude, that there had been no intention of keeping it. As good citizens, he and his friends had considered it their duty to recover the money from the English criminals and return it to Don Carlos. 'The police didn't believe him any more than I did,' Everard said.

'Did they recover the money?' Colin asked.

'Most of it. There was some missing, according to Gonzales. No doubt they kept that as expenses.'

But it was Juanita, not the money, who had been Everard's concern; and of Juanita Pablo had stoutly denied all knowledge. So had his friends — insisting that they had not been near the village since Rossiter had driven them away earlier in the day. The woman — two women — had been there, and another man. If Rossiter was dead, the men said, then one of those three had killed him.

Despite harsh interrogation by the police, they had stuck to their story, with Everard growing steadily more impatient. If they were telling the truth, then Juanita was with Corbett, the man whom he believed to be primarily responsible for the kidnapping. There was no alternative. But where had he taken her? Not down to the road, or they would have been seen;

and certainly not towards Guadix. Incredible as it seemed, they must have gone up the mountain. When he put this to the police lieutenant and suggested an immediate search, the lieutenant was unresponsive. Pablo and his friends were lying, he said; just a little more pressure and they would change their tune. The señor would see. Besides, how could one search the mountain in the dark?

Everard was uncertain how, but he knew it had to be done. It was the magic of Don Carlos's name which finally persuaded the lieutenant to co-operate; Don Carlos was influential. Once committed, he acted swiftly. Yet to the anxious Everard it seemed that many hours had passed before he and Ramon, together with three policemen and several volunteers from the town (the lieutenant stayed to continue his interrogation) had set out on their improbable task. 'We made quite an impressive posse,' he said finally. 'Even so, I doubt if we'd have found them had not Smith and Johnson stumbled on them first and drawn Corbett's fire. It was that which attracted our attention.'

'What were they doing there?' Colin asked. 'Smith and Johnson, I mean.'

'According to Smith, they had come to the conclusion that Pablo and his gang might not, after all, have been responsible for Juanita's disappearance. That left Corbett. Corbett, he said, was a mean fellow who had certainly killed once and probably twice. He couldn't bear to think of Juanita in the hands of such a man, and he persuaded Johnson that they must look for them. Quite by accident, they found them.' Everard gave a harsh, ironical laugh. 'He said that in a desperate attempt at rescue he was shot in the arm. He dragged himself down an adjacent gully and, under constant fire from Corbett, persuaded Johnson to make a second attempt. All lies, of course. They were trying to escape. It was their bad luck that they tangled with Corbett. Juanita says he imagined them to be me.'

'What happened to them?' Colin asked.

'Johnson was dead when we found him. Corbett died later, on the way to hospital.'

'And Smith?'

'In gaol. Madrid, I think.'

'Carabanchel Prison, probably,' Morgan said. 'Grim. He won't like it there.'

'That at least is something to be thankful for,' Everard said.

'And Juanita, John? She's all right?'

'She will be. The wound in her shoulder was only a scratch, but she's suffering from shock and exposure. That's why the doctor wouldn't let her come home with me. She's worried about her father, naturally — he's better; still hasn't regained his speech, but she thinks he recognizes her — but Tommy is her main concern. I wouldn't be surprised if a cable arrives tomorrow or the next day to say she's on her way.' He looked challengingly at Morgan. 'Be nice for her, won't it, to find her husband in prison? Or can one get bail on a charge of murder?'

'It would be most exceptional.' The superintendent shifted the acid-drop he was sucking from one side of his mouth to the other, and looked at Colin. 'Well, now! Let's turn to the home front, shall we, my Lord? That's been your department, I believe.'

'Good lord, no! I'm as much in the dark as you are.' Colin looked hard at Everard in the hope that he would understand.

'H'm! That's a pity. I was hoping you might substantiate some of the charges you made against Tasker in that anonymous letter you wrote the police.'

'Well, I can't. I — ' Colin bit his lip, annoyed at being surprised into self-betrayal. 'How the hell did you know I wrote that letter?'

'We're not quite the numbskulls of Mr Everard's belief. We have our moments.' Morgan decided he was being pompous, and balanced the words with a much practised smile. 'I wouldn't want you to incriminate yourself, of course.'

'Of course. But it's getting late. How about that dinner date of yours?'

'I've had that, I'm afraid.' The superintendent sighed. 'A pity. The A.C. keeps a good table. But duty must come first.'

'All right.' Colin could seldom resist a challenge. 'But put me in the witness box and I'll deny every word. Is that clear?'

Morgan nodded. 'It couldn't be clearer.'

Without mentioning names or places, Colin described how he and two friends had waylaid Tasker and persuaded him to tell them where Tommy was being held. 'We were mad as hell to find that we'd missed him by only a few hours,' he said, with an apologetic glance at Everard. 'But that's how it was. And there was nothing we could do about it.'

Everard frowned. 'But you hadn't missed him,' he said, trying to hide his disappointment. 'I mean, he was never there. If the woman was right in saying the child had been at the flat for three weeks, then it wasn't Tommy. It couldn't have been. Tasker was lying.'

That was how it had looked to him, Colin said. But Tasker denied it. He said that the Prices had a son of their own, just about Tommy's age. On the day of the robbery Mrs Price had taken her son to her mother's, asking her to look after him while she and her husband took a short holiday. Tasker had then handed Tommy over to her, and she had gone back with him to the Clapham flat.

'No-one there seems to have suspected the switch,' Colin said, pausing to light his pipe. 'When we called at the house later (I thought the couple might have returned) the woman we saw previously admitted she had not seen the child over the week-end, although she had heard him crying. Anyway, I dare say one small baby looks much like another to the casual observer.'

A week ago Everard would have disputed that statement. Now he disregarded it. He said, 'This man who called for them. Didn't Tasker know who he was?'

'He said not. He said the couple had been given instructions to sit tight until they heard from him.' Colin shrugged. 'He could have been lying, of course.'

'He wasn't,' Morgan said, and winced as his teeth cracked the last sliver of acid-drop. A bad molar there, he thought. 'The caller was a policeman. You don't have to worry about Tommy, Mr Everard. He's safe and well in an L.C.C. nursery.'

The two men stared at him. Everard's relief was so great that he felt suddenly faint and light-headed, and he slumped on the bed with a muttered 'Thank God!' The superintendent, after a pause to enjoy their astonishment, went on to explain; but Everard heard his voice only as from a great distance. Mrs Price's mother, Morgan said, alarmed when her grandson was taken ill, had gone to the police; could they help her to trace the parents, who were on holiday she did not know where? The first move of the police had been to visit the Prices' flat in the hope that a neighbour might know where the couple had gone. And there they had found the Prices — and Tommy.

'We claim no credit,' he concluded modestly, with a glance at the recumbent Everard. 'But it does stress the wisdom of consulting the police in such matters. Every copper in the country had been alerted when your wife and son disappeared. And that's a lot of coppers, Mr. Everard.'

Everard's relief had been replaced by anger. He sat up slowly.

'And you let me sweat it out when you could have told me this at the beginning?'

His body was trembling. 'Good God, man! Don't you damned policemen understand the meaning of humanity?'

Morgan was unperturbed. 'We even practise it sometimes, sir. But had I told you about Tommy when I arrived you would have wanted to dash off to see him. That wouldn't have suited me at all.'

Everard glared at him. 'You know damned well you wouldn't have let me go.'

'That's beside the point, sir.'

Despite the superintendent's politeness, Colin guessed that the antagonism between the men was mutual. To close the breech he said quickly, 'Do I finish what I was saying about Tasker? Or have you both lost interest?'

'Not me,' Morgan said, and popped another acid-drop into his mouth. 'Let's have the rest of it.'

Everard nodded. He was still too angry for speech.

Although the attempt to rescue Tommy had failed, Colin said, he had not yet done with Tasker. There was, he knew, a great deal more that the man could tell him. The difficulty had been to drag it out of him. 'Very reticent type, Cyril George,' he said. 'But we managed to persuade him eventually. He — '

'Was it Mr Cope or Mr Ballantyne who did the persuading?' Morgan asked. His voice was grave, but the corners of his mouth twitched in a smile. 'I understand they both have a way with them.'

Colin was not to be drawn. 'Do they, indeed?' he said. 'Interesting — but irrelevant.' And continued his narrative unruffled.

For some months Tasker and Corbett had been considering means of reprisal against Everard for what Tasker called their 'savage and unjustified dismissal.' 'I don't know about Corbett,' Colin said to Everard, 'but Cyril George is obviously one to feed a grudge until it swells real big. They installed Tasker's son (a bit actor, not a critic; Laroche was his stage name) in the bungalow with instructions to become friendly with you and Juanita, and so find an opportunity to obtain an impression of your front door key. This he did; and he and his father then carried out the burglary. They had made no plans to dispose of their haul; but the bungalow was costing them money they could ill afford, and Laroche (who seems to have been a very shady character indeed) suggested they sell the stuff. It was he who introduced them to Rossiter. Rossiter disposed of the silver, but he refused to handle the pictures.'

'Tricky things, pictures,' the superintendent said. 'The ordinary fence won't touch 'em. Incidentally, we found yours in the Melwich cottage, Mr Everard.'

Everard nodded. That once-prized collection seemed unimportant now. He was thinking of what lay ahead. Juanita and Tommy were free, they would soon be going home. But not with him. Even if the charge of murder were reduced to one of manslaughter (a prospect in which he had little faith) he still faced a term of imprisonment.

'Thank you,' he said stiffly.

It was the association with Rossiter, Colin said, which led to the wages snatch. It was his baby, and he and his men carried it out, with Tasker and Corbett supplying the information. But the basic plan — to hi-jack Juanita, and gain admittance to the works by forcing her to act as driver — was soon augmented. Corbett and Tasker wanted Juanita to be held prisoner for a few weeks; that, they thought, would cause Everard more concern than the robbery. Rossiter had no objection, but suggested to Tasker that there was little point to a kidnapping without a ransom; if they were going to stick their necks out it might as well be for profit. Juanita's father was a wealthy man, and the obvious course was to smuggle her into Spain and get the money — big money — from him. 'I don't know why Corbett wasn't in on this,' Colin said. 'Tasker didn't explain. With him, revenge had obviously become subservient to the profit motive. Perhaps Corbett thought differently.'

'He said they *forced* her to drive?' Everard asked, with a sidelong glance at the superintendent. To Everard, the significance of that incriminating note found in the Jaguar after the raid had been the suggestion that Juanita and

Laroche were lovers. He had forgotten what to the police would be its more important imputation — that Juanita had been a willing accomplice, and as such was liable to arrest on her return.

Colin hesitated. He too looked at Morgan.

'Couldn't we skip this, Superintendent?' he asked. 'From now on it's rather personal.'

'Mrs Everard's association with Laroche, my Lord, is no news to me. Or is it Mr Everard's visit to Melwich that worries you?' Morgan shrugged his broad shoulders. 'I fancy I know more about that than either of you. However, it's for Mr Everard to decide.'

'It's all right, Colin,' Everard said. Nothing Colin might tell them could harm Juanita more than that damned note, and his own pride had long since been deflated. 'Go ahead.'

'Well, if you say so.' Colin looked and felt unhappy. It was damnable to hurt a friend the way he knew this would hurt Everard. 'No, they didn't force her. Not according to Tasker. Laroche told them it wouldn't be necessary. Mind you, I don't believe a word of this, but — well, Tasker said Laroche told him she was in love with him, that she'd been pestering him to take her and Tommy away. He wasn't interested — he was stuck on some other girl — but he had played up to her because he liked you no more than Corbett or his father did, and he knew how this would hurt.' Colin saw the agony on Everard's face. But he could not stop now. He had to go on. 'Anyway, Laroche told her he was broke, that he couldn't afford an elopement unless she helped in the robbery; and Juanita was so infatuated, Tasker said, that she agreed. So now the gang had to consider what to do with Tommy. It was Rossiter who suggested they held him in England as an assurance against failure in Spain.

'At the start, Tasker said, the arrangements worked smoothly. He, Rossiter, Johnson and Smith met Juanita as arranged. Tasker offered to look after Tommy while the job was on, and promptly handed him over to Mrs Price; and afterwards he picked the others up at a prearranged spot, where they abandoned the Jaguar and drove to Melwich. It was then that Juanita realized how she had been tricked. They had told her that Tommy and Laroche would be waiting at the cottage. Neither was there.'

Despite his own misery, Everard was able to feel sympathy for his wife at that moment. Poor Juanita, he thought — separated from her baby, abandoned by her lover. How she must have loathed herself!

'Not Laroche?' Morgan asked.

'No. He and his girl friend arrived the next afternoon, when the coast was clear. The others kept Juanita there overnight, and then carted her off to Spain in an aircraft laid on by Rossiter.'

Morgan fumbled in his pocket. Acid-drops were a poor substitute for a good dinner, but they had become a habit.

'You didn't discuss this with your wife, Mr Everard, before leaving Spain?' he asked.

'I couldn't. She was shocked and overwrought. No emotional strain, the doctor said.'

Colin said earnestly, 'All I've given you, John, is what I got from Tasker. It doesn't have to be true. I'm damned sure it *isn't* true.' Inspiration came to him. 'Dammit! Isn't that just what the bastard would do? Twist the truth around to make it as bad for you as he could? It's all part of his mania for revenge.'

'Maybe,' Everard said. 'Thanks for trying, anyway. But don't stint the Superintendent. Give him full value.'

Tasker had got his share of the robbery, and it wasn't until the Saturday afternoon that he realized how easily Rossiter could, and probably would, bilk him out of any money he got from Don Carlos. So he decided to hold Tommy to ransom. 'It was another blow at you, John, and could be profitable,' Colin said. 'That he was undermining Rossiter's insurance didn't bother him at all. He found someone to deliver the ransom note to your house, and then returned to Melwich to tell his son what he had done — unaware, of course, that in the meantime Laroche had tried his best to double-cross the lot of them. He arrived at the cottage to find his son's body being carted away in an ambulance.'

Everard shuddered. Morgan said thoughtfully, 'I was there too, checking up on Laroche. The fact that he had vacated the bungalow on the same day as the robbery made me suspicious. A pity I missed his father.'

'He took good care that you did. It wasn't until everyone had gone that he went in and talked to the girl. It was from her description, John, that he recognized you as — well, as — '

'His son's murderer,' Everard said grimly. 'No need to beat about the bush, Colin. It's common knowledge.'

'Manslaughter, John. If that. You had every right to hit him.'

'We'll discuss that later,' Morgan said. 'Incidentally, it was the girl who telephoned you, Mr Everard, under instruction from Laroche. He was afraid you might recognize his voice.' He turned to Colin. 'Go on, please, my Lord.'

To Tasker, everything now became subservient to revenge. Everard must not be allowed to escape the consequences of

351

his act, and Tasker made it his business to track his enemy down and ensure that the law took its course. Obviously Everard would shun his home and the works; the police would be watching them. But Juanita had told Laroche of her husband's friendship with Colin, and for want of a better lead he tried the gym. 'He was in luck,' Colin said. 'He arrived as we were leaving and followed us to the flat. After that — well, you know what happened then.'

'I don't,' Morgan said.

'It's your story, John,' Colin said. 'You tell him.'

Listlessly, Everard complied. With so much to occupy his thoughts, his visit to the works that Saturday night seemed distant and unimportant now.

Morgan turned to Colin. 'You and your friends must have worked overtime to get such a complete confession out of Tasker,' he said.

'We did.' Colin grinned. 'But he took pains to point out that it had been obtained under duress, and as such was valueless. A lot we cared!'

'And you trussed him up, dumped him in his car, and rang the local police telling them where to collect him. But it came unstuck, eh?'

'It did,' Colin agreed ruefully. 'Some chance pedestrian set him free before your chaps turned up. He drove off like a bat out of hell. One of my friends was watching, but he couldn't interfere. Have you picked him up yet?'

'Not yet.'

'He's an ugly devil. Conspicuous too, with that pock-marked face and the goatee beard and the bulging eyes. He'd be difficult to miss.' Colin hesitated. 'What happens to me now, Superintendent? Are you going to arrest me?'

'I don't see how I can, my Lord.' Morgan caressed his chin with a well-manicured hand as he considered the problem. 'Apart from your own statement there's no evidence, is there? Of course, if Tasker chooses to bring a civil action, claiming damages for assault — ' He shook his head. 'We'll have to wait and see.'

There was an uneasy pause while he

stood up and carefully adjusted tie and cummerbund. Colin made a show of examining his pipe, and then slowly tapped it out on a heavy glass ashtray. He knew what must happen next.

So did Everard. He slid off the bed. 'Do I go with you now?' he asked.

'If you wish, sir.'

'If I wish? Good Heavens, man! Have I a choice? Aren't you arresting me?'

Morgan took his time in replying. He knew that he should have given the answer to that question at the start. But he disliked Everard; in all their dealings the man had gone out of his way to denigrate the police. He had felt no sympathetic urge to allay his fears.

'No, sir, I am not arresting you. I know this is a familiar theme, but had you gone to the police when you found that Laroche was dead you could have saved yourself a deal of worry. He had a weak heart, you see, and under the threat of violence it gave out. You didn't kill him, Mr Everard — he died of heart failure. He was probably already dead when you hit him.'

# 21

Juanita returned two days later. Everard was waiting for her at the airport, and when she saw him she smiled happily and broke into a run. He moved to meet her, but there was no answering smile on his face; and gradually her steps slowed, and she walked sedately up to him and lifted her face to be kissed.

'How are you?' he asked, pecking at her cheek with his lips. His tone was coolly polite. 'No worse for the journey?'

She shook her head, her eyes searching his face. The bruise on her forehead had yellowed, she wore the wounded arm in a sling. Everard thought how tired she looked — tired and bewildered — and his heart ached for her. He knew that his greeting had been like a slap in the face, and he wanted to take her in his arms and comfort her as he had done that night on the mountain. But to do so now would be to commit himself unreservedly, and that he would not do. Not until the truth had been established. If they were to have a future together it must be based on considered judgment, not on emotional impulse. He would not write a blank cheque on forgiveness.

'How is Tommy?' she asked.

'Fine. I've left him with Mrs Chater.'

He had taken Tommy home the previous morning. He had not warned Mrs Chater they were coming, and their arrival had shaken her out of her habitual calm. She had clung to the front door when she saw them, her faded grey eyes asking innumerable questions that she was too startled to voice. But by the time she had put Tommy to bed and made coffee she was her composed self again. Seated on the edge of a chair, her back straight, she had listened quietly to what he had to say. Only when he spoke of finding Juanita on the mountain did she interrupt.

'But why didn't she come with you?' she had asked; adding quickly, 'She is not seriously hurt, is she?' And once more he had explained that only on the doctor's insistence had Juanita been persuaded to stay behind; that because she needed complete rest he had not even been allowed to question her, but that he expected her back in a day or two. Mrs Chater's obvious relief had touched him. She and Colin, he thought. What would he have done without them?

Because silence between them was even more difficult than speech, he mentioned this to Juanita as they walked to the car.

'I am glad you can trust someone,' she said. He had not meant to hurt her, but her voice told him that he had. 'It seems you do not trust me.' She waited for his denial, but he made none. 'Why, John? I have done nothing to hurt you. If you would listen — '

'I will,' he said quickly. 'But not now. Later.' Good news or bad, he did not want to hear it there. Emotionally he was in too unstable a condition to accept either calmly. They had to be alone when they discussed it. Completely alone.

'If you wish,' she said quietly.

As they drove from the airport he asked after her father, and she told him that he still had not regained his voice. 'He seems more aware,' she said, staring out of the window, her voice flat, emotionless. 'And he can move his arms a little. But that is all.'

'The doctor said it might take time,' he said. 'Don't expect too much at once.'

He thought back to that last day at the estancia. For most of it she had been under sedation, but towards evening he had been allowed to see her. 'She has something to tell you,' the doctor had said; 'but no questions, Señor, no emotional disturbances.' He had sat by the bed, her hand in his, and listened to what she had to say. It was much what he had expected to hear. She had set out with Tommy that Friday morning to do the week-end shopping, and some way down the lane a car had swerved in front of the Jaguar, forcing her to stop. There were four men in the car — Rossiter, Smith, Johnson, and Tasker — and Tasker had taken Tommy from her and driven him away. The others had got into the Jaguar, and Rossiter had told her that she was to drive the car for them in the hold-up; when she refused he had added that Tommy's future depended on her co-operation, and that unless she ensured the success of the venture she was unlikely to see him again. Against that threat she had had no defence. She had driven them to the works and smiled at the gateman, had waited in the car while they robbed the van, and then driven them away to where Tasker was waiting in their own car. But Tommy was not with him; and despite her desperate pleading they had taken her to some place in the country, where they had kept her overnight before flying her to Spain. 'I knew you would understand about the robbery, that they forced me to do it,' she had said, gently squeezing his hand. 'But Peter had told me he would be away for a while, and I was afraid you would think, when I did not come back, that I had gone with him. You were so terribly jealous, John.' She blinked her long lashes at him. 'Did you think that?'

'For a little while, perhaps,' he had answered. 'Not for long.' And that was true. But he had not told her that

Laroche himself had settled that doubt, nor that Laroche was dead. That must wait until she was well again.

'Poor John,' she had said, with a faint smile. 'It was so unnecessary. Don't you know that I love you?'

He had answered that he did. He had even believed it. But Colin had given him Tasker's version, and in the subsequent hours of troubled thought doubt had returned. Much as he loved and wanted her, he could not shut his mind to the knowledge that Tasker's version fitted the facts — and that Juanita's did not.

They had travelled some way in silence when she said, 'Do the firm know that you are back?'

'They do if they read the newspapers. I was pestered by reporters for most of yesterday. But I haven't contacted them, if that's what you mean. They were too damned quick to prejudge me. It's up to them to make the first move.'

She said quietly, 'You too were quick to prejudge, John. And with less reason.'

'I didn't prejudge you,' he said, knowing that he had. 'I've tried to keep an open mind. It is just that the facts — '

'It is just that you did not trust me,' she told him.

He did not answer. He had remembered that this was not only a domestic issue; the police were also concerned. Grudgingly, and somewhat to his surprise, Superintendent Morgan had acceded to his request that the police should not meet Juanita at the airport, that he be given a few hours alone with her first. But they might well be waiting at the house. And before they put their questions he had to know the answers, for her sake as well as his.

He turned down a side road and stopped the car. Surprised, Juanita looked up at him. He took a piece of paper from his wallet and handed it to her.

'What is it?' she asked.

'One of the reasons why my trust in you didn't come up to scratch. Go on, read it.'

There were furrows in her brow as she read. She turned the paper over, saw the reverse side was blank, and read it again. Everard could feel the steady thumping of his heart as he watched.

'I don't understand,' she said. 'What does it mean?'

'It's a copy of a note the police found in the Jaguar after the robbery. It was in an envelope addressed to you.'

'To me? But I have never seen it before. And who — ?' She caught her breath as she understood. 'Oh, no! You mean they believed that I had actually *arranged* to meet those men and drive the car for them? But that is absurd! Did you not tell them — ?' Her voice hardened. 'No. No, you did not. You believed it too. Just as you believed that Peter and I were lovers. John! How could you!'

'Very easily,' he said stiffly, annoyed that somehow she had managed to switch the blame. 'Mrs Chater recognized the envelope as one she had taken up to you with your breakfast that morning.'

'But I tell you I have never seen it before! Mrs Chater must have confused it with another letter.'

'Did you have another letter that morning? On brown paper — in a brown envelope?'

'I don't remember. No, I don't think

362

so. But I did not have that one.'

'Then what was it doing in the car?'

'How can I tell?' she protested. 'Perhaps one of the men put it there.'

It was possible, he thought. A fancy touch by Tasker, a final garnish to the harm and misery he and Corbett had already planned. Tasker would know that the note must be found. And what more hurtful to a man than to throw mud at his wife?

Possible — but unlikely. It did not fit the facts, it was out of the pattern.

'You were not intending to go away with Laroche?' he asked.

'No! No! No!' she cried, punctuating each denial with a fist on her knee. 'Peter amuses me, but I do not love him. I do not even like him very much. It is simply that — ' She sighed, unclenched her hand, and leaned to place it on his knee. 'Oh, John! Why can you not understand?'

He nearly succumbed then. There was the misty look of tears in her eyes, her voice was tremulous. But he resisted her appeal. If the questions were not put now they must be put later. And later would be still more agonizing.

'I'm trying to understand,' he said unhappily. 'Believe me, Juanita, I *want* to understand. But why take a suitcase if you were only going shopping?'

'But I did not!' she protested. 'I took nothing. Did you ask Mrs Chater? She would know.'

'Mrs Chater didn't see you leave. But some of your clothes were missing. And your passport. And how did they come to be in that cave if you did not take them with you?'

'The men brought them,' she said, shuddering at the memories his question evoked. 'I suppose they called at the house and told Mrs Chater I wanted them.' She frowned. 'She must have thought that strange.'

'No-one called,' he told her. 'Mrs Chater would have said so.'

'Then they stole them while she was out.'

Some of the load lifted from his heart as he realized that that too was possible. Mrs Chater had been in London that day, she had returned on the same train as

364

himself. And the men would have had no need to force an entry; Tasker had had a key to the house, they had used it for the robbery. Had he (and the police) jumped too hastily to conclusions Tasker and his crew had intended they should? Had Juanita been completely truthful about her association with Laroche?

No. Not completely truthful. She might not have planned to run away with Laroche, but she had certainly meant to spend the day with him. Why invent the invitation from Molly Walker if not to account to Mrs Chater for her absence?

When he asked her that she shook her head.

'I am sorry, John, but I have no idea what you are talking about,' she said wearily. 'What invitation?'

'You told Mrs Chater that Molly had telephoned to invite you and Tommy over for the day. But that was a lie, wasn't it? I checked with Molly, and she said she hadn't spoken to you for weeks. So why, Juanita? What were you planning?'

'Nothing. I told you, I was going shopping. There was no telephone call, and I did not — ' She sat up and clutched his arm. The weariness had gone from her voice as she asked quickly, 'Mrs Chater said that? That I told her Molly had telephoned?'

'Yes.'

'But I did not!' The grip on his arm tightened. 'John, I'm scared! Why should Mrs Chater lie to you about me? What was she trying to do?'

Something of her fear communicated itself to him. 'You are sure it was a lie?' he asked.

'But of course! And she could not have been mistaken. She knew I was going to the shops. She *knew* it, John. So why should she tell you otherwise? I don't understand.'

'I'm beginning to,' he said grimly. Careful of her wounded shoulder, he bent to kiss her. 'Darling, I'm sorry. I was a fool and a brute to doubt you. Please forgive me.'

'Of course,' she said, her cheek against his. 'It was not easy for you, John. I know that.'

He kissed her again and drew away. 'I'll

make it up to you,' he promised, pressing the starter. 'I've learned my lesson, believe me. But right now we have to get back to Tommy. And fast.' He put the car into reverse and backed erratically to a turning. 'What a fool I was to leave him with that damned woman!'

'Why? Because she lied about me?' She gasped as he swung the Jaguar on to the main road, narrowly missing a passing car. 'But she is fond of Tommy. She would not harm him.'

'I hope you're right.' He changed into top, and pressed firmly on the accelerator. 'But unless I'm mistaken she's in league with that devil Tasker. That's enough to damn any woman.'

'No!' She seemed to shrink into her seat. 'Oh, hurry, John! Hurry!'

'I'll hurry,' he promised.

He thought about Mrs Chater as he drove. He knew he was right; he had to be. The way she had stimulated his jealousy by stressing Juanita's friendship with Laroche, her pretended recognition of the note found in the Jaguar (Tasker or Laroche must have put her up to that), the lie about Molly's invitation; they all added up. No doubt it was she who had told Tasker that Juanita always went shopping on a Friday morning, and who had packed Juanita's clothes and handed them to the men; there had been no need to steal. It would be Mrs Chater whose silhouette he had mistaken for Juanita's in Laroche's bungalow; perhaps she had gone there after talking to him in the kitchen, taking the china ornament so that he would see it. For she had known that he would go. She had put the idea into his head with the cunning insinuation that Juanita might be there.

Why had she done it? For money, presumably. Laroche would have reported to his father that Juanita had engaged a housekeeper, and been told to bribe her. And quite obviously he had succeeded.

They were approaching a series of bends. Ahead of them was a transporter, and as they came up to it Everard hesitated, trying to judge the distance. He swung out to overtake, realized he could not make it, and stamped on the brake.

'Damn!'

Juanita stirred restlessly, regretting her injured shoulder. She was a better driver than he, and she knew that had she been at the wheel there would have been no hesitation, they would have been safely past the transporter before the first bend. But she made no comment. She did not want him to take chances. Better delay than an accident.

As they crawled through the bends, with Everard muttering curses under his breath, she said, 'You told me she was pleased to hear that I was not badly hurt, that I would be home soon. That does not make her sound wicked, John.'

'I got it wrong,' he said. 'She was pleased, all right. But not at your quick recovery. What mattered to her was that I hadn't been allowed to question you. She knew that for the time being she was safe — just as she knows that by now we'll have talked it over and discovered the truth.' The road straightened, and he pressed impatiently on the horn. 'Get over, damn you!'

As he swept past the transporter he

glared savagely at the driver. Yet he knew that no matter how fast he drove it would not be fast enough. The most ominous portent of all was that Tasker had not incriminated Mrs Chater to Colin. The others, yes. That was why it had never occurred to him that she was lying. But now it could mean only one thing. She was Tasker's trump, and he was keeping her up his sleeve, meaning to use her if opportunity offered.

And he, Everard, had thoughtlessly given him that opportunity.

They covered the last three miles in four reckless minutes. The gravel flew as they slid up the drive to a stop. Everard did not wait for Juanita. He ran to the front door, found it unlocked, and hurried through to the kitchen.

There was no-one there. There was no-one in any of the rooms. Mrs Chater had gone, and Tommy with her.

# 22

Even Everard had little criticism to make of the speed and efficiency with which the police acted. But, as Morgan pointed out when he arrived later that evening, the woman had had five hours in which to disappear, and in that time she could be many miles away. Already there had been several reports of a woman answering to Mrs Chater's description and carrying a baby, and all were being investigated. 'But it's like looking for one particular straw in a haystack,' he said. 'Women carrying babies aren't exactly scarce. We can hope for a lucky break, Mr Everard, but don't expect it. At worst, this could be a long haul.'

'I've run out of luck,' Everard said. He stood with his back to the room, staring out at the gathering night. 'You realize that devil Tasker's behind this, I suppose?'

'I think it's highly probable.'

'She must have known where to

contact him, and he came down to collect her. They wouldn't have risked using public transport. So isn't this concentration on trains and buses rather superfluous? It's Tasker you should be looking for. Find him, and you'll find my son.'

'We're looking for him, sir, believe me. But we mustn't neglect the alternatives.'

'You've been looking for him for days.' Everard turned slowly. The despair in his voice was reflected in his lined face. 'What makes you think you'll find him now?'

'I said it might be a long haul,' Morgan reminded him gently. Despite his dislike of the man he felt considerable sympathy for him. It was cruel luck that he should have had to suffer this final blow. 'But there's one encouraging aspect. Up to now Tasker has probably holed out with an accommodating pal. Hasn't had to move around. With Mrs Chater and Tommy on his hands it may be different.'

Colin Sievewright came in with coffee and sandwiches. He had learned of Tommy's disappearance when he telephoned to congratulate Everard on his wife's return, and had hastened to help. For some hours the two men had toured the district, leaving Juanita in the care of the doctor. Only the coming of night had forced them to desist. Colin, restless in idleness, had transferred his energies to the kitchen.

'A welcome sight, my Lord,' Morgan said. 'I missed out on lunch.'

'Help yourself. How about you, John?'

Everard shook his head. 'I'm not hungry. What do you think he's after, Superintendent? Ransom? Or is it sheer bloody malevolence?'

Morgan shrugged. 'If it's ransom we'll soon know,' he said, munching his way through a sandwich. 'Otherwise — well, he can't hold the child indefinitely.'

'And the third alternative?'

Morgan knew what he meant. 'No, sir, I don't think so. It didn't happen before, and it's unlikely to happen now. Particularly with the woman around. Didn't you say she was fond of the child?'

'We thought so. But then we thought she liked us too,' Everard said bitterly.

Morgan made no comment. Bitterness

was natural under such circumstances. But because there was nothing he could say or do to alleviate the other's distress he felt uncomfortable, and as soon as he had finished his sandwich and gulped down a cup of coffee he said goodnight.

'Not a bad chap, really,' Colin said, as the sound of the car died away. He helped himself to a sandwich and pushed the plate hopefully towards his friend. 'How's Juanita?'

Everard ignored the sandwiches. 'Sleeping, thank God!'

Juanita had collapsed on hearing that Tommy had gone. Weakened physically by what she had already endured, her nerves stretched to breaking point, she had nothing in reserve with which to meet this new disaster. In a state of complete exhaustion she had wandered hysterically from room to room, the tears pouring down her cheeks in a flow she had no power to check. Unable to comfort her, Everard had telephoned the doctor. Only under sedation had she been able to achieve the rest which brain and body demanded.

Everard himself had little sleep that night. Around five o'clock he came out of a doze to find Juanita awake beside him. The rest seemed to have calmed her, and for a while they talked, watching the dawn banish the shadows from the room. Hitherto Juanita had seemed reluctant to discuss her period of captivity; now she did so compulsively, as though by reliving one harrowing experience she could shut her mind to her present agony. She did not minimize her sufferings, but he noticed that when she spoke of her captors she did so with no great bitterness.

'Doesn't the very mention of their names sicken you?' he asked curiously.

She considered this. 'Not really,' she said. 'At first they terrified me — not because of what they did, but because of what I feared they might do. Later, up in the mountains, I think I was more angry than afraid. They were wicked men, but they were not completely wicked. Johnson was kind in his way, and Rossiter had a certain code. He allowed no-one to molest me, and he risked his life to save mine. I did not like the one they called Connie, but he was too afraid of Rossiter to be really unpleasant.'

'And Corbett?'

'He was an angry, bitter man. At first he ignored me. I felt sorry for him when his wife was killed, but afterwards — ' She shuddered, and he saw the tears start in her eyes. 'Oh, it was horrible! Horrible!'

Colin cooked breakfast. They ate in the kitchen, and in near silence; there was no news of Tommy, and open speculation was too painful. As she nibbled at a piece of toast Juanita said listlessly, 'It is not right to impose on Lord Dunmour like this, John. Perhaps Mrs Long — '

She trailed the sentence into the air. 'I'll go see her after breakfast,' he promised.

Colin said hastily, 'I'll go with you.'

'No. Stay and keep Juanita company.'

Colin looked doubtfully at the girl. They were almost strangers. He admired her; but he was shy with women, and the prospect of being alone with her embarrassed him. Yet he did not demur. He knew that Everard was right, that she should not be left on her own.

It had rained for most of the night, and a steady drizzle was falling when Everard left the house. As he strode down the drive, shoulders hunched and raincoat collar up, a police car stopped at the gate and Morgan got out and stood waiting. Despite the weather the superintendent managed to look impressively dapper; he wore a smartly fitting raincoat, and his narrow-brimmed felt that was at just the right angle. Raindrops glistened on the highly polished leather of his shoes, poised precariously before sliding off.

'Going anywhere in particular?' he asked. And, when Everard explained, 'Mind if I join you? Exercise isn't much in my line, but I could use some this morning.'

Everard did not want company. He needed to sort out in his mind the problems still confronting him; apart from family worries, there was his position with the firm to be resolved. But he nodded agreement. It would have been difficult to refuse.

After an interval of silence Morgan said, 'Your image of the police worries me, Mr Everard. Like most people, we like to be liked. Is it of long standing, or has it evolved recently?'

'Recently, I suppose. Their performance since my house was burgled hasn't exactly impressed me.'

'Perhaps not. But one can't build bricks without straw, sir, and you and Lord Dunmour withheld the few straws that might have helped. Even so we didn't do too badly. We got Tommy for you, and we'd have got Laroche if you hadn't got to him first with a lucky short cut. Given Laroche, we might well have got Tasker and Mrs Chater also. He only had to talk a little.' Morgan sighed. 'Believe me, Mr Everard, with co-operation from you this present misfortune could have been avoided.'

Everard knew he was right. Yet they had walked some distance before he could bring himself to admit it. Eventually he said, 'I'm not arguing, Superintendent. Who am I to throw stones? I've made a sorry mess of things myself. And if I crowded you somewhat — well, I'm sorry.'

Morgan stroked his massive chin. 'Matter of fact, sir, I owe you an apology also. You were right to bawl me out at the hotel. I should have told you at the start that you were in no danger of arrest, and that Tommy was safe.' He gave an odd, jerky laugh. 'I'm burdened with a high horse too, you see.'

' 'Burdened' is right, Superintendent.'

They were approaching the path which led to the Laroche bungalow. Everard slowed and stopped. 'Mind if we go this way? It's shorter, and I've a morbid desire to take another look at the damned place. It may not be strictly true to say that this is where the trouble started, but that's how it seems to me.'

'Carry on, sir.'

The path had become a series of puddles, water dripped steadily from the trees. As the bungalow came into sight Everard thought how drear it looked — almost sinister, with its drawn curtains, and the tall trees hemming it in, and the dark tiles of the roof merging in

379

the dull light with the foliage beyond.

He shivered. Morgan said, 'Anything wrong?'

'Not really. A ghost trampling on my grave.' He walked on slowly, to halt before the front door. 'Gloomy, isn't it? I never realized that before. Last time I came — on the Saturday, the day after I'd seen you — I was mad as hell at what I thought had happened here. Yet it didn't strike me as an evil place. It does now.'

'What brought you here? Laroche had already gone.'

'Yes. But I didn't know he'd gone for good. It was the tidy way he'd left it that told me that. You know — covers on the beds, the kitchen looking like it had never been used, no books or papers or personal belongings lying around.' He turned away. 'Come on, let's go.'

They had walked only a few paces when Morgan stopped him with a heavy hand on his arm.

'One moment, sir.' The superintendent's normally soft voice had an edge to it. 'You had a key to the bungalow?'

'Certainly not. I peeked through the windows.'

The grip on his arm tightened as Morgan pulled him round. 'Take another look at the windows.'

Everard looked. It took him a second or two to get the superintendent's meaning.

'The curtains! They've been drawn! But not by Laroche — he was dead. Hell! Do you think — '

'Could be. Laroche left here on Friday, and he didn't arrive at Melwich until the Saturday afternoon. He could have spent Friday night with his father, and given him the keys. He'd finished with them, and they weren't on him when we found the body.' Morgan had slackened his grip on the other's arm. Now, as Everard started impetuously forward, he grabbed him again. 'No, sir. Not that way.'

'But dammit, man! If they're in there with Tommy — '

'We'll see they stay there. But don't let's take unnecessary risks. Not with a man like Tasker — and perhaps a child's safety at stake.'

'All right, all right!' Everard jerked his

arm away. 'What do we do?'

'Go back to the house and tell my driver to bring the car. Tell him to leave it on the road. Then ring Inspector Challen and ask him to collect whatever men he has available and get them here pronto. I want the place surrounded before we move in.'

He started to walk towards the road. Everard said sharply, 'Aren't you staying to keep an eye on them?'

'Of course. But if Tasker happens to be watching I want him to think we're both leaving.'

Everard ran the few hundred yards to the house, his heart pounding as he raced up the drive; two cars were there now, and with relief he saw that both belonged to the police. In the hall Colin was talking to Inspector Challen, with Juanita watching tired-eyed in the background. When she saw her husband and read the look on his face she hurried to him.

'What is it, John?' she cried, clutching his wet sleeve. 'Have they found Tommy?'

'I don't know. Perhaps.' Juanita's slim fingers were feverishly kneading his arm as he gasped out the news. He guessed what was in her mind. As Challen turned to leave he added, 'Hold it, Inspector! My wife and I are coming with you.'

'Me too,' Colin said.

The inspector's hesitation was only momentary. They had a right to be there, and if he did not take them they would come on their own. But as they scrambled into the car he uttered a word of warning to Everard.

'Keep Mrs Everard in the background, please, sir. Just until we've flushed him out.' And added, 'If he's there, of course.'

On his instructions the drivers coasted the last few yards. Superintendent Morgan was waiting near the bend in the path, and as they paused to gaze speculatively at the bungalow he came out from the trees to join them. Quickly he made his dispositions: the inspector and one constable at the rear, himself and the other constable at the front. 'And no impetuous interference from you and Lord Dunmour,' he told Everard, stern authority in his voice. 'Keep out of the way. We'll call on you if we need you.'

Everard nodded. 'Any sign of them?' he asked anxiously.

'None,' Morgan said, and walked briskly away, to pause outside the front door while the others took up their positions. Juanita thought with relief how solid and dependable he looked. Clinging tightly to her husband's hand, she closed her eyes and prayed.

'Don't bank on it, darling,' Everard said. 'We could be wrong.'

Morgan strode to the door and knocked loudly. Seconds passed, but the door remained closed. He knocked again, and stepped back to watch the front windows. There was no movement of the curtains, nothing to indicate that the bungalow was inhabited.

'Open up, Tasker!' he shouted. 'This is the police.'

Everard moved a few paces forward, his eyes fixed on the door, willing it to open. It stayed closed, and with a sigh he looked down at Juanita. She had released his hand and was nibbling at her broken nails. When he put his arm round her she did not relax against him. Her body was taut under his hand.

Morgan spoke to the constable, and they moved from door to window. Everard saw the constable raise a bent elbow, and guessed that they were about to break in. But the glass remained intact. Without warning the door was flung open and a man came out, dodged past the two policemen, and started to run down the path — saw Colin and the Everards barring his way, and turned to race across the clearing towards the trees. Everard let out a bellow and sprinted after him. But Colin was quicker. He caught the fugitive a few yards from the trees, hurled himself forward in a flying tackle, and brought the man down with a body-racking thud.

For a few seconds both lay still. Then Colin rolled clear and sat up. As Morgan and the constable reached him he said cheerfully, 'Sorry about the impetuous interference, Superintendent.'

Morgan grunted, and helped the constable haul the man to his feet.

'Is this Tasker?' he asked.

'That's him,' Colin said. 'He's shaved off the beard, but he couldn't do much with that corrugated pan.'

Everard stared hard at the glaring Tasker, knowing that the fury in those bulging eyes was reflected in his own. It seemed incredible that so much hatred could exist between two comparative strangers; for although the pock-marked face was vaguely familiar he knew that he would not have recognized it had they passed in the street. Then anger was swamped by anxiety, and he turned away and ran into the bungalow.

Juanita was there before him; she had scarcely looked at Tasker, all her thought had been for the child. She sat on a settee with Tommy in her arms, murmuring softly as she hugged him to her. In the centre of the room Mrs Chater stood watching. She looked at Everard over her shoulder as he came in, but made no move to escape. He had meant to pour his anger over her in a flood of invective. But the grey, lifeless look on her face stopped him. Something told him that words at that moment would be ineffectual.

Tommy was crying fretfully. 'Is he all

right?' he asked, bending over the child.

Juanita looked up. She was smiling, but her eyes were bright with tears. Mrs Chater said evenly, 'He's perfectly all right. But he's hungry. I haven't fed him yet.'

Morgan and the inspector were in the room now. The inspector was talking to Mrs Chater, cautioning her, but she appeared not to be listening; she was watching Juanita. Barely waiting for him to finish, she said, 'I want to explain.'

'You can make a statement at the station,' the inspector told her.

She shook her head. 'I want to make it now, while Mr and Mrs Everard are here.'

Challen looked at Morgan, who shrugged. 'Take Tasker to the station and charge him,' he said. 'I'll bring her along later. And send in my driver, will you?' And, to Mrs Chater, 'You understand the meaning of the caution?'

'Yes. May I sit down?'

Everard sat down also. He was suddenly inexpressibly weary.

She spoke in a near monotone, with only the restless movement of the entwined fingers in her lap betraying her nervousness. Soon after Laroche became friendly with Juanita, she said, the latter had mentioned that she was thinking of engaging a cook-housekeeper, and it had occurred to Laroche and his father that an accomplice installed in the house could be useful. So Tasker booked her in at the local pub, and Laroche brought the Everards there one evening so that she might introduce herself to them and cautiously disclose that she was looking for a job. They had hoped Juanita would engage her immediately. In fact this did not happen until after the burglary.

'And if Mrs Everard had chosen someone else?' Morgan asked. 'What then?'

'I was only an embellishment to their plans,' she said. 'Not a necessity.'

Everard wondered at the bitterness of her tone. What had she to be bitter about?

Her task, she said, had been to foster Everard's jealousy of Peter Laroche. That was all. It was not until later that she learned of the plan to kidnap Tommy and Juanita. At first she had objected; but

Tasker had assured her that they would be well cared for, and that it would be only for a week or so. After they had left the house she was to pack some of their clothes, which Laroche would collect. He would not return to the bungalow, so that Everard would assume they had gone away together. It would, said Tasker, be a more subtle form of revenge than the robbery; and in case Everard still doubted his wife's infidelity an incriminating note would be left in the abandoned Jaguar. It would be in a brown envelope, and if she were shown it she was to pretend to recognize it.

'And the lie about Molly Walker's invitation?' Everard demanded. 'Whose subtle touch was that?'

'Mine.'

'H'm! Very friendly. And I suppose it was you I saw at the bungalow with Laroche on the Wednesday evening?' She nodded. 'Did you take him that china ornament my wife kept on her dressing-table?'

'Yes.'

'Anxious to make a good job of it, eh?'

There was bitter contempt in his voice. 'I hope they paid you well.'

She shook her head. 'They paid me nothing.'

'What? Not even your share of the robbery?'

'They didn't tell me about the robbery.' The admissions of guilt had come in a near whisper, but her voice was firmer now. 'They knew I wouldn't agree. The first I heard of it was from you, Mr Everard, after Mr Morgan's visit on Friday. And by then it was too late.'

Everard looked his disbelief. Morgan said, 'You could have told the police what you knew. It wasn't too late for that.'

She sighed. 'I was afraid. They said no-one would believe that I wasn't involved. And not only that. They threatened to harm Mrs Everard and Tommy if I exposed them.'

'Exploiting your well-known devotion to the Everard family, eh?' Everard sneered. He was sitting next to Juanita, and he felt her hand on his arm. She shook her head when he looked at her. But he could not interpret the look, and he went on, 'If you felt so strongly about theft, Mrs Chater, why did you agree to work for them when you knew they had already burgled my house?'

'They told me they would return the things later.'

'And you believed them, of course.'

'Yes, I did.' She looked him full in the face, her gaze unflinching. 'You ruined their lives, Mr Everard. But the law couldn't punish you, so they had to do it themselves. I knew how they felt, and I believed them when they said that all they wanted was to settle the score. I didn't regard them as criminals. Not then.'

Very impressive, thought Colin. But is it true?

Morgan said quietly, 'Yet you continued to help them, Mrs Chater, even after you knew them for what they were — an unprincipled band of crooks. Isn't that so?'

Yes, she said. But from fear, not sympathy; so that when Everard told her that someone had telephoned offering to sell information about his wife and son she had tried first to dissuade him from investigating and, when that failed, to warn Tasker. She had no idea who the caller might be, but she was afraid that if Everard were successful the truth would come out, and that Tasker might implement his threats before the police could intervene. But Tasker had not answered her call, and it was not until the evening that she managed to contact him, and learned who the would-be informant must be.

'He rang me back later,' she said, looking at Everard. 'Much later. He wanted to know if you were home. He said he had gone to Melwich to warn Peter you were on your way because he could get no reply on the telephone.' She hesitated. 'He said that Peter was dead, and that you had killed him.'

Everard said nothing. He had already told her that Laroche died of heart failure. He remembered that the telephone had rung while he was upstairs with the girl. He had not answered it, but it would have made no difference if he had. By then Laroche was already dead.

'Tasker was wrong,' Morgan said. 'Mr

Everard did not kill Laroche.'

'I know. But I did not know it then.'

Everard said sharply, 'You knew about his death when I rang you from London, then?' She nodded. 'And that ransom note you read to me. Where did you get it?'

'A messenger brought it after you had left. At Lord Dunmour's request I handed it to the police.'

'Very co-operative of you.'

'Yes, it was.' She almost snapped the words at him. 'You see, I hated you as much as the others did. Perhaps more. Only by then it had all gone sour, and the ransom demand for Tommy was the last straw. It wasn't just the money, it was the implications. I didn't think they'd harm Tommy; but there was no mention of Mrs Everard in the note, and that frightened me. Cyril Tasker believed you had killed his son, and I knew what that could do to him; Peter wasn't much of a person, but Cyril didn't see it that way.' She sighed. 'I was too cowardly to take positive action, but I *wanted* the police to find them.' With a pitiful attempt at defiance, she added, 'You won't believe me, I know. But it's the truth.'

'You're right,' Everard said. 'I don't believe you.' But her first remark had puzzled him. What harm had he done her that she should hate him?

Before he could ask, Juanita said quietly, 'I think I believe you.'

A slow flush spread over Mrs Chater's pallid face, and to hide her embarrassment she burst into rapid speech. For three days, she said, she had waited anxiously for news. Then, on the Tuesday evening, Tasker had arrived without warning and demanded shelter; he was in an unpleasant mood, and she had been too frightened to refuse. 'And then you returned, Mr Everard,' she said. 'When I told him that Mrs Everard and Tommy had been rescued without any ransom being paid he was so mad I thought I'd never get him out of the house. What moved him eventually was this crazy notion that he could still get even with you. But he had to be free to do it, so he came here. To plan, he said. Peter had given him the keys.'

Everard swore under his breath. 'Are

you telling me that he was actually in the house when I arrived?'

'Yes.'

Morgan said, 'Why didn't you go to the police then, Mrs Chater? Tommy and Mrs Everard were no longer in danger.'

She had been thinking of herself, she said. Luck had been with her in that Everard had been unable to question his wife in Spain, but it would run out when Juanita returned; and Tasker swore that if the police picked him up at the bungalow he would hold her responsible, and would see that she was fully implicated in everything that had happened.

'I was afraid,' she said. Her face was very pale. 'I knew I could go to prison for a long, long time. But when Mr Everard told me yesterday that he was collecting his wife from the airport that afternoon I had to do *something*. I couldn't stay there. I decided to take Tommy to Mrs Long's, and call in here on the way to tell Cyril I was going.'

'And why didn't you do just that?' Everard demanded angrily.

Tasker had forestalled her, she said. He

had seen Everard leave, and guessed what would be in her mind. 'He was waiting for us in the woods,' she said, 'and made me bring Tommy here. He said he didn't trust me, that Tommy and I were to stay with him until he had decided what to do. The thought of your dismay when you returned and found Tommy missing made him almost cheerful. He said we would lie low here until the hunt spread farther afield, and then make our escape. He didn't mention Tommy, but I think he planned to take him with us.'

'And you agreed?'

'What else could I do?' There was a hint of passion in the quiet voice. 'I told you, I was afraid of him; afraid for myself, and afraid for Tommy. I kept hoping that someone would come; the house agent, perhaps, or some passer-by who had heard Tommy crying. But no-one did.'

There was a short silence. Morgan said, 'Is that all?' And, when she nodded, 'I'm taking you to the station, Mrs Chater. You will be formally charged, and your statement will be typed and given to you to read and sign. Are your things here or at the house?'

'Here,' she said. 'Cyril and I collected them.'

'One moment, Mrs Chater,' Everard said, as she stood up. 'You said just now that you hated me. I want to know why.'

She looked surprised.

'I thought I told you. My real name is Manning, not Chater. Alice Manning. I'm Tom Manning's widow.' She paused while they gaped at her in shocked dismay. 'I loved my husband, Mr Everard. He was a good man. But he was too conscientious, and when you sacked him he couldn't face up to what was left of his life. I don't suppose you considered yourself responsible for his death, but I did. I still do. Left to myself I doubt if I would ever have done anything about it, but when the others asked me to join them I did so gladly. Now — ' She sighed, and shook her head. 'Now I'm sorry. Not for hating you — I couldn't help that — but for letting myself be dragged into this vendetta. None of us has gained by it. There have been only losers.'

Juanita eyed her compassionately and shifted the child in her lap; with her arm in a sling he was not easy to hold. But her husband was still too angry to feel compassion. Manning's widow! So that was it! And yet . . .

'You didn't become Mrs Chater just for our benefit,' he said. 'Your previous employers knew you by that name. So when did you change it?'

'After Tom's death. It seemed disloyal, but I wanted to avoid publicity.'

There was an uncomfortable silence until she and the two policemen had left the room. Then Colin said, with forced cheerfulness, 'Well, that's that. Been quite a party, hasn't it? But all's well that ends well — to coin a phrase.'

Everard was frowning. 'Had she any justification at all, do you think, for saying I was responsible for her husband's death?' he asked.

'Of course not. It was an unfortunate chain of events, that's all.' Colin slapped his knees and stood up. 'I'll fetch the car. You two wait here. You must be just about jiggered.'

They were not sorry to be alone. Juanita said, 'Don't blame yourself too much, John. And don't try to rationalize her hate. A woman in love is seldom rational. It is over, darling. Forget it.'

He bent to kiss her.

'She was right in one thing,' he said. 'Nobody profited from all this hate and villainy. Nobody.'

'No,' she said. She leaned back and stretched, and then sat staring at the floor, her head cupped in her hands. 'But I keep thinking about Johnson. I am sure he was trying to rescue me. Why else would he have been where they found him? And the police told Ramon it was the only place where the cliff could be climbed.'

'Coincidence,' he said. 'More likely he was looking for cover from Corbett's gun. A scoundrel like that doesn't risk life and freedom in an heroic gesture.'

'I suppose not.' She sighed. 'But I like to believe it. Just as I like to believe that Rossiter's attempt to save my life was not as mercenary as he pretended, and that Mrs Chater really did worry about

Tommy and me. People are not just all good or all bad.'

A car horn blared loudly on the road. Everard took Tommy from her and stood up.

'Then you believe it, my darling,' he said. 'Come on, let's go home.'

## THE END